Theater Shoes

by
Noel Streatfeild

Bullseye Books • Random House

New York

A BULLSEYE BOOK PUBLISHED BY RANDOM HOUSE, INC.
Copyright 1945 by Noel Streatfeild
Copyright renewed 1973 by Noel Streatfeild and Random House, Inc.
Cover art copyright © 1994 Diane Goode

All rights reserved under International and Pan-American Copyright
Conventions. Published in the United States by Random House, Inc., New York,
and simultaneously in Canada by Random House of Canada Limited, Toronto.
Originally published in the United States by Random House, Inc., in 1945.
Library of Congress Catalog Card Number: 94-29776
ISBN: 0-679-85434-7
RL: 5.3
First Bullseye Books edition: December 1994

Manufactured in the United States of America   10 9 8

Contents

About This Book

Some years ago Random House published my story of Pauline, Petrova and Posy Fossil, three English children who were brought up together as one family. That story finished with Pauline leaving for Hollywood, Petrova settling down near an aerodrome in England, and Posy off to Czechoslovakia to train for the ballet. Since the beginning of the war, innumerable children in America have very kindly written to ask me how the Fossil children are getting along; particularly, since the German occupation of Czechoslovakia, I have had anxious inquiries about Posy. I have answered all these letters, but it now happens, owing to the help the Fossil sisters are at present giving to some other children, that in this story I am able to give news of them.

You may find the way Alice speaks a little puzzling. Rhyming slang, as it is called, is a way some Cockneys have of expressing themselves. The rhyming slang that Alice uses came into existence about a hundred years ago. It is said that rhyming slang is understood anywhere within the sound of London's Bow Bells, but as a matter of fact, it is believed that it began as thieves' jargon, which I am sure Alice does not know and would be very shocked if she did.

This book is dedicated to all you children in America who have asked so kindly after the Fossil sisters. It has been very nice of you to take such an interest.

Noel Streatfeild, 1944.

Chapter I

Tea with the Bishop

It is very difficult to look as if you minded the death
of a grandfather who, though you may have spent
your holidays in his house, certainly seldom remembered that you did. It was like that with the Forbes
family. Their mother had died when Holly, the
youngest, was quite little. Before the war they had
lived in Guernsey with their father. As soon as war
was declared, their father, who had retired from the
Navy to have time to bring his family up properly,
rejoined the Navy, and the children were sent to
England and given to their grandfather to look after.

Grandfather was a clergyman, vicar of a village
called Martins. But Martins, though he did his duty

3

by it, was far less important to him than a reference book he was writing on animals mentioned in the Bible. He was so absorbed in this reference book that when Sorrel, Mark and Holly first arrived at the vicarage all he said was, "There were four beasts." At the time Sorrel and her brother and sister, not knowing about the reference book, thought this both rude and inaccurate, but after a very little while they understood that he honestly did not realize they were there.

Holidays came and went and Sorrel and Mark and Holly scarcely ever saw their grandfather except in church. Sometimes they saw him on his bicycle going to visit somebody in the village, but mostly he was shut in his study. He even ate his meals there. Then, two years later, he spoke to them again. He told them about their father. This time he was not so much vague as buttoned-up looking. It was as if he had fastened an extra skin around him as a covering against feeling miserable.

"The telegram says 'missing.'"

"Nothing about 'presumed drowned'?" Sorrel asked.

"Nothing."

"Then he could easily be a prisoner in the hands of the Japs," she persisted.

Grandfather looked at her. "Quite possibly," he said and shut his study door.

Sorrel was just a little over twelve at that time. Mark was nine and a half and Holly eight and a quarter. The telegram talk had taken place in the hall. Mark swung on the banister.

"I bet he's a prisoner."

"If he's a prisoner or..." Sorrel broke off, she did not believe her father was drowned, so she was not going to say the word. "Whom do we belong to? Grandfather?"

Holly smelled something good cooking. "Let's ask Hannah."

Hannah was what made holidays with Grandfather bearable. She had been looking after him for years and years, and she treated him with a mixture of affection and rudeness, but never with respect.

"I give respect where respect is called for," she would say to Grandfather, "and it's not called for when you wear your suit so long you can see your face in it, and it's green rather than black. And it's not called for when, instead of taking an interest in decent Christian things, you get creating about eagles, lions and the like, which aren't what a person expects to hear about in a vicarage."

Hannah treated Grandfather as if he were a piece of furniture, flicking him over with a duster or a feather mop.

"Look at you, looking like something thrown away for salvage! Dust everywhere!"

Perhaps because she had always liked them, or perhaps because she had lived so long in a vicarage, Hannah was a great singer of hymns. All day long snatches of hymns came from her, often with bits that were not hymn stuck on and sung to the same tune or something like it.

"We plough the fields and scatter the good seed...drat the butcher, that's a wretched piece of meat!"

On the morning when Grandfather had his telegram Hannah was not singing. She knew what was in the telegram and she was very fond of Mr. Bill, as she called Sorrel's and Mark's and Holly's father. All the same, singing or not, she was comforting looking. She was all curves: a round top piece which was pushed in a little in the middle, only to bulge out enormously down below. Her legs had great calves, which curved only slightly at the ankles before they became feet. She had a curving face finished off with a round bun of hair. Usually her face was red but that morning it was almost pale.

Sorrel looked at her and quite suddenly she began to cry, and when she cried the other two did too. Hannah knelt on the floor and made room for them all in her arms.

"Do you think he's drowned, Hannah?" Sorrel hiccuped.

Hannah hugged them all tighter.

"Of course I don't. Nor does them at the top that sent that telegram. Gentlemen of few words they are in the Navy. If they mean drowned they say drowned, and if they mean missing they say missing. Why, we're used to your father being missing. We're always missing him."

After that the three felt better. Hannah said worrying made you cold inside and she gave them all cups of cocoa and, as if there were no such thing as rationing, two spoonfuls of sugar in each cup. While

6

they were drinking their cocoa Sorrel asked Hannah what was going to happen to them. Hannah did not see at first what she was worrying about and when she did she gave a big laugh.

"You never thought your father didn't arrange for something like this, of course he did. You'll go on just the same until he comes back. You and Holly at Ferntree School for Girls, and Mark at Wilton House."

Mark frowned when he was puzzled. "But who pays for us if Daddy can't?"

"Who says your father can't? Of course he's provided for you and, as a matter of fact, your grandfather pays your school bills and always has."

Mark took a big swallow of cocoa. "Why?"

Hannah was cooking the lunch. She looked over her shoulder at him.

"What a boy for questions! Your father lost money when the Germans took the Channel Islands, but your grandfather had enough so that was all right."

Sorrel had a long bob. She fiddled with a strand of hair when she was worried. She was fiddling now.

"He doesn't seem to get much for it. I mean, we aren't what you'd call a pleasure to him."

"I wouldn't say that," said Hannah. "There's pleasure comes from knowing you're doing your duty. When he takes his mind away from his lions and snakes and all that, he knows you're safe here or safe at school and he can go back to his work feeling there's nothing more he can do."

In August Grandfather died. He finished writing

his reference book, and it was as if that was what he was waiting for, because he just ruled a neat little line under the last animal's name, and then he was dead.

"If only we had the coupons for decent black you couldn't want anything more seemly," said Hannah.

The people who lived in the parish were always very nice to Sorrel and the two children. And when Grandfather died they were nicer than ever, asking them to so many meals that they could have had two or three lunches and teas every day. The family did not go to the funeral but they had tea afterwards with the Bishop. Hannah had been so pleased that the Bishop was taking care of the funeral, and so sure that the furniture ought to be given an extra polish because he was coming, that Sorrel and Mark and Holly were prepared for somebody they would simply hate. But the Bishop was not at all "hateable." They had tea in the dining room with cucumber sandwiches and a jam sponge, and he was just as openly pleased about the sandwiches and the jam sponge as they were. It was when the last sandwich had been eaten that he began to talk about the future.

"I suppose you three have got on to the fact that you won't be living here any more."

They had, of course, realized that a new vicar must be coming. Mark said so.

"Hannah thought I was the person to tell you about your future," the Bishop began. "Hannah has a very great respect for gaiters. She thinks where there are gaiters there must be great intellect. It's not correct, of course. I'm just an ordinary person of whom you may ask ordinary questions. So stop me if I tell you something stupidly and you don't understand what I'm saying. How much do you know about your mother?"

Sorrel and the two children thought.

"I can remember a little, I think," said Sorrel. "I'm not certain, though. I may just think that I do."

"Did your father never talk to you about her?"

"Oh, yes, of course," said Holly. "She was so beautiful that people used to turn and stare in the streets."

Mark leaned forward. "She was very gay. When she was in the house it was as if the sun were always shining."

Sorrel flicked back a lock of hair which had fallen forward.

"In Guernsey everything lovely in the house was something she had chosen and Daddy never would have anything moved from where she had put it."

The Bishop nodded. "Very lucky children to have had such a mother, but she was even more interesting than you know. She was a Warren. Adeline Warren."

He said Adeline Warren as if it were something that tasted good. Holly said:

"We knew her name was Adeline. Daddy called her 'Addie.'"

"But you didn't know she was a Warren, or what the name Warren means. The Warrens are one of the oldest and most distinguished theatrical families in this country."

The three of them were so surprised that for a moment they said nothing. Never once had their father said anything about the theater.

"Do you mean our mother's father was an actor?" Sorrel asked.

"Her father was an actor, and her mother was and still is an actress. Her brothers and sisters are all on the stage. So were her grandparents and great-grandparents. So was she for just one year. Lovely Adeline Warren! I had the good fortune to see her."

Mark liked his facts clear. "Did she stop acting because she married?"

The Bishop looked at each of them in turn to be sure they were attending.

"She was eighteen and your grandmother was very proud of her, so proud that she thought she ought to have the very best of everything, especially husbands."

"And she chose Daddy," said Holly.

"No. She chose somebody else. I mean, your grandmother chose him. A very important man. Your mother was very young and perhaps a little afraid of your grandmother and she did not say 'I won't marry him, I love somebody else,' so preparations for an enormous wedding went on. And then, when everybody was in the church, including the bridegroom, a message came to say that she was sorry she was not going to be married that day, and never to that bridegroom. She was going to marry your father."

"And so she did," said Holly.

"Yes, but it wasn't as easy as all that. Your grandmother was very angry and she never saw your mother again."

"What, because she married Daddy?" said Mark. "I should think she ought to have been jolly pleased to have Daddy in the family."

"I know, perhaps she should. Perhaps she's sorry now, but at that time she felt she'd been made to look foolish, and she lost her temper. Very understandable, you know."

"I don't think it was very understandable," said Sorrel. "To be angry at the time is all right, but fancy never seeing our mother again!"

"Your mother didn't live very long after you children were born. I expect your grandmother was heartbroken when she died. I feel sure she was."

Sorrel eyed the Bishop suspiciously. "Why do you want us to like our grandmother?"

There was a long pause before he answered. "Because we have been writing to her. You are going to live with her."

Questions burst from them all.

"Where does she live?"

"Does she act now?"

"When are we going?"

"I don't think she is acting in anything at the moment. You are going next week. She lives in London."

Chapter II

In the Train

It was when they were in the train traveling to London that Hannah broke the news. The train was an inconvenient place to talk in because there were fourteen people in their carriage. Sorrel and Mark were on the same side; Hannah and Holly faced them, Hannah's curves taking up nearly two seats. On one side of Hannah there was a thin woman who looked as if she were wearing tin underclothes, she was so stiff and held-in looking. She was clearly a woman who knew her rights, and her most immediate right was that having paid for a seat, she meant to have the proper space to sit on. She fought so hard to prevent even a quarter of an inch of Hannah from bulging into her piece of seat that she dared not open a book or take out a piece of knitting for fear she should relax and Hannah's curves win. Because of this woman Holly had to do all the giving way to Hannah's curves, and she had less than a quarter of a seat and was pushed so far forward that she was almost in the middle of the carriage.

The train had been bumbling along for about half an hour when Hannah, taking a deep breath as if she were going to blow up a balloon, said:

"You aren't any of you going back to school."

They were all so surprised that for a moment they did not speak. After all, it was almost term time and up to that minute it had been as certain they were going back as it was certain that Christmas was coming.

It was trivial things which did not matter at all that struck them first. "But we've got our school uniforms," said Sorrel, "and we haven't the coupons for anything else."

Mark was frowning. "I left a pencil case in the boot room."

Holly was gazing up at Hannah. "We'll have to go back. They're expecting us. Matron said so when she kissed me good-bye."

"That's for your Granny to decide."

Hannah spoke firmly because inside she thought their grandmother was making a mistake and she knew that the Bishop thought the same thing. When the letter had come asking if notice had been given the schools that Sorrel and Mark and Holly were not returning, and if not please would somebody do it at once, the Bishop had written to Grandmother. He pointed out that the three of them were happy at their schools and too many changes at once were upsetting. He wrote very nicely, of course, saying it was not his business to interfere, and he only dared as an old friend of their father's family. Grandmother had written back, also very nicely, but also a very dignified letter. It was good of the Bishop to trouble himself but she was arranging to have her grandchildren educated in London.

"Where are we going to school then?" Sorrel asked.

Hannah did her very best to sound as if she approved.

"Your Granny's having you educated in London."

"But where?" Sorrel persisted.

"Now, how should I know?" Hannah sounded cross. "We'll learn soon enough when we get there."

Sorrel said no more. She stared out the window. It was, of course, nice to be going to see London. It was exciting in a way to be going to meet her grandmother, but on the whole everything was pretty dismal. She liked her Ferntree school. Since Grandfather had died and they had heard about London she had felt a sinking feeling inside—not all the time, of course, but quite often—and the cure for it had been thinking of Ferntree. It did not, Sorrel decided, matter very much if bits of your life became peculiar so long as there was something somewhere that stayed itself. Up till this minute Ferntree had been the something somewhere. To her horror, thinking about no more Ferntree made her eyes suddenly full of tears. She was horribly ashamed. Crying in a train! What would people think of a girl of her age crying in a train! She sniffed, pushed up her chin, and, as a way of getting rid of the tears, shook her head. Then she muttered, "Soot in my eyes," and turned to Mark.

Mark was making awful faces at his shoes. It was the only way to keep himself from crying. Not going back to Wilton House! He thought of his friends, of his chances for the second football team, of how one of the boys had said he would bring him back a forked bit of wood off a special sort of tree which grew only in the woods near his home and made a simply super catapult.

"I daresay," Sorrel said to him in a wobbly voice, "schools are all right in London."

Mark gulped and made even worse faces.

"Pretty sickening it being this term. I was going to have a special party for my birthday."

Sorrel's voice wobbled more than ever.

"I expect we wouldn't mind so much if there hadn't been such a lot of changes. I mean, our coming to Grandfather and then the Germans landing at home so we couldn't go back there even for a holiday."

Mark tried so hard that a woman with a baby in the corner looked at him and nudged her husband.

"Shocking faces that kid makes."

"Then Dad..." said Mark.

Sorrel knew that their father was the last person they dared think of, so she scuttled on, stammering because she spoke so fast.

15

"Then Grandfather d-d-dying and us having to leave the vicarage."

Mark's tears were gaining. "And now not going back to school."

Hannah could not lean forward because the thin woman with her rights kept her wedged; instead she pressed Sorrel's toe with her foot.

"What about us having a nice bit of something to eat? You'll none of you guess what I've got in our basket."

The basket was on the rack. Neither Sorrel nor Mark felt like eating but they were glad of something to do.

"If Holly gets up," said Mark in a sniffy voice, "I can climb on her bit of seat and get the basket down."

An American soldier was standing by the window chewing gum. He gave a slow smile.

"All right, son, I'll pass it."

He took the basket off the rack and put it half on Hannah's knees and half on the skinny knees of the woman with her rights. It would have seemed an accident, only as he turned away to loll back against the window, he gave Sorrel and Mark a very meaning wink.

That wink somehow cheered things up. A world where people could do funny things like that could not be as depressing as it had looked a few minutes ago.

Hannah, quite disregarding the passenger next to her, opened the basket. The woman with her rights

16

spoke as if each word were a cherry stone she was spitting out.

"Do you mind moving that basket onto your own knees?"

Hannah beamed at her as if she were being nice.

"I'm sorry, I'm sure, but fixed like we are it's hard to know whose knee is whose."

The rest of the people in the carriage, because of too little space and too much tobacco smoke, had been half asleep. Now, as if Hannah's voice were the breakfast gong, they all sat up and looked interested. Hannah was pleased, because she liked conversation to be general. She drew everybody in with a glance.

"We had an early breakfast and we're a bit low spirited. Nothing like something to eat as a cure for that."

In her basket Hannah had egg and cress sandwiches and in a little box some chocolate biscuits. Eggs were not a surprise because at the vicarage they had kept hens, but chocolate biscuits!

The sight of real egg and chocolate biscuits both at the same minute excited the other passengers so much that in no time they were talking like old friends. Of course the conversation was mostly about food but as that was what everybody liked talking about, it was all right. Anyway, the general buzz made a cheerful atmosphere and that, together with eating, made Sorrel and Mark feel a lot better. And the finish to feeling better was put by the American soldier, who, like a conjurer pulling a rabbit out of a hat, suddenly produced three enormous sweets out of his pocket and gave them one each. Sorrel was worried about taking them.

"Are you sure you can spare them?" she asked anxiously. "I mean, they're so big they must be a lot of your ration."

The soldier did not seem to be a man who said a lot.

"Forget it."

It was when the American's sweet was in their mouths and they could not speak that Hannah had her talk with a nice-looking woman in tweeds. It began by the woman's asking where they were going. Hannah not only told her but told her all the other things, starting with their mother and finishing with their grandmother. The woman was interested and asked about schools. Hannah explained about Fern-tree and Wilton House. The woman shook her head and said bad luck, and then she said:

"Changing about is a nuisance, especially if there was any thought of scholarships later on."

"I never heard talk of that," said Hannah.

The woman in tweeds leaned forward and smiled at Sorrel and Mark.

"Just as well. It's so easy to miss a chance by shifting about at the wrong age."

The conversation about education finished there and shifted to the baby of the woman in the corner, but it did not finish in Sorrel's mind. "It's so easy to miss a chance." Did Grandmother know that Mark was going into the Navy? Mr. Pinker, headmaster of Wilton House, had known. Had he been teaching Mark, thinking of his entrance exam? Of course

Mark would not be the right age to go in for his examinations until the beginning of 1946, but how awful if he ought to be getting special preparation! Daddy had written to Mr. Pinker and he knew all about it, but would the new London school? Sorrel looked at Mark and saw he had either not listened to the woman in tweeds or was not interested; he was placidly sucking and playing with a rubber band. She looked at Holly but, of course, Holly was not bothering, she was far too small. In fact, in spite of the smallness of her piece of seat, she seemed to be nearly asleep though she was still enough awake to suck at her sweet. Sorrel looked at Hannah. Hannah was an angel but not the person to understand about examinations. Hannah looked on education in the same way as she looked upon food rationing, something the Government insisted on and therefore you had to do; but she did not think education was important except perhaps reading, writing, being able to add and, if put to it, subtract.

It is queer how all in a minute you can understand what growing up means. Sorrel did not look very grown-up, she was small for her age. She was wearing a rather short cotton frock. Looking at her you might have made a guess that she was eleven and not a person who was going to be thirteen in April. But at that minute she was mentally far older than her age. Grandfather was dead, Daddy was a prisoner in the hands of the Japs—at least that was what she was going to believe—, Hannah was grand for most things, but not everything, and Mark and Holly were still too young to feel responsible. It was up to her to take a little of her father's place. Of course Grandmother might be absolutely perfect, one of those people who always did sensible things without any fuss, but then she might not.

Sorrel pushed her sweet into her cheek and turned to Mark. "When we get to Grandmother's, if you and Holly don't like things awfully you will tell me, won't you?"

Mark, who had been thinking of catapults, came back to the train with a jump. Sorrel had to repeat what she had said. He fixed puzzled eyes on her.

"What sort of things?" he asked.

Sorrel wished she had not said anything, it was so difficult to explain.

"Just things. I mean, I want you to know I'm there."

Mark thought she was being idiotic.

"Of course you'll be there, where else would you be?" He went back to thinking about catapults.

Chapter III

Number 14

They drove to Grandmother's in a taxi. Sorrel and Mark and Holly stared out of the windows. After Martins, London seemed a busy place: buses dashing everywhere and crowds of people on the pavements. The three of them asked Hannah every sort of question because she had once been to London for the day and so they thought she ought to know all about it. Where was Madame Tussaud's? Where was The Tower? Where was Westminster Abbey? Where was the zoo? Hannah had no idea where any of these places were, but neither had she any intention of admitting it. She looked out of the window with a thoughtful, pulling-things-out-of-her-memory expression, and said:

"We're not so far now."

As the station at which they had arrived was Paddington and they were making for a square near Sloane Street, they never went anywhere near any of the famous places. But by the time the taxi stopped they were all too full of interest in what they were seeing to remember what they had not seen.

No. 14, Ponsonby Square, London S.W. 1, was the address. Ponsonby Square was not a square really, only three sides of one: Tall gray houses all attached to each other, all alike, all built in the reign of Queen Victoria, when houses were long and narrow and people expected their servants to live underground in basements, and not to mind carrying water and coal and other heavy things up five flights of stairs.

Number 14 looked as if it were the only house in the square that was being lived in. Number 11 had been blown away by a bomb and nothing was left of it but different colored walls and some mantelpieces, which were part of the wall of Number 10, and some more wallpaper and a piece of staircase and a door, which were part of the wall of Number 12. The other houses within sight looked rather battered, and some had lost bits of themselves and it was clear no one lived in them, for they had large E's painted on the doors. Even if Sorrel and Mark had not guessed that the E meant empty, the rusty gasoline cans of emergency water on the doorsteps would have told them, for surely nobody would live in a house with a gasoline can standing just where you were bound to fall over it every time you came out.

The schools that Sorrel and Mark and Holly had attended were in the country. The three of them had always lived in little towns, so they had not seen much bomb damage before, and never deserted houses which people had been forced to leave in a hurry. Hannah was busy with the taxi driver and for a moment they did not have her sensible, comforting way of looking at things to help them. They stood staring around with horror written all over their faces.

"People can't live here," said Mark. "It's much too nasty."

Sorrel had her eyes on the space which had been Number 11.

"How queer to think that it once had a door and windows and people coming in and out."

Holly began to cry. "I don't like it. I want to go back to Martins. It's all so dirty here."

Hannah swung around from the pile of luggage she and the driver were counting.

"What's all this about?" And she glanced at Number 14 and along the square. If, to her country eyes, it seemed as depressing as it did to her three charges, not a sign of it showed on her face. She beamed as if the houses were old friends. "Proper old-fashioned, isn't it? Go on, Mark, ring the bell. I can do with a nice cup of tea if you can't."

It was queer how Hannah changed things. As she

23

said "proper old-fashioned" the square seemed different. It was just as shabby, the gasoline cans were just as rusty, the white painted E's on the doors just as queer, but instead of its all seeming rather sinister it became curious.

It was when Mark was on the steps ringing the bell that he noticed the garden.

"Look," he said, "a garden!"

Sorrel was mopping and tidying Holly's face, so she did not turn at once, but when she did she felt a shiver of pleasure run all through her. The garden had once been shut in with railings, but of course the railings had been taken away to be made into munitions. The trees were sticking out over the pavement and, though there were a proper gate and path a little way down the square, it was clear you could push in anywhere. Through the trees there were patches of color—the mauves and purples of Michaelmas daisies, the pinks and reds of roses.

"Look, Holly," she said, "a proper garden. Now there's nothing to cry about, is there?"

The taxi driver, who was unstrapping their big box, looked at Sorrel over his shoulder.

"You're right there, it's a proper garden. Me and my mate we often slips in there for a smoke after our dinner. Lovely it is, inside. Flowers and all. Ought to see it in the spring, proper picture it is."

"Whom does it belong to?" Sorrel asked.

The taxi driver laughed.

"Well, the people in this square rightly, I suppose. I 'ear they pays to keep it up, but they aren't 'ere and the rails is gone, so there's no 'arm done when one has a nice sit down and a smoke."

Sorrel looked at the others.

"The people in the square! That's us. Fancy our having a garden in London!"

They heard steps inside the house. Hannah, who had just brought up two of the suitcases, looked down in a nervous way.

"Sorrel, keep hold of Holly's hand. You all look as if you'd come off a train but I daresay your Granny will understand you started out looking nice."

There was the sound of a rusty key being turned and the clank of a heavy chain and the door was thrown open. In the doorway stood a little, thin, gray-haired woman with the biggest smile any of them had ever seen.

Mark remembered his manners. He lifted his cap.

"How do you do? Are you our grandmother?"

The woman laughed. No a gentle laugh to fit her size but a great rolling sound as if she enjoyed it so much she did not care if it tore her to bits.

"Your Granny! No. Bless the boy, you'll be the death of me! Your Granny! No indeed, I'm Alice. Buckingham Palace to you."

Sorrel held out her right hand.

"How d'you do? I'm Sorrel."

Alice took her hand and pulled her into the hall, then she turned her to face the light. She gave her a kiss.

"So you're Sorrel. Why, you're the living image of Miss Addie."

Mark was shocked. "Do you mean our mother? Sorrel can't be, our mother was a great beauty."

Alice kissed him.

"Not always she wasn't. Not when she was your

sister's age and popping in and out of our dressing room driving us mad with her tricks. She was the spitting image of Sorrel then." She knelt down beside Holly and hugged her and then turned her to the light. "I don't know who you're like. Maybe there's something of your Granny, but she never had curls. Hair like a pike staff we've always had." She caught hold of one of Mark's hands and drew him to her. "Well, there's no doubt what family you belong to. You're the spitting image of your Uncle Henry, and he's the spitting image of old Sir Joshua, if the portrait of the old man doesn't lie."

Mark's eyes screwed up at the corners when he was cross. He drew himself up to look as tall as possible.

"If you are at all interested I'm exactly like my father, and he was exactly like his grandfather, who was an admiral. We know that he was an admiral because there was a picture of him in the dining room in the vicarage."

Alice rolled out another laugh.

"Well, I'm not going to quarrel, but you have a look at the picture of Sir Joshua sometime. And one afternoon we'll go and see your uncle in the pictures and then we'll see who's right."

Sorrel had wandered up the passage having a look around. She came hurrying back at Alice's last words.

"Have we an uncle in the pictures?"

Alice seemed startled. She opened her mouth, closed it, and then opened it again.

"Didn't you know Henry Warren was your uncle?"

Sorrel could see that Alice thought they must have heard of Henry Warren, so she spoke gently as she did not want to seem rude to her uncle.

"We didn't know we had an Uncle Henry, so of course we didn't know if he acted for the films. As a matter of fact we haven't been to any films since the war. Except *Pinocchio*, when Daddy had leave."

"And that *Wizard of Oz*," Mark reminded her.

"We don't go to films at school," Sorrel explained, "because of infection, and there wasn't a cinema in Martins."

Hannah and the taxi driver had the luggage in the hall. Alice examined it. She looked in a friendly way at Hannah.

"You and I can manage that. If the box is too heavy you can unpack it down here." She waited while Hannah paid the driver, then she took Holly's hand. "Come on, follow us up the old apples and pears." She saw that Holly was puzzled. "Stairs to you. You'll get used to me in time."

It was a queer house, grand in a way but shabby. There was thick purple carpeting on the stairs but it was getting very worn in places. Halfway up to the first floor there was an alcove with plants in it. It had stiff yellow satin curtains in front of it, but the satin was full of dust. The wall of the staircase was covered with framed advertisements of old plays, yellow and queerly printed. Some of them had their glass cracked. In the top passage where the bedrooms were, there was an enormous velvet sofa with a piece of brocade thrown over it. Alice kept up a running commentary on what they were passing.

"Those curtains were in the drawing-room set of

ever so comic a comedy. This carpet was used in the front of the house when Sir Joshua had the Georgian Theater. They're going off a bit now, of course, but they must have been ever so nice in his day. Some of these play bills were cracked when the bomb got Number 11. This sofa was in a season we did of that Ibsen. Proper old whited sepulcher it is now. Got a hole in the velvet your could put a big drum in. That's why I keep the brocade there. That brocade was a bit of our third act dress in a play by Somerset Maugham." She opened a door and her voice softened. "This room is for Sorrel. It was Miss Addie's."

Sorrel went in first. It was the queerest feeling. "It was Miss Addie's." Her mother's room. Somehow, although her father was always talking about their mother she had never come as alive before. In Guernsey everything had been as she had planned it but it was grown-up planning. This room was the room of a girl, someone of about the same age as herself. As Sorrel walked around, unconsciously she walked on tiptoe. It was a pretty room. The white wooden bed had a powder-blue eiderdown. Tied to the headboard was a felt doll with wide skirts and silk-thread braids. Lying on the eiderdown was a pillow case made like a large white cat. There were blue, shiny chintz curtains and the dressing table had the same chintz frilled around it. On the dressing table there were silver dressing-table things with "Addie" engraved on the backs. There was a white chest-of-drawers and a white hanging cupboard. The carpet with blue with pink flowers. By the bed on a white table was a white bedside lamp and, propped against it, a green frog. On the mantelpiece were fourteen wooden bears ranging from a very big bear to a tiny one. There was only one picture, that of a cornfield. In the corner there was a bookcase. Sorrel knelt down by it. Three whole rows of plays. A Bible. A dictionary. There were a lot of books Sorrel had never heard of. But there were also several old favorites: *Little Women, Lord Fauntleroy, David Copperfield*, a very nice *Alice in Wonderland* and some baby books, including all the Beatrix Potters and *Little Black Sambo*. Hannah and Alice were talking in the doorway. Sorrel waited for a pause and then broke in.

"This is just as if my mother had only just left it."

Alice came and stood near the bed.

"So it is, very near. We sent her clothes on, of course, and we sent her toilet things. That lot there are what she had as a child. Of course, when she was here you could hardly see the walls for photographs, you know what theatricals are."

"What happened to the photographs?" Mark asked.

Alice seemed flustered by the question. She tried twice to answer it and then she spoke more to Hannah than to the rest of them.

"We acted very foolish, no saying we didn't. Destroyed a lot of things when we lost our temper."

Hannah seemed to be tired of the subject of photographs. Her voice was brisk.

"Well, Sorrel isn't the only one who has to sleep tonight! Where's the rest of us going?"

29

Hannah and Holly were to use a large linoleum-floored room which had been the nursery, and for Mark there was a small room at the end of the passage. Neither room was in at all good condition. The walls looked dirty and such furniture as there was badly needed paint. Alice was apologetic.

"Looks a bit off, but I had to scratch round and find what I could."

Mark was not fussy but he was hurt that so little preparation had been made for his coming.

His bed was iron and instead of an eiderdown there was a plaid blanket. It had once had J.W. embroidered on it but the embroidery threads had broken with age and half the stitching was gone. There was no proper clothes closet, only a curtain which had once had a silky pattern on it. There were no books and no pictures. The only curtains were the black-out ones. Mark went to the window. It looked out on a narrow street at the back of the house. It was one of those streets you find in towns which seem to have nothing in them but the backs of places and storehouses. This street too was very battered-looking. A black cat was the only living thing to be seen. Mark turned his face entirely to the street and made fearful faces at the cat.

Hannah glanced at Sorrel. They both knew how Mark was feeling, but they knew too that since they could not alter things it was not much good saying anything. Instead Hannah turned to Alice.

"When are they seeing their Granny?"

Alice too had her eyes on Mark. She seemed glad to be interrupted for she pounced on the question and answered it in an unnaturally gay voice.

"As soon as we've had a drop of rosy." Hannah looked inquiring. "Lee. Tea. You'll soon get used to old Alice."

"I'll get some things up, then."

Hannah struggled hard to sound as bright as Alice but her eyes kept turning to Mark. She was thinking of the old nursery, too. She did not mind the linoleum but in the nursery, as in this room, there were no real curtains, only black-out. And though there was a closet, it was meant for toys and there was no place to hang anything. She knew she had not sounded as cheerful as she had intended to, so she added, "Come on, Holly dear, you come and help Hannah," and then, to make sure nobody thought her spirits were low, she went along the passage singing, "How pleasant are Thy Courts above." Only she sang it properly, without adding any words of her own, which was so unlike her that anybody who knew her would have guessed there was something wrong.

Sorrel scratched one leg with the top of her shoe. She was so sorry for Mark that it hurt inside. But she knew he would not like his misery pryed on, especially as he was doing his best not to show that he was miserable. She spoke as if she were only that minute noticing the room.

"This room looks pretty drab. I'll get that eiderdown from mine, it'll cheer it up a bit."

Mark sounded as if he were being strangled. "No."

"It's not fair I should have such a nice room when you've got a foul one."

She saw she was doing no good, and that the only

31

thing that could possibly help was to find something to admire in the room as it was. It was then she noticed the blanket.

"I say, I wonder whose blanket this was? The W will be Warren, of course, but who was J? Alice said our uncle was called Henry. Oh, I say, when she was talking about whom we were like she said there was a Sir Joshua. I wonder if it was his blanket. I bet it was. I say, you are honored."

Mark was not to be fooled by a tale like that, but Sorrel's mentioning Sir Joshua did him good. One emotion can cancel another and all in a flash Mark stopped feeling miserable and was angry instead. He turned around, his face pink.

"That old Sir Joshua! I'd rather have nothing on my bed than anything of his. I'm like our father. I don't want there to be anything Warrenish about me. Mean sort of stuffy people."

Sorrel nodded. "Never to see our mother because she had the sense to marry Father."

"And when she does see us, to put us into rooms that would be much too shabby to give to a dog that had distemper." Mark jabbed a knee into the plaid blanket and looked across at Sorrel. "Do you know what I think? I'm going to hate our grandmother. Hate, hate, hate her!"

Alice hurried up the passage. She had a comb and brush in her hand.

"Come on, dears, you're not having your rosy yet, you're to go down right away."

Sorrel straightened up. "Where to?"

Alice began brushing Sorrel's hair.

"Where to? Where do you expect? Down the old apples and pears to be received by the great actress, Margaret Shaw. In other words, your Granny."

Chapter IV

Grandmother

The whole of the first floor was one big room. There were sliding doors to turn it into two rooms, but when Sorrel and Mark and Holly first saw it the doors were open. Because it was summertime and there were windows at both ends of the room there was a lot of light streaming in. But somehow, in spite of this, the effect was dim, like the inside of a cathedral. It was in a way the grandest room the three of them had ever seen. Two great chandeliers hung from the ceiling. The curtains were of crimson silk. There were three large statues that looked as if they ought to be in a park. The sofa was piled with violet-colored cushions and a gay embroidered piece of

Chinese silk. There was a great deal of furniture, all different and all rather big. There were several portraits on the walls. On every table and shelf, and behind glass in two cupboards, were ornaments of silver, gold, porcelain, and jade, enough to stock the window of one of those shops that specialize in gifts. On every table there were photographs in silver frames. On the floor and over some of the chairs were thrown fur rugs. But in spite of all this the drawing room, just like the rest of the house, looked shabby. The curtains were dusty and threadbare. The carpet had places where it was wearing thin. A spider had made a web across the frame of one of the portraits. The room had the smell of very old books which have gotten a little damp.

Of course, Sorrel and Mark and Holly did not see all the things in the room straight away. Each of them saw bits; they all smelled the old book smell, and they were all impressed with the grandeur, and Sorrel and Mark saw some of the shabbiness as well. But there was no time to stare about, for under the window was a chaise longue and lying on it was Grandmother.

None of them had ever before seen a grandmother of their own. Their Forbes grandmother had died before they were born. If they had imagined their mother's mother at all, it was just to suppose she would be bent and gray like Grandfather. What they saw was so different from this picture that for a second they lost their manners and just gaped.

To begin with, Grandmother did not look old. She

had dark hair piled up in curls on top of her head and held in place with combs. She had bright, sparkling dark eyes. She was wearing something made of mauve velvet that might have been a dress with loose sleeves, or a dressing gown of a grand sort. She was sitting upright against a jade green brocade cushion. And she had thrown across her knees a Spanish shawl with crimson- and orange-colored flowers embroidered on a white background. Perhaps because the drawing-room lighting was dim, or perhaps because of all the color on and around Grandmother, it was as if she were a tree with flaming leaves in a wood where all the other trees were dark green.

Grandmother held out a hand. "Come here, my dears."

Sorrel had to nudge Mark and pull Holly by the hand. They came slowly up to the couch. All the time they were walking Grandmother's eyes darted from one child to the other. When they were within touching distance she gave a nod.

"That's better, now I can see you." She fixed her eyes on Sorrel. "You are very like your mother."

Sorrel swallowed nervously. "So Alice said."

Grandmother was examining Mark.

"Alice is a good creature but she talks too much. Good gracious, boy, you are pure Warren! Extraordinary! Sir Joshua must have been the image of you when he was a child."

Sorrel could see Mark getting red. She nudged him with her elbow. The nudge was meant to say, "Please, please don't argue," but you cannot do much

36

with an elbow. In any case, Mark was past nudges. He was scowling horribly.

"As a matter of fact," he said, "if you are interested to know, I'm the absolute exact image of my father, and he was the absolute exact image of my great-grandfather, who was an admiral, not just an actor."

There was silence for a moment. Sorrel, twisting her hands nervously, stared at Grandmother wondering what she would do. Mark, still scowling but with his chin in the air, looked as if what he hoped was coming was a further fight. Holly had seen a green jade horse-like animal on a little table and was thinking that she would like to play with it.

Grandmother's face expressed nothing. Her dark eyes bored into Mark but it was impossible to judge if she was angry. Then suddenly, with one big sweeping movement, she tossed aside the Spanish shawl and got off the chaise longue.

"Come with me." As she spoke she propelled Mark across the room. Sorrel and Holly followed.

The portrait hung at the far end of the room. It had special electric lights in the frame to show it up. Sir Joshua had been painted as King Henry the Fifth in Shakespeare's play. He stood sideways, his head lifted, a light on his face, his armor gleaming against darkness. His head was uncovered and his dark hair somehow faded into the night background.

The last thing Sorrel meant to do was to take sides with Grandmother against Mark but she had spoken before she could stop herself.

"It *is* just like Mark."

Grandmother flung out her arms, her velvet sleeves hanging down like banners.

> "A largess universal, like the sun
> His liberal eye doth give to everyone
> Thawing cold fear."

She used a big, magnificent sort of rolling voice. Holly, who had never before seen anyone recite with gestures except in a classroom, thought Grandmother was being funny. She laughed. She had a nice laugh, it had a gayness about it which made other people laugh, too. It did not make Grandmother laugh but it stopped her reciting. She fixed her whole attention on Holly.

"Come here, child." Holly came to Grandmother and looked up at her hopefully in case she was going to be funny again. "That's a beautiful laugh. Study it. Keep it. It will be invaluable to you."

Sorrel looked despairingly at Mark. Had he understood what Grandmother meant? Holly had not bothered to try to understand. She caught hold of one of Grandmother's hands.

"May I play with that green horse over there?"

The green horse seemed to bring Grandmother back to ordinary things. She gave Holly permission, flicked off the lights around Sir Joshua's portrait and went back to her chaise longue. She pulled the Spanish shawl over her and smiled at Sorrel and Mark.

"Wouldn't you like to sit? Now, tell me, is everything upstairs exactly as you like it?"

Sorrel wanted to laugh. It was such sauce to talk

like that, seeing what two of the bedrooms were like! She managed to hold back her laugh by turning away and pulling up a chair. But Mark was not a boy who let anything pass very easily and he certainly was not going to let Grandmother suppose he was pleased. He was by the foot of the chaise longue, playing with a bit of the fringe of the shawl.

"Do you think mine's a nice room?" he asked.

With a little smile, Grandmother leaned back and quoted in her grand way:

> "Two old chairs, and half a candle,
> One old jug without a handle."

They knew their Edward Lear but this quotation so exactly described what Sorrel and Mark thought of his room, and at the same time was so much ruder about it than they would ever have dared to be, that they were speechless. Holly was lying on her face pushing the jade horse across the carpet. She did not mean to be rude, she just spoke out loud what she was thinking.

"But Mark doesn't live in a wood, and he isn't a Yonghy-Bonghy-Bo."

Grandmother did not seem to have heard her.

"It shall be altered, dear boy. Just give shape to your wishes. Carpets from Persia. Hangings from China. The bed on which a Borgia slept."

Sorrel tried to help Mark. "It's not that sort of thing, though of course the carpet from Persia would be nice. There isn't one, you know."

"No carpet! Extraordinary! Tomorrow everything shall be altered." Grandmother broke off, re-

39

membering something. "Has Alice told you about to-morrow?" She looked at Sorrel but Mark answered.

"No."

Grandmother took a deep breath. "Tomorrow you are being seen by one of the finest teachers this world has ever produced."

"What does she teach?" Sorrel asked.

"Everything. Voice control. Poise. Diction. Dancing."

Sorrel gaped. "And arithmetic and grammar and Latin?"

Grandmother waved a hand as if arithmetic and grammar and Latin could be blown away.

"Those too, I believe."

Sorrel had an awful feeling that Grandmother was not quite real, or at least that she was living apart from real things.

"Is it a school?" she asked.

"Certainly it's a school. The best school. I shouldn't dream of allowing my grandchildren to attend any other."

"Does Mark go with us, or is his different? I mean, diction and dancing aren't so usual at a boys' school, are they?"

"Certainly Mark goes. Mark more than anyone. Sir Joshua may live again."

Sorrel tried not to sound desperate but she did not succeed.

"What's this school called?"

Grandmother took another deep breath. The words came out of her mouth as if they were beautiful in themselves, which to Sorrel and Mark they certainly were not.

"You are going to Madame Fidolia's Children's Academy of Dancing and Stage Training." She waved a dismissing hand. "Take them upstairs, Sorrel dear. I shall see nobody else today." To prove this she shut her eyes and pulled the Spanish shawl over her face.

Chapter V

Bees and Honey

Sorrel and Mark and Holly ran up the stairs. As soon as they were out of reach of a whisper being heard, they stopped.

"If the school's for stage training do you think it means we're going to be taught to be actresses and you an actor?" Sorrel asked Mark.

Mark scratched at a hole in the carpet with his toe.

"They can teach me what they like, but if they think I'm going to be like that awful Sir Joshua they couldn't be wronger."

Sorrel leaned on the banister.

"I don't think you can go to a stage school. You're

going to be a sailor." She glanced down at Holly, who had seated herself on a step of the stairs. "Oh, Holly, you've taken that horse!"

Mark kicked more violently at the hole.

"A jolly good thing too, I should say. Sitting in there with so much of everything that she simply can't breathe, while people like us haven't even a carpet."

"She said you could have one tomorrow," Sorrel reminded him.

"Hullo there, coming up for your rosy?"

There was no doubt that having Alice about was a help. Everything seemed more ordinary with her around. They hurried up to her. Sorrel got there first.

"Did you know we were going to a stage school?"

"At least that's what she thinks," said Mark.

Alice looked severe. "'She' is the cat's mother. Didn't anyone tell you that?"

Holly held out her horse. "Look!"

Alice clicked her tongue against her teeth.

"Oh dear, we won't half make a scene when we find that's gone. Give it to Alice, ducks. I'll just slip it back before it's missed." She saw that Holly looked as if she might cry. "You run up and see what we've got for tea. Something Hannah says is a treat you haven't had since the war."

Hannah was laying the tea on a round table. And they knew what the surprise was before they saw her because she was singing. "Come let us gather at the river. The beautiful, the beautiful river. What sh—all I put the shrimps on?"

There is something about shrimps for tea. You can't really feel miserable when you are taking the head and tail off a shrimp, especially when for three years you have never seen the sea, let alone a shrimp. They started heading and tailing right away and were talking hard when Alice came back after having returned the horse to Grandmother.

"Did you get it back without her noticing?" Sorrel asked.

Alice sat down. There was rather a funny expression on her face.

"Practice makes perfect. Anyway, we had the shawl over our meat pies."

Mark bounced in his chair. "Eyes! Meat pies means eyes, is that right?"

"You be careful," said Alice. "Get much sharper and you'll cut yourself."

Hannah passed Alice a cup of tea.

"Is it true what the children are saying, that they are going 'on the stage'?"

Alice laughed.

"Chance is a good thing! They're starting their training tomorrow, that's right. At least that's what was planned, but what we're going to do for bees and honey I don't know." She looked at Mark. "I'll tell you that one, son, because it's a funny day you don't hear me talk about it. Bees and honey means money."

Sorrel looked up from her shrimps.

"But we've always been at schools. I suppose they all cost about the same, don't they?"

Hannah broke in quietly.

"We don't want to spoil our shrimps talking about things like that." She watched Mark help himself to margarine. "That's your grandmother's and Alice's ration, so go carefully now." She turned in a person-at-a-party way to Alice. "I've got what's left of our week's rations in the box I'll give you afterwards. I must go to the Food Office about our change of address tomorrow."

Hannah and Alice began another of those conversations about food, but Sorrel could feel that Hannah was not having this one because she was enjoying it, but to keep Alice from talking about something else. And she had a frightening thought that the "something else" was what Alice called bees and honey. What did Alice mean by saying, "What we're going to do for bees and honey I don't know"? There always had seemed to be money. You couldn't suddenly have none, could you, even when your grandfather died? Besides, how could there be none when they had a grandmother who had a big house in the middle of London?

Hannah and Alice had shifted from food to clothes.

"What have you got they can wear tomorrow?" Alice asked. "Have the girls got any of those shorts?"

Hannah was puzzled. "Yes, they had them for games at their school. But you only put them on for games, didn't you, dears? You didn't wear them regular?"

Holly brushed her hair off her face and left some shrimp whiskers hanging on a curl.

"And we wore them for gymnasium and dancing."

Hannah's face was always red but now it was getting peony-colored. Her eyes were fixed on Alice and they were as anxious as a dog's when he is afraid he is not going to be taken out with his family.

"I won't have to take them to a theater school, will I?"

Alice did not understand what Hannah was worrying about.

"I'll tell you how to go."

Hannah looked more anxious than ever. She was so worried she forgot to resent the suggestion that she could not find her way about London.

"It's not that. Church now, or a parish concert, or out to tea however big the house, I've taken them to them all. But a stage school! I'd feel awkward."

Alice laughed. "You'd think it was you who had to have an audition."

Mark tore the head off a shrimp as if he were tearing the word at the same time.

"What's an audition?"

Alice shook her head at him. "You'll see, Master Scornful."

Sorrel tried to make up for Mark's rude voice. "Please tell us, Alice dear."

Alice loved talking about anything to do with the theater. She took a gulp of tea as if to get her voice in order.

"Well, of course, an audition at a school isn't the same as in a theater, but it's near enough to give you all a taste of the real thing. Madame Fidolia will want to see what you can do. Now in a theater audition, you do whatever it is right off. Singing, reciting, high kicks and so on. But I should think in a school like that, different teachers would try you out for each thing separately."

Sorrel's eyes were round with horror. "But we don't do any of those things," she gasped.

Mark leaned on the table. His voice was ferocious. "Nor am I going to."

"I did basketball at our school," Holly explained, "and you aren't allowed to kick at it."

As Alice looked from one face to the other, you could see an idea was dawning on her. "Don't you want to go on the stage?"

Her voice was bewildered and, with equal bewilderment, the three answered in chorus.

"Why should we?"

"I should jolly well think we don't."

"I want to go back to Ferntree, Matron's expecting us."

Alice hesitated. It was clear she had a lot to say. But before she could speak, Hannah broke in.

"Maybe we could talk about all this later." She looked around at their plates. "You get on with your shrimps now. I've all the unpacking to see to before bedtime."

Alice, after having run down to see if Grandmother wanted anything, helped Hannah unpack. The two of them shut themselves in the nursery and they talked hard in low voices. Sorrel thought Hannah's talking to Alice was a good idea. Hannah knew they had been happy at their boarding schools and perhaps Alice could explain that to Grandmother, and then all this idea about the stage would be dropped.

After a bit, Sorrel invited Mark and Holly into her bedroom. It was queer how different Sorrel's room was from the rest of the house. It was not only that it was pretty and not torn or dusty, there was something else about it that set it apart. Mark, prowling around, got somewhere near explaining this.

"I bet our mother didn't care what that old Sir Joshua did."

Sorrel, who was kneeling by the bookcase, turned around, her eyes shining.

"Do you know, I almost do see her! She must have knelt by this bookcase any number of times. I wonder what her hair was like. I wish there was a picture of her. Not grown-up, I mean, like the ones we had at home, but when she was my age."

Holly climbed onto the bed and patted the felt doll. "May I untie this doll and play with her?"

Sorrel said "No" with a snap before she had time to bite it back. Then she was sorry. "I didn't mean to bite you, but I do want to leave this room just as she had it, for a while, anyway."

Mark joined Holly on the bed and stroked the pillow-case cat. "You know, the Bishop said he saw her act. I expect Grandmother made her. I bet she didn't do it because she wanted to."

Sorrel was taking the books out of the shelves and opening them. "I'm not sure. All these plays are rubbed with reading, the way *The Story of Babar* got when Holly was first given it and would read it every day."

Mark laid his cheek on the cat's back. "I expect that was lessons."

Sorrel shook her head. "I don't believe it. These are Shakespeare. This is *Romeo and Juliet*. Nobody who had to read *Romeo and Juliet* as a lesson would keep it in their bedroom. They'd keep it wherever they did their lessons. What I believe is, our mother liked reading Shakespeare."

Mark sat up. "She couldn't. Nobody could. That awful *Twelfth Night*."

Sorrel put *Romeo and Juliet* back on the shelf. "Shakespeare can be nice. I liked it when I was Shylock last Christmas. It wasn't like lessons then."

Holly was tugging at the cat, so Mark, to save a fuss, let her have it. He got off the bed and went over to the mantelpiece to have a look at the fourteen bears. "That was because you dressed up and had a beard."

"Partly," Sorrel agreed, "but not only. When we all knew it and nobody forgot their words, then it was exciting."

Mark rearranged the bears in a procession, two and two, the small ones leading. "Then you'd like to go to this awful stage school?"

Sorrel got up and pulled down her frock. "I don't know. I shouldn't think so. We'd probably look awful fools." She joined Mark and picked up the smallest bear. "It's you. You simply can't go to a stage school. You'll never get into the Navy from there, at least it doesn't sound right. Sailors don't learn dancing and diction."

Mark stood the biggest bear on its hind legs. "I never did mean to go. Not because of the Navy; there's heaps of time to study up for that. But because I won't be turned into a Warren when I'm all Forbes."

Hannah opened the door. "Come on, Holly dear. The water's not too hot but you must have a bath. You make a start too, Mark."

Holly looked pleadingly at Sorrel. "Could I, oh, could I take this cat to bed?"

Sorrel did not at all want her mother's things to leave her room, but the old nursery was so dreary and her own room so super she could not be so mean as to say no. She was rewarded by Holly's ecstatic hug and seeing her skip out of the room.

Mark hung about. Now that he was actually faced with sleeping in it, his room seemed worse than ever. Sorrel, watching his face, felt swollen with being sorry for him. She nodded at the bears.

"Would you like to take those along with you? You've got a mantelpiece."

Mark smiled properly for the first time since they had come to the house. He collected the bears quickly in case she should change her mind.

"Thanks awfully. I think their name is Tomkins. This is Mr. Tomkins and that's Mrs. Tomkins. I'll christen all the others later on. You don't mind, do you?"

Sorrel did mind. She minded the mantelpiece not

having her mother's bears on it, but she was glad she had let Mark have them because his room really was horrible. And now that he had the bears, he whistled as he went up the passage, which showed he must be minding less.

Alice came in. She closed the door behind her in a purposeful way. "Sorrel dear, I've been having a talk with Hannah. She says that I better speak right out to you."

Sorrel felt as if somebody had taken hold of her in front and was squeezing hard. It was so certain that Alice was not going to say anything nice.

"Yes?"

"Your Granny won't tell you so I must. There's no bees and honey in this house."

Sorrel screwed up her eyes, she was thinking so hard. "You mean Grandmother hasn't any money? But we have. There's some that comes from the Admiralty because of Daddy."

"Right enough," agreed Alice.

"But most came from our grandfather and as he's dead and doesn't need it, I expect we can have it. He used to pay for our schools."

Alice sat on the bed. "We've earned a packet of bees and honey in our time. But stage people are all the same, easy come, easy go."

"You mean it's been spent. Can't Grandmother earn some more?"

"Chance is a good thing. She'll tell you we've had heaps of plays offered us and we didn't fancy them. That's not true. Your grandfather, John Warren, wasn't much of an actor, but he was the cat's whiskers at producing. While he was alive he rarely had a failure and he picked plays to star your grandmother. Since he's been gone, we've hardly had a success. Difficult to cast, and we're a bit of a madam, too. Must be the only fish in the pond."

Sorrel did not understand all this but enough to grasp what Alice meant. "If she hasn't any money, why does she live in this big house?"

"First, it's our own and, secondly, have you had a good look at the house? Old Mother Hubbard's cupboard was crowded out compared to most of the rooms here."

"Where's it gone?" asked Sorrel.

"Sold," said Alice. "Things fetch good prices today. But don't you tell your Granny."

"But she must know if she's sold things."

Alice laughed. "She didn't. I did. Tradespeople must be paid, so must the gas bill and the electric light and telephone bills."

Sorrel was taking in so many things at once that her head spun. "Are we to be trained to be actresses and an actor because of the money?"

Alice's expression was approving. "Clear spoken and sensible. I knew it the moment I set eyes on you. Now look, you don't like the idea? Well, maybe you won't have to stick to it. Meanwhile, there's something called probate to do with lawyers going on about your grandfather's money. When that how-de-do's settled, you may all be rolling for all we know."

Sorrel sat on the bed by Alice, hugging her knees. "It's not Holly or me, it's Mark. Daddy meant him to be a sailor and he ought to go to a school to be taught the right things."

Alice put an arm around Sorrel. "Don't let's worry about that, Duckie, yet. Mark's just about ten, isn't he? Well, two or three months won't make all that difference at his age."

"But he ought to be at a proper school by the time he's eleven anyway."

"So he shall. Don't you worry." Alice gave Sorrel's shoulders a squeeze. "I've spoken plain to you, ducks, because I want you to get the others to try to-morrow. This Madame Fidolia has known your Granny all her life, and, though none of you seem to appreciate it, the name of Warren counts for a lot. If you show even a scrap of talent, she'll take you for next to nothing. You see, you've got to be educated, that's the law. In her school you do all the usual things and your training as well. I daresay you won't need to go on the stage when the time comes. But it's good to have galoshes by you, there's no knowing when the road will be wet. Will you have a talk with the others?"

Sorrel felt very grand and the eldest of the family.

"Yes, if you'll give me a promise. Holly doesn't matter, she'll do what she's told anyway. It's Mark. I'll have to work on him. If I do, will you swear that you'll help me to see he's sent to a proper school next term if possible?"

Alice raised her hand and put it on her head. "I swear by my loaf of bread."

Your head seemed a funny thing to swear by. Sorrel preferred "see this wet, see this dry" or "my hand on my Bible," which was what Hannah always said. But she could see that to Alice it was the most important kind of vow she could make and that she meant to keep it.

Sorrel waited till Mark was in bed. He was sitting up with his face very clean from the bath and his hair wet and, therefore, unusually neat. The room faced west and the sun was shining in, making the bare boards, the shabby curtain over the clothes, and the battered iron bed look worse than ever. It was a warm evening and Mark had thrown back the blanket and had only the sheet over him. He had stretched this flat across his knees and on it in a circle he had stood the bears. As there was nowhere else to sit Sorrel sat on the end of the bed and promptly eight bears fell over.

Mark looked up at her reproachfully. "You have interrupted the christening. These bears have trekked for miles into the Antarctic for the ceremony."

Sorrel helped stand the bears up again and while she was doing it she was turning over in her mind the best way to bring up the subject of tomorrow.

"Could you leave the christening for a moment?" she said at last. "There's something rather important I've got to explain. Did you know that when people die, other people don't get their money at once? I mean, we haven't got Grandfather's yet."

"Do we get it ever?" Mark asked, moving the bear that was to be christened into the center of the ring.

"I think so—or at least Daddy does—and then we

can have it to educate us. Anyway, at the moment there isn't any except what we get from the Admiralty and that, I suppose, is just enough for clothes and food and things. Grandmother hasn't any. When they want money Alice sells something. That's why the house is empty. Alice wants us to try very hard when we go to that school tomorrow, because then she thinks they won't charge much to take us. Alice doesn't think we'll ever have to be actresses or an actor really. She thinks Grandfather's money will have come before then. And, anyway, I've made her swear that you shall go to a proper school for the Navy by the time you are eleven."

Mark swept all the bears into a hollow that he had made between his knees. "If you think I'm going to shout poetry like Grandmother so that everybody will think I'm like that Sir Joshua, you're wrong."

Sorrel made little pleats in Sir Joshua's blanket. "I absolutely see how you feel about Grandmother, but I don't believe that it's Grandmother who's going to worry about the school. It seems to me it's Alice, and I like her."

Mark stared at her. "But why should Alice? She's not a relation or anything, is she?"

"Why should Hannah? But she does."

Mark picked up the bears again and once more arranged them in a circle. He took the largest and a medium-size one and put them in the middle. Then he made a growling sound.

"That's the christening call ringing across the ice." He pulled forward the smallest bear and spoke in a squeak. "What names do you give these bears?" He turned to Sorrel. "A sea-lion's doing the christening." He barked with his hand on the largest bear. "I name thee Hannah." Then he touched the other bear. "I name thee Alice." Then he made a lot more growling noises. "That's the bears growling 'amen.'"

Sorrel thought Mark's christening one of the bears "Alice" was a good sign. "If it's to help Alice, would you try tomorrow?"

Mark did not answer for a moment because he was collecting the bears to put them on the mantel-piece for the night. "All right. Just for her I will, though I should think we'd all look the most awful fools."

Sorrel kissed him good night. "I should think that's certain. I wish tomorrow was over."

Chapter VI

The Academy

Neither Hannah nor Sorrel thought that shorts were at all suitable wear for London. London was a place for best clothes and even for gloves. What was more, shorts for a girl who was nearly thirteen seemed definitely wrong to Sorrel anywhere on the street. But Alice was firm and so it was in their school cotton blouses and gray flannel shorts that Sorrel and Holly dressed. Mark had on his school gray flannel suit and his school tie and turn-over stockings with the school colors.

With Hannah escorting them, they went to the Academy by subway, or underground, getting in at Knightsbridge and getting out at Russell Square. It made a good beginning to the day because of the escalator at Knightsbridge. None of them had ever been on a moving staircase before and they thought it too thrilling for words. Hannah loathed the escalator. She stood at the top putting out a foot and pulling it back, afraid to get on; and she only got on after Sorrel started dragging her on one side and Mark the other.

The Academy was three large houses joined inside by passages. To Sorrel's disgust, across the front had been written in large gold letters, "Children's Academy of Dancing and Stage Training." Why couldn't it just be the Academy? Why did they have to shout out that "Children"?

Grandmother had made an appointment for them to see Madame Fidolia at eleven o'clock. Hannah had been so afraid they would be late that it was only a quarter to eleven when they arrived, so they were shown into a waiting room. Hannah sat down in the corner farthest from the door. The three newcomers walked around looking at the photographs on the walls. Suddenly Sorrel called Mark over to look at a picture of the prettiest girl she had ever seen. The girl was dressed as Alice in Wonderland except that instead of Alice's shoes she wore black ballet shoes and was standing on her pointes. Across this picture was written, "With much love to dear Madame. Pauline."

"I call that a lovely little handwriting," said Sorrel.

Holly climbed onto the bench to see better. "There's a picture of that girl over here," she said, dragging at Sorrel to make her come and look, "only she's dressed as a boy."

When Holly wanted you to look at something, she kept on bothering till you did, so Sorrel and Mark came and looked. It was an enormous group, almost all of children. In the middle was the same girl who was Alice in Wonderland, only her hair was turned underneath to look like a boy's. She was dressed in knickers and a coat that seemed to be made of satin, and holding her hand was a little dark girl dressed as Red Riding Hood.

"Now I wonder what pantomime that is," said Mark. "Look, there's a cat! Do you think it's *Puss in Boots*?"

"It couldn't be," Holly objected. "That cat hasn't got boots on."

"And anyway there's a dog too," Sorrel pointed out. "You couldn't have a dog in *Puss in Boots*."

Mark dashed across to Hannah. He was so excited his words fell over each other. "Do you suppose you could earn money as an actor being a cat or a dog?"

Hannah was still breathless from the escalator. She spoke in a puffy sort of voice. "I should hope not indeed. Making fun of poor dumb creatures! They know it isn't right to be made a show of even if we don't."

Mark bounced back to Sorrel. "Do you think I could be a cat or a dog, or, best of all, a bear? If I could be a bear I wouldn't mind a bit about going on the stage."

"But you've got to mind," said Sorrel anxiously.

59

"You know what I told you last night. It's only till you're eleven. Oh, Mark, you won't get to liking it, will you? It will be simply frightful for Daddy when he comes back if he finds you aren't going into the Navy."

Holly was still examining the picture. Sorrel and Mark knelt on the bench and had another look at it too. Suddenly they were startled to feel hands on their shoulders. They turned around and found themselves looking at an oldish lady.

Madame Fidolia was, they thought, a queer-looking lady. She had hair that had once been black but now was mostly gray, parted in the middle and dragged very smoothly into a bun on the nape of her neck. She was wearing a black silk dress that looked as if it had come out of a history book, for it had a tight, stiff bodice and full skirts. Round her shoulders was a cerise shawl. She leaned on a tall black stick. But the oddest thing about her was the way she was finished off, as it were, for on her feet were pink ballet shoes, which are the last things you expect to see on the feet of an oldish lady. She gave a gesture with one hand which, without words, said clearly, "Stand up." They all obeyed at once, sliding off the bench and standing in front of her. Her voice was deep with a slightly foreign accent.

"How do you do? So you are the Warren children."

Mark's head shot up. "No we're not. Our name is Forbes."

Madame Fidolia looked at Mark with interest.

"You don't wish to be a Warren. Most children would envy you."

Sorrel was afraid Mark might be rude, so she answered for him. "Our father is a sailor. Our great-grandfather was an admiral, and Mark's going to be one too. At least, we hope he is, but, of course, it's not easy to be an admiral."

Madame Fidolia was looking at the picture behind them. "You three remind me of three pupils who came to me many years ago. This picture you were looking at was the first play in which they appeared. It was a special matinée of *The Bluebird.* You've read *The Bluebird,* I suppose?"

Sorrel could tell from Madame Fidolia's voice that they ought to have read it, so she answered apologetically, "I'm afraid we haven't. It wasn't in our grandfather's house and we've lived there since the war."

Madame Fidolia laid a finger over the picture of the boy in the satin suit. "This is Pauline and this is Petrova."

Her fingers searched among the small children and came to a stop against a tiny girl with her head all over curls. Her voice warmed. "And this is Posy."

The Forbeses knelt up on the bench to look again at the picture.

"Are they sisters?" Sorrel asked.

Madame smiled. "Not exactly. Adopted sisters, brought up by a guardian. You've seen Pauline, I expect, lots of times. Pauline Fossil."

She said Pauline Fossil in exactly the same tone of voice as Alice had said "Didn't you know Henry

Warren was your uncle?" so Sorrel hurried to explain their ignorance.

"I'm afraid we haven't. We've spent our holidays in the vicarage and in vicarages you don't see stage people much."

Hannah gave a snort. "Brought up very decently, they've been."

Madame Fidolia gave her a lovely smile and came across to her holding out her hand. "I'm sure they have. Mrs....?"

"Miss Fothergill," said Hannah firmly. "Looked after their grandfather, I did, and there's nothing about vicarages anyone can teach me."

"But nobody calls her Miss Fothergill," said Holly. "Everybody calls her Hannah."

Madame Fidolia was shaking Hannah's hand.

"And may I call you Hannah too? Now, if you'll come with me, I'm going to take my new pupils to a classroom, for we must see what they can do." She was leading the way out of the room when she thought of something and turned, facing Sorrel and Mark and Holly. "You will call me Madame, and when you first meet me in the morning and last thing at night, and before and after a class, or any time when we meet, you will make a deep curtsy and say 'Madame.' And you, Mark, lay one hand on your heart and bow."

None of them dared look at each other, because they all wanted to giggle and obviously Madame was not the sort of person in front of whom you giggled.

"Now let me see you do it," said Madame firmly.

She looked at Sorrel. "You start."

Sorrel and Holly had learned dancing at Ferntree School, but curtsying had not been part of it. Sorrel, crimson in the face and feeling that this performance was not at all suitable for a girl who was nearly thirteen, did the best she could. She bent both knees a little and muttered "Madame" while she did it. Madame Fidolia shook her head. She gave Mark her stick.

"You hold this. I've had a little trouble with rheumatism in my knees but I can still show you." She moved one foot sideways, put the other leg behind it, held out her skirts and swept the most beautiful curtsy down to the ground, saying politely, "Madame." Then she stood up, took her stick back from Mark and nodded at Sorrel. "Now, my dear, try again."

Shorts are the most idiotic things to curtsy in, but Sorrel was quick and did her very best. Madame seemed quite pleased. Then she looked at Holly.

"Now you."

Holly had been charmed by the way Madame's skirts billowed around her and it was no trouble at all to pretend that she had skirts too. So instead of holding out her shorts as Sorrel had done, she lifted her hands as if she were holding up silk, and swept down to the floor.

"Madame," she said politely, and then added as she got up, "I'm wearing pale blue with little stars all over it."

Madame laughed. "I could see you were wearing

something very grand. Now, Mark."

Sorrel prayed inside her, "Oh, please God, don't let Mark argue."

But Mark, oddly enough, did not seem even to mind being made to bow. He swept a really grand bow when he said "Madame." The only thing he did not do very well was saying her name. He spoke it in a low, deep growl. Madame's eyes twinkled. She took Mark's chin in her hand.

"And what did you have on when you bowed to me?" Mark wriggled, but she smiled down at him, holding him firmly. "Tell me."

Mark looked cross for a moment and then something in Madame Fidolia's face made him feel friendly.

"I was wearing a bearskin. I was a bear in the Antarctic who'd traveled miles to call on the queen there."

Hannah was thoroughly ashamed. "Really, Mark, what a way to talk!"

But Madame did not seem to mind at all. She took Mark's hand in hers. "And a very nice thing to be," she said cheerfully. "We'll lead the way, shall we?"

In a long room, a lot of small girls and boys were doing dancing exercises. A tall ugly girl with a clever, interesting face was teaching them. As the door opened this girl and all the children stopped work and bowed or curtsied, saying "Madame." Madame beckoned to the girl, saying to Sorrel as she did so:

"This is Winifred, who teaches dancing. We're very short of teachers now but we're allowed to have

Winifred because she teaches lessons as well." She turned to Winifred. "This is the Warren family." She smiled at Mark. "Their name is really Forbes and Mark, at any rate, wants to be called Forbes. This is Sorrel, this is Holly, and this is Mark. You might try them out and see what they know. But I imagine, with their tradition, acting is more in their line." She turned to the rest of the class. "Sit, children." The children, without a word, ran to the side of the room and sat cross-legged on the floor.

There was a piano at the far end of the room on which a fat woman in a red blouse had been playing. Winifred went over to her.

"You might play that Baby Polka, Mrs. Blondin." She came back to the middle of the room. The piano struck up a gay little polka and she began to dance. It was only one, two, three, hop, but she did it so well that it seemed a quite important kind of dancing. As she danced she held out her hand to Mark and Holly. "Come on, children, you do it too." And she beckoned to Sorrel with her head.

Sorrel felt the most awful fool. She could not forget the eyes of all the children sitting cross-legged on the floor, watching her. What must they think she looked like! Prancing about in her shorts. She was so conscious of the eyes that she danced worse than she need have done, and twice she fell over her feet.

Mark put on his proudest face and folded his hands behind his back while he danced. He did not pick up his feet very much but slithered from one step to the other. And Sorrel, watching him out of the corner of her eye, could see that he was not minding dancing because he was not a boy dancing in a room full of children, but a bear skating in the Antarctic.

Holly had learned the Baby Polka at school and she liked dancing, so she held out imaginary skirts and pranced around the room.

Winifred suddenly called out, "Stop." She came over to the new arrivals and one by one lifted first their right legs and then their left legs over their heads. Then she went to Madame and curtsied.

"Elementary."

Madame nodded. "But watch Holly, Winifred. You never know. I thought there might be a something."

Winifred gave Madame a respectful but affectionate smile. "Another Posy?"

Madame shook her head. "One can't expect to find two Posies in a lifetime, but I shall always go on looking. Come along, my dears."

She stood in the door and Winifred and all the children curtsied and said "Madame." The fat woman at the piano just sat and stared.

"I suppose she either doesn't quite belong," Sorrel thought, "or else she's too bad a shape for curtsying. Lucky her!"

Madame took Sorrel and Mark and Holly into her own sitting room. It was a charming room but so full of photographs hung on the walls that the quite lovely blue-gray of the walls scarcely showed. Madame sat in an armchair. Hannah sat on a small upright chair behind the door, looking respectful. It was quite a little chair and she bulged over both sides.

"Now," said Madame, as if she were in for a treat, "let us see if there is any of the Warren talent, or Margaret Shaw's charm, or your own mother's genius about you. I don't want you to recite. Instead, go outside the door and think out a little story—a fairy story, anything you like—and come back and act it."

In the passage outside the three leaned against the wall and tried to think what they could act. Sorrel knew right away that Mark would have to be a bear as he was in that sort of mood, and Holly would have to pretend that she was well dressed. But for the life of her she could not think at first of a story that would fit these characters.

Then suddenly Sorrel thought of just the thing. "Let's do a kind of Red Riding Hood. Let's have a little girl sent out to look for strawberries in the woods because they're hungry at home, and there's nothing to eat. And in the wood the little girl meets a bear and she's terrified and runs home. Then the bear follows her and he turns out to be a prince, so he marries the little girl's mother and they live happily ever after."

"Where was the little girl's father?" asked Mark.

"He died of smallpox," Sorrel invented, "and that's why they're hungry, because there's no one to work for them."

"Pretty rotten for the bear having to turn into a prince," Mark argued.

Sorrel lost her temper. "All right, then, think of a better story yourself. I've made you a bear and Holly can be as dressed up as she likes to think she is, and all I am is just an old mother cleaning the house. I think you're jolly selfish."

"Keep your hair on," said Mark. "We'll do your story. Only I shouldn't think you're as old as all that, otherwise why does the prince marry you? Princes don't."

Sorrel was so thankful to have gotten a story settled that she did not bother to argue with him. "Come on," she said nervously. "Let's do it just once before we go in."

As soon as the door had shut on Sorrel and Mark and Holly, Madame Fidolia went to her desk and picked up a printed list and gave it to Hannah. Hannah was carrying a large brown bag with a zipper fastener. She undid it, took out her spectacles, put them on and read the list:

"Rompers, two (pattern to be obtained from the Academy). Tarlatan dresses, white, two. Knickers, frilled, two. Sandal shoes, white satin. Black patent-leather ankle-strap shoes. White socks, six pairs. Face towels, rough, two. Overalls, two (to be obtained from the Academy)." And at the bottom in large letters, "Everything must be clearly marked with the pupil's name."

Hannah knew just what state the family coupon books were in so she just stared at the list, looking hopeless.

Madame did not give her time to worry long. "That's an old list, of course, from before the war. As

68

you probably noticed at the elementary class we've just come from, all the children's things are made of different colors and a lot of them were wearing shorts. Have the children got bathing dresses?"

"The little girl has, and Sorrel. But Mark's are only a pair of drawers."

"Well, with their shorts and shirts and their bathing things I expect they can manage. But they must have tunics of some sort for ballet. It's hard for a pupil to be graceful in a bathing dress. So we have designed a short tunic with plain knickers underneath. It can be made out of anything. The children's grandmother must have some old dresses put away that could be altered."

Hannah was perfectly certain that she was not going to approach Grandmother. She did not mean to sound grumpy, but she did rather.

"I couldn't say, I'm sure. There wasn't nothing in the vicarage suitable, I do know."

Madame smiled. "Never mind, I'll write to Miss Shaw."

The night before Alice had explained to Hannah that actresses were usually known by their stage names. And so, though to Hannah Grandmother was Mrs. Warren, she accepted the fact that Madame would call her Miss Shaw.

"What about these overalls?" she asked, tapping the list. "They've got the cotton frocks they had for school."

Madame smiled. "There we are fortunate. The overalls have always been made of black sateen from a Russian design, and have wide black leather belts.

Black-out material is not rationed and these overalls are still made. The belts and the buttons we get from our old pupils. The real difficulty is shoes."

"Both the girls have sandal shoes. They had them for their school dancing. And Mark's got a pair of plimsolls, if that'll do."

Madame shook her head. "No, they will not. But I expect we shall manage. Old pupils send us shoes secondhand and if the girls have sandals, that's something." She looked at Hannah with a sweet smile. "You think it all a lot of nonsense, don't you?"

Hannah squeezed her bag tightly in her hands.

"It's none of what I'm used to. I give respect where respect is due and I'm sure you mean well, Madame, but all this dancing and so on isn't what was meant. The Reverend took a lot of looking after, what with being busy with his Bible animals and all that, and his clothes were a perfect disgrace with all my trying, but I could see what we were at. He was never a minute late for his services and he never missed a call from the village. Where we're living now isn't what I'm used to. No good pretending it is."

Madame nodded. "I know, but you have to look at their grandmother's point of view. Nobody knows if the children's father will ever come back."

Hannah's hand shot up to her mouth. "Oh, don't say that, Madame! Such a nice gentleman! And the gentleman in the Navy only said missing and they've never said worse."

"I certainly shall not say it to them," said Madame, "and I'm full of hope that we shall hear from him. But meanwhile they must be looked after. They come from an immensely famous theatrical family and blood tells. It would be a curious thing indeed if none of them had any talent. Of course, they will probably never need to earn their living. Their uncles and aunts are doing well and their grandmother has money and..."

Hannah had to interrupt.

"I don't know about the uncles and aunts, Madame, we haven't seen them. But the old lady hasn't any money. Alice, it's her that looks after the old lady, she hasn't known where to turn."

Madame leaned forward, her voice startled.

"Really! I had no idea! Well, in that case..." She broke off and held up a finger for at that moment Sorrel and Mark and Holly came back.

The charade was rather fun. Holly was very pleased with herself as the child, and Mark made a really grand bear, but it was Sorrel who surpassed herself. Somehow, seeing Holly off into the wood to look for strawberries because there was nothing to eat in the house was so like what was really happening to them that it made her voice full of anxiety, and you could feel that she honestly minded. Then at the end, when Mark proposed, Sorrel was quite overcome, it all sounded so nice, and she said, "Oh, goodness, yes, I'd simply love to marry you. Thank you so very much for asking me," with such fervor that even Hannah smiled and Madame went so far as to clap.

When the charade was over Madame went to a cupboard and took out a tin marked "candies."

"These were sent me from America. From that

Pauline whose picture you were looking at downstairs. I want to talk to you about those three sisters, so you each take a sweet and listen very carefully. The Fossils were brought to me because their guardian had gone away and not left enough money to look after them. Gum, they called him. It was short for Great-Uncle Matthew. A very nice person called Sylvia brought the three little Fossil girls up with the help of someone called Nana."

"Was Nana like Hannah?" Holly interrupted.

"In a lot of ways, very like her. The children did well at my school. Pauline was, and is, lovely, and while she was still quite a child she went to Hollywood and became a very great film star. One day I will take you to see her in the pictures. But to me the most exciting of the three was Posy, the youngest. Even as a tiny child she had talent, sometimes I thought genius. When Posy was eleven she went to Czechoslovakia to study under the greatest living ballet teacher. Manoff. Before the Germans took Czechoslovakia, Monsieur Manoff and most of his pupils, including Posy and Nana, who was with her, escaped to America. There Posy and Nana joined Pauline and Sylvia in Hollywood. They had, of course, nothing but what they stood up in and I'm afraid poor Monsieur Manoff went through a bad time. But finally he succeeded in starting a ballet school of a sort in California and, of course, Posy attends the classes when she can. Posy, under another name, is dancing in the films." Madame laughed. "She detests it, the naughty girl. I must read you her letters sometime."

"What happened to the middle one?" asked Mark.

"Petrova?" Madame said the word affectionately. "Funny little girl! She is a countrywoman of my own. I am Russian. Petrova went away and lived with Great-Uncle Matthew and learned to fly. She is now a pilot. You know, what they call the Air Transport Auxiliary."

Sorrel moved her sweet to the side of her mouth. "How old are they now?"

"Pauline will be twenty-two this December. Petrova is just twenty and Posy will be eighteen this month. Have another, do."

They all bent over the box and chose carefully.

"Now listen carefully because this is where you come in," went on Madame. "Pauline and Posy have both felt that they ought to be back in England doing something important, like Petrova. At least, I don't suppose Posy thinks that because Posy would dance if there were nothing but smoldering ruins left to dance on. But all the same they would both like to help, and so they suggested something. They have sent me sums of money for two scholarships, Pauline's for someone who shows promise in acting, and Posy's for a dancer. So far I have not granted these scholarships, since the money only reached me last month. I have no hesitation at all, Sorrel, in saying that I think that Pauline would like her scholarship to go to you. It will pay all your fees and it will provide such clothes as we can manage and—they were both very particular about this—some pocket money." She looked at Holly. "I'm going to start Posy's scholarship by giving it to you. I shall write and explain to her why. She asked me to find a little girl who was very clever at dancing. I can't say that about you yet. Perhaps if you work hard I shall be able to later on." She leaned forward and picked another sweet out of the box and put it in Mark's mouth. "As for you, my friend, we shall have to see. But I should not wonder if we found a scholarship for you, too."

Mark looked up. He spoke very indistinctly because of the sweet in his mouth. "What, from the one who flies?"

Madame got up to show them that the interview was over. "I should not wonder. There was a very noticeable thing about the Fossil family, and that was the way they all stood together."

Chapter VII

The First Day

Sorrel and Mark and Holly started at the Academy the very next day. Before they got home, Madame had telephoned Grandmother. Alice told them all about it when she brought up their lunch.

"So you're in, and scholarships too! We pretend we aren't pleased, but are we? 'Alice,' we said, 'look through my clothes and find something of soft satin that'll cut up into tunics for the girls.'" She put a stew in front of Hannah. "When you take them to the Academy tomorrow, you're to bring back the pattern, and we're to get down to it right away."

Hannah took the lid off the stew and sniffed it with a pleased smile. "I must say it's a treat to eat something I haven't cooked myself."

"Mostly vegetables," said Alice. "We'll do better when you've got your meat coupons. Fancy," she gave a luxurious sigh, "a scholarship from Pauline Fossil. That really is something, that is."

"Have you seen her in the pictures?" Sorrel asked.

"Have I! I should say I have. Lovely, she is. She was in that picture all about that civil war the Americans had. You should have seen her at the beginning in a crinoline, and a big hat. Made your heart stand still. I don't think I've ever missed her in anything yet."

Holly, who considered Posy her property, was jealous of all this talk about Pauline. "Have you seen Posy Fossil?"

Alice looked surprised. "What, a sister of Pauline? No, I never knew she had one."

Holly was furious. "But she's every bit as important, more important, I should think. Madame said so."

Alice gave a tolerant smile. "Oh well, Madame's got a bee in her bonnet. I expect this Posy dances."

"She does," said Sorrel. "I think she's a star like Judy Garland in *The Wizard of Oz,* only she mostly dances."

Alice laughed good-temperedly. "No harm in thinking, but I don't mind telling you that a film star old Alice hasn't heard about isn't shooting very far."

That night, and on the way to the Academy the next morning, they all talked a lot about the Fossil sisters. It seemed so remarkable to think that they had once been just ordinary Academy pupils like themselves.

"I bet Pauline would be sorry for me," said Sorrel, "having to go on my first day to the Academy in just shorts and a blouse. I bet she started with all the proper things."

Holly ran her fingers through her hair. "It's funny, Posy and I both having curls. It makes us alike somehow."

Mark was rather grand about Petrova. "She's the only sensible one. Pretty good for a girl to be a pilot. She's the only one I'd like to know."

Hannah had implored Alice to think of some way by which they could get to Russell Square other than on the escalator. But Alice only laughed and refused to treat Hannah's fears seriously.

"May as well learn first as last. You can't live in London and never get on a moving staircase."

"It's not Christian," Hannah said stubbornly. "We were meant to move our feet for ourselves, not have them dragged down the stairs for us."

Alice giggled.

"If my plates of meat," she winked at the three, "feet to you, had to carry the weight yours do, I'd thank my stars for anything that would move me along, without my having to trouble myself." Then her face grew serious. "All the same, we can't have you going every morning with them. Sorrel's nearly thirteen. She's old enough to lead the troops and you and I will find plenty to do here. Half my morning's gone getting us up, and I'll be glad of an extra pair of hands, I don't mind telling you."

Sorrel was a little startled to hear they were going about alone in London. But there was so much that was startling going on that it did not make the big sensation it once would have. After she and Mark had dragged Hannah onto the escalator for the second morning, they agreed that it was really a very good thing that Hannah was not going to do it every day. For after she had been on it she did look terribly like a large pale green jelly that had forgotten to set.

The first day in any new school is confusing. Everybody else knows where to be, and what they ought to be doing, and new students feel as if they are running very fast and never being quite sure they are in the right place at the right time. At the Academy there were a lot of things in which Sorrel and Mark and Holly could not take part, because they did not know any of the work that the other pupils did merely as a matter of routine. Their great prop and stay was Winifred, who was an explaining sort of person and seemed very anxious that none of them should feel worried. She told them that the term proper did not begin until next Monday, and that what was going on now was holiday classes.

"In term time you do ordinary school lessons in school hours," she said, "just as you would anywhere else, except that sometimes you have a special dancing or acting class in the afternoon, and then you make up your lesson time after tea. There's Madame Moulin who takes you for French. There's Miss Jones for mathematics. There's Miss Sykes for English literature, and you have me for everything else. We've got about seventy students here this term, so you'll be about fifteen or twenty in a class. This afternoon I'm going to set you a little examination paper to see how much you all know, but this morning you'll come to my dancing class. We all have lunch together sent in from the restaurant across the road."

There was never one second in that morning when Sorrel felt she was learning anything. She was in a different dancing class from Mark and Holly, and she found herself doing what they called bar work, with a lot of girls rather younger than herself. All the girls had on silk or satin tunics, split up at the sides, and she felt an awful mess in her shorts and blouse. Besides which, although she tried very hard to copy what the girl next to her was doing, it was impossible for her feet to keep pace with the feet of the rest of the class. Winifred, in her practice dress, stood in the middle of the room and rattled off instructions.

"Left hand on bar. Body erect. Don't stoop, Biddy. Right arm extended. Relax your elbow and wrist, Mildred. Don't stick your hand out like that, Poppy. All I want is a perfectly natural position. Knees bent. Now a nice arm sweep. Knees straight. Don't wriggle, Pansy. Head and eyes straight in front of you. Do you call that a first position, Agnes? Now, plié, six times. Now then, second position."

At intervals Winifred came over to Sorrel and tried by pushing to get her into the right position. But even as she pushed she was still being nice.

"Don't worry. I think you'll be in this class. But I'm going to give you special coaching to bring you up to the others. They're only beginners."

"Beginners!" thought Sorrel desperately. "What in the world can it be like when you stop being a beginner?"

The acting class was no better because it was all taken up with a performance that was going to be given for the soldiers at some hospital. It was not only acting, a lot of it was dancing, and some of it was singing. The class was taken by a Miss Jay and she tried very hard to be nice to Sorrel, but Sorrel wished she would leave her alone. The others who were going to perform for the soldiers seemed so terribly efficient, she knew she could never be in the least like them. All she wanted was to be left quietly in a corner, watching. But Miss Jay would not hear of it; she came and sat down beside her.

"I think you're going to work with this class, so we must fit you into the concert if we can," she said. "What do you do?"

Sorrel fidgeted with a strand of hair. "Well, I was Shylock once, and twice I've been an angel at Christmas in a Nativity play, and we were children in *Cranford*, in a play in the village."

Miss Jay looked puzzled. "But don't you do anything when your Granny gives a party?"

Sorrel turned scared eyes up at her. "I didn't know she ever did give a party, and I couldn't do anything if she did."

Miss Jay made a funny sniffing sound. "Very unlike your cousin Miranda."

"My what!" exclaimed Sorrel.

Miss Jay looked puzzled. "Surely you knew Miranda was a student here?"

"I didn't know I had a cousin Miranda."

Miss Jay broke off a moment to tidy up a hornpipe, which was being accompanied by a group of young performers who could whistle. Then she turned back to Sorrel.

"Miranda is the daughter of your Aunt Marguerite."

"Yes," said Sorrel politely.

"You must know that you have an Aunt Marguerite," went on Miss Jay.

"No, I didn't."

Miss Jay evidently thought it was time that somebody explained her family to Sorrel.

"Your grandmother had five children: Henry Warren, the film star; Lindsey, who married Mose Cohen, the comedian (their daughter Miriam is coming here next term); Marguerite, who married Sir Francis Brain, the Shakespearean actor (and they have a remarkably clever child called Miranda); Andrew, who died, and your mother, Adeline."

Sorrel could not possibly take in all these uncles and aunts at once, so she fixed on her cousins.

"What's Miranda like?"

Miss Jay used a funny voice—it was as if she were being nice when she did not want to be. "Good-looking and got the Warren voice, speaks blank verse beautifully."

"And Miriam?" prodded Sorrel.

Miss Jay shrugged her shoulders.

"I only saw the child for a moment or two. She's about eight, I think, a tiny dark little thing. You'll meet them both on Monday."

She got up and went over to rearrange the whistlers, but she evidently had Sorrel on her mind for later on she suddenly clapped her hands. "I know! Lambs! Come here, Sorrel."

Sorrel got up unwillingly and went toward her, glaring at the floor, conscious that all the other girls were staring at her.

"In that spring number we can do with an extra lamb," explained Miss Jay. "We'll run through that number now." She selected two girls. "You two put Sorrel between you, and she can copy what you do."

What followed seemed to Sorrel perfectly idiotic. They played what seemed to her just follow-my-leader, of a rather silly kind, hopping and skipping. She could not see that any of it was the least like lambs. Try as she would she was always late, never getting in a hop at quite the same time as the others.

But Miss Jay seemed pleased. "That'll be splendid," she said in a satisfied tone. "With your long bob, and in a black tunic, you'll look very nice indeed." And then she added, perhaps seeing rather a sullen look on Sorrel's face, "There's nothing like getting used to the feel of a stage. Never mind making a start in a humble position."

The tap dancing class was just dull. Sorrel was not wearing the right shoes and in any case the class was being taken through what the teacher called "a routine." The routine was part of the concert for the soldiers and it did not need Miss Dane's cheerful, "I think this is too much for you to pick up, Sorrel dear," for Sorrel to be certain that she could not even pretend to copy in this class. The steps went very fast with taps from toes and heels in time to the music. There was one place, which the class practiced over and over again, where the music stopped and was carried on only by the rhythm of the tapping of the girls' feet. Sorrel, sprawling on a bench, was filled with admiration but also with horror. Surely these could not be just ordinary girls like the ones at Ferntree School. They must be exceptionally talented. She could not believe, however many special classes she attended, that she would be able to use her feet like that.

There was no class going on that morning suitable for Mark and Holly and so they were tacked on to a children's special holiday class. The children were all quite small, mostly from outside London, and had been brought to their classes by very proud mothers who were sure that their children were remarkable. The first class was with Miss Jay and it was dancing and miming of nursery rhymes.

"Now," said Miss Jay, "we're going to start with 'Mary, Mary quite contrary.'" She looked around the class and selected a child with black curls and a very short white muslin frock. "You shall be Mistress Mary, Shirley."

Mark was not so much disgusted at finding himself supposed to take part in such a childish entertainment as he was incredulous that he was going to be so insulted. To keep his mind off Miss Jay's instructions, he looked at the parents. He saw at once which was Shirley's mother, for the moment she heard that her child was to be Mistress Mary she looked around at the other mothers with an expression which clearly said, "Talent will tell."

He came back to the class with a start to hear Miss Jay saying, "Come along, Mark, don't dream. You're the tallest, so you must be the leading silver bell."

Mark flushed. "If it makes no difference to you, I'd rather watch."

Miss Jay's eyes twinkled. "Oddly enough, it does make a difference to me and I'd rather you were a silver bell." She came over to him and then quite suddenly she whispered, "Pretend it's a children's party and you're helping to amuse the little ones."

Miss Jay could not have said anything better. There had been lots of children's parties in the village at home, and Mark had helped at one of them, giving assistance to the head Sunday School teacher. She was tall and gray-haired and thin and wore pince-nez, and had tried so hard to make the party a success that she never stood still for a minute, but kept saying things like, "Splendid, splendid!" or "Isn't it fun?" The moment Miss Jay said, "Help to amuse the little ones," this woman came back into Mark's mind and in a moment he was being her and not minding the class any more.

"Mary, Mary" was followed by "Baa, Baa, Black Sheep" and, finally, "A Frog He Would A-Wooing Go" with Mark as the frog. Ordinarily Mark would have enjoyed being a frog. But by the time they got to this nursery rhyme, he was so full of being the

Sunday School teacher that he could not quite get rid of her. And though he saw himself clearly in a bright green frog suit, he also saw a gray bun of hair on the top of his head, and pince-nez on his nose. And he still had the anxious smile of somebody who is going to fight very hard to make a party a success. Somehow the mixture of these two characters came out and it was funny. The parents laughed, the children laughed and Miss Jay, who had a cheerful laugh, gave a hearty roar.

Winifred, though of course she had to take an interest in all her pupils, was giving her especial attention to Holly. She had known about the Posy Fossil scholarship and it had astonished her that Madame should grant it to Holly, who obviously had scarcely learned dancing and, therefore, showed no ability at all, let alone talent. Had Madame sensed some quality in Holly which she herself had missed? To Winifred all new pupils at the Academy were interesting, and these Forbes youngsters—or rather Warren, for that was how Winifred thought of them—really were exciting. What a history! There must be talent. There absolutely must. What fun if one of the three proved even better than their cousin Miranda, Winifred also thought—for she could be very human at times—and what a comedown for Miranda if they were!

But though Winifred watched with the utmost care and gave Holly some especial chances to show what she could do, she could not see any sign of remarkable talent. She dismissed the class feeling disappointed and low of heart.

The written examination papers in the afternoon were easy and so were the verbal questions. Sorrel and Mark and Holly had been well taught in their schools and all of them were ahead of their ages. Winifred corrected the papers and then looked at the three with a smile.

"Very nice indeed." Then she sighed.

Mark got up and stretched himself, he was so cramped from writing.

"Why did you sigh if our papers are good?"

Winifred thought about his question. "One of the difficulties of this sort of school is to fix the classes. It's much easier to put you in a class and leave you there for everything. You can see for yourselves that it must be. Now what am I going to do with Sorrel? She is very well on for her age in lessons but she has done no ballet at all."

Sorrel got up and pushed her chair in against the table. "Well, you haven't got to decide until Monday."

Winifred flicked over Sorrel's papers. "As a matter of fact I've already decided about you. For everything except ballet, you will work with the upper middle. The girls in that class are rather older than you but about your level in work. It'll be interesting for you because in your class you will find your cousin Miranda."

Chapter VIII

Cousins

Sorrel and Mark and Holly had all noticed one point about the Academy. The right thing for a proper pupil to carry was a little brown brief case. In it you carried all your belongings to hang up in your locker; in it you carried things like your towel, shoes and spare socks for your classes, and in it you took home any of your belongings which needed to be washed. None of the Forbes family wanted or expected the full Academy wardrobe. They were so used to coupons, or rather lack of them, that they knew they could not have clothes just because they needed them. But a brief case was different. It did not require coupons, and having one was the sign of being a real pupil rather than just somebody who came in merely for holiday classes.

They decided not to explain about the brief cases to Hannah. Hannah could not be made to see that anything to do with the Academy really mattered. She looked upon the whole business of their going to the Academy as something that would pass, like having measles. Instead they told Alice. Alice was the sort of person who understood how having just one of the right things could make all the difference.

Alice lived up to their expectations. "That's quite right, that is. That's just what you do need. I'll have a word with Hannah about bees and honey and then you can go shopping Saturday morning."

Saturday morning was wet. Hannah had a great deal to do and only terrific cajoling could get her to go out at all. Alice advised trying the Kings Road, Chelsea. They could walk to it, which meant no escalators to put Hannah off. The morning was a dismal failure. They splashed along in the wet, Hannah absolutely refusing to hurry, and they went into every single shop in the Kings Road, including Woolworth's, that could possibly sell brief cases. But it was not until they got to the far end where the shops finished that they faced the awful truth. Cheap brief cases were one of the things you could no longer buy. In a few places were grand little cases of leather costing a lot of money, but the cheap kind could not be bought anywhere.

On Monday morning when they set out each was carrying a brown paper parcel which contained their belongings. The nearer they got to the Academy, the worse they felt about the parcels.

"If only it was boxes!" said Sorrel. "A little box would be neat and you could carry things about in it."

Mark angrily kicked a stone off the pavement. "Even that awful Shirley who did Mistress Mary and was only a holiday pupil had a brief case."

Sorrel slowed up because the Academy was in sight.

"I wouldn't mind if it weren't for our being Grandmother's grandchildren. People expect us to be good at everything because of her and because we have scholarships. It's bad enough that we aren't good, but when we haven't got anything but brown paper parcels as well we really look most peculiar."

The Academy was quite a different place now that the term had started. Winifred was standing at the students' entrance with some lists in her hand, and she told the girls to hurry up and put on their black tunics with their white socks and dancing sandals, which they would wear for lessons. Sorrel and Holly had lockers side by side in one changing room; Mark's was in the boys' room down the passage. Sorrel opened her locker quickly and pushed her parcel inside and tried to unpack it in there. There did not seem to be many of the girls about whom she knew. But all the same she thought she would like to get her parcel undone and everything hung up before anyone noticed. All round the room there was a flow of chatter.

"Hullo! Had a good holiday?"

"Hullo, Doris! Have you come back to live in London?"

"Have you heard Freda will not be back until half term? She's still with that concert party in Blackpool, lucky beast."

Then it happened. Somebody hurrying by tripped over Sorrel's feet and the back half of her that was sticking out of her locker, and a voice said:

"Oh, bother! I nearly fell." And then added, "One of the new girls grubbing about with a paper parcel."

Holly was sitting on the floor changing her socks. She did not so much care what anybody said to her but she would not have anyone being rude to Sorrel. She raised her voice to what Ferntree School, which did not approve of such behavior, would have called a shout.

"We would have brief cases if we could but we can't because there is a war on. Perhaps you didn't know that."

There was a lot of laughter and then somebody said, "That's put you in your place, Miranda."

Miranda! Sorrel got up, her cheeks crimson. What an awful start she had made with her cousin! What an even worse start Holly had made, shouting like that. Miranda was walking up the line of lockers, so Sorrel ran after her and caught hold of her arm.

"Are you Miranda? I—I mean we—are your cousins. We're Sorrel, Holly and Mark Forbes. Mark isn't here just now, he's in the boys' room changing."

Miranda turned and Sorrel gave a little gasp of surprise, because Miranda was so very much like what Grandmother must have been when she was her age: The same brown hair—it hung down at the back, of course, but the top part was piled up into curls; the same dark eyes; the same effect of being a patch of color in a dull room. Only Grandmother was like a sparkling bit of color and Miranda was more like the last smoldering red cinder lying in the gray ashes. Miranda was evidently not a person who minded if she had been rude to her cousins or not. Rather she seemed to have forgotten it for she put on a very grown-up, gracious air.

"How do you do? I heard you were coming. We'll be quite a family gathering this term, for Uncle Moses is sending Miriam—did you know? You're a beginner, aren't you? I'm afraid that means we shan't see much of each other."

Sorrel wished most heartily that this were going to be the case, but she remembered what Winifred had said about their both being in the same class. Quite time enough, however, for Miranda to find that out if it happened. So she just smiled politely and admitted to being a beginner and went back to her changing.

Sorrel and Holly had just gotten into their overalls and were fastening their belts when the changing room door was thrown open and a little girl dashed in. She had on a frock of bright orange linen, against which her thin little face looked pale and yellowish. In fact there seemed to be scarcely any face at all, it was so surrounded by a fuzz of black hair. In one hand she carried a grand leather brief case of the sort which costs pounds and pounds. She glanced imperiously round the room.

"Which is my cousin Holly?"

Holly felt shy at being called out in front of all the big girls and she spoke in a very small voice. "Me."

The child dashed over to her, put her brief case on the floor and gave her a kiss. "We're cousins. I'm Miriam Cohen. You're just a tiny bit older than I am. I won't be eight until the end of this month."

This was so insulting that Holly forgot to be shy. "If you don't mind my saying so, I'm a great deal older than you. I shall be nine at Christmas."

Miriam seemed to be a person who did everything quickly. She snapped open her brief case and threw everything in it out onto the floor.

"Never mind, let's be friends. Mum says if we're friends I may ask you to tea. I can't come to you because we're not on speaking terms with Grandmother just now. We hardly ever are, you know, except at Christmas. Of course we always go to Grandmother's then."

Sorrel and Holly rather liked the look of Miriam, who was, at any rate, friendly. Sorrel knelt down beside her and began collecting the things that Miriam had upset.

"I'm a cousin, too. I'm Sorrel. Do you know which your locker is?" She picked up a white satin tunic and knickers and gave them a shake. "These will get awfully dirty on the floor."

Miriam got up and began taking off her orange linen frock. "Mum's made me two tunics and two knickers. She cut up one of her best nightdresses. I think that was pretty decent of her, don't you? She said I'd have to have two; she knew I wouldn't be clean a minute if I had only one. I've got the locker next to Holly; they told me at the door."

Sorrel hung up Miriam's tunic and knickers and her linen frock and helped her into her black knickers and tunic. Holly passed Miriam her dancing sandals, then said:

"Are you absolutely new, like me, or have you learned it before?"

Miriam sat on the floor to put on her sandals. "Learned what?"

Holly crouched down beside her. "All these routines and things the big girls do, and that tap and that work at the bar."

Miriam tied the tapes of one of her sandals. "I began tap when I was three," she said. "Then I started acrobatic work; you know, flip flaps and all that. I learned to sing when I was four. I did some shows with Dad for charity when I was five. I don't really ever remember a time when I wasn't learning, but mostly I went to special classes or learned at home. That's why they've sent me here. It's to see which way I'm heading, at least that's what Dad says. He thinks it's time I specialized. He says I'm too plain for the glamour type and I ought to do a lot of acrobatic work and become a comedienne. But I shan't. I'm going to dance. He knows that, really." She tied the tapes of her second sandal. "There's no doubt about it, I'm a bitter disappointment."

A bell clanged in the passage. At once there was a

crash of locker doors and everybody hurried out. Winifred was standing at the foot of the stairs with a list in her hand.

"Get in line, please, and come past me slowly."

Sorrel leaned a little way out of the line and looked up the passage for Mark. Boys were easy to pick out in that mass of black tunics and white socks. Mark had changed into his sandals, but otherwise he was dressed exactly as he had started out in the morning. He saw Sorrel and gave her a grin. It was a cheerful grin but she knew that inside he was feeling very much as she was, sort of sinking and wishing they were not so new.

Winifred had stopped Miranda and told her to wait. She was standing at the foot of the stairs when Sorrel arrived at the head of the queue. Winifred laid a hand on Sorrel's arm.

"I expect you've met Miranda in the changing room." She looked at Miranda. "I want you to look after Sorrel. You two are in the same form."

Miranda gaped at Winifred. "But she's younger than I am and she's never done a thing."

Winifred spoke nicely but you could not help feeling she was not sorry to be able to say what she did.

"She is nearly thirteen, not so young as she looks. And from the paper I set her, she's well up to the standard of work in the upper middle. What's more, Madame has granted her the scholarship Pauline Fossil has given for dramatic work."

This last remark seemed to stun Miranda into silence. She caught Sorrel by the hand and pulled her up the stairs after her. It was only when they were outside the door of the practice room that she suddenly stopped.

"I didn't know you could act; nobody told me."

"I don't know that I can," admitted Sorrel.

"What did Madame see you do?"

Sorrel was just going to tell her, then she thought better of it. Perhaps Madame had been over-generous in granting her the scholarship. Perhaps she had not really seen very much talent, but if that was so she was certainly not going to let Miranda know about it. Like a distant light at the end of a long tunnel, a thought shaped in Sorrel's head. She had not ever thought of being an actress but she was the daughter of one and the grandchild of an actor and an actress, and the great-grandchild of a very great actor indeed, if all they said about that old Sir Joshua was right. Anyway, there was every bit as much reason why she should be an actress as why Miranda should. Why shouldn't she see if she could be a good one? If she could really be worth Pauline Fossil's scholarship?

So she answered Miranda casually, "Oh, just a bit of a play that she asked us to do. Is this the classroom?"

In the next few weeks, Sorrel and Mark and Holly were all so busy that they had no time to think if they liked London or the Academy, or living with Grandmother or anything else. So far as the lessons were concerned, they found things easy. The Academy standard was reasonably high but nothing like as high as it had been at their previous schools. And some subjects, such as Latin, were dropped altogether. But, of course, other things took their place. There was a tremendous lot of history of dancing and of the theater and any amount of time given to music. The music teacher was a Dr. Felix Lente, who came every afternoon and taught the whole school.

The Forbeses could have kept pace with all the ordinary school subjects, even the music, for, as a whole, the pupils were not exceptionally musical. But it was the dancing they found so difficult. In spite of extra coaching and the fact that all three were quite intelligent, they were taking a long time to catch up. Sorrel, in fact, was obviously never going to catch up with her age, and when she was finally put to bar work with a class, it was with girls of Holly's age.

In addition to all the dancing they had to memorize; each of them had two or three acting parts. And in those first weeks they frequently found themselves trying to do three things at once: have a bath, say a part out loud, and stick out one foot, murmuring with half their minds, plié and rise, plié and rise.

Everything was much more difficult for Sorrel than for Holly and Mark. Mark took his dancing lessons very lightly. He tried to remember all he could but he felt it was a shocking waste of time for somebody who was going into the Navy. Holly had only to compete with the new little girls who knew no more than she did, and very soon she began to like dancing and became one of the best in her small class. It was not saying much but it was something to show for the person who held the Posy Fossil scholarship. But for Sorrel life was pretty difficult. Every girl of her age had been learning dancing for at least two years, and most of them had been working on their pointes for a number of months. Of course the majority had been evacuated for about a year during the heavy bombing, but they had kept up fairly well by working under a local ballet teacher. Sorrel could see that however hard she worked and however many extra classes she had, she was never really going to be a dancer. It was not even as though she had any especial talent. She was light on her feet and quick at remembering, but it took more than that to make a dancer. Sometimes, in the night, she thought desperately of going to Madame and asking if she could not drop all this dancing, but even before she had framed the thought she knew it would be hopeless. Madame's Academy was primarily for dancing. Once you were inside those doors, you had to dance.

What Sorrel did find, as the weeks went by, was that she looked forward to all the acting classes. Mime, where you acted scenes with no words spoken at all, she loved. Then there were her speaking parts. She had the part of the queen in a French version of *The Sleeping Beauty*. She had a scene or two of Rosalind's in *As You Like It* and she had Friar Tuck in *Robin Hood*. She liked acting more and more. She found that things happened to her. One day, quite suddenly, she knew what her hands should be doing. Another time, she discovered how she should get from one place to another across the stage. She found that she knew what it meant when Miss Jay said, "You were nicely in the scene, Sorrel dear." She began to know how to act and yet how to sound natural. A lot of these things she could not possibly have explained, but they were each becoming clear thoughts, so that she knew that presently each one would be sorted out and she would be able to say, "I did that because…"

All the time, in front of her at the acting classes, there was Miranda to watch. Miranda in the school, or Miranda at a dancing class, or Miranda listening to an Appreciation of Music lesson, was just an ordinary schoolgirl. But Miranda acting was something so special that you forgot she was Miranda. It did not matter to her that she was dressed in a black Russian overall and white socks and black sandals and looked just like all the other girls, for when she was acting she became the person she was meant to be. As the very young princess in *The Sleeping Beauty*, you knew that she was very young and wearing stiff satin, and that she had never heard there were such things as needles in the world. And when the needle pricked her, though there was no needle there, you could see that it had gone in and had hurt her, and you could watch her going to sleep and know it was not just an ordinary sleep but would last for a hundred years. In her Rosalind scenes she took the words and they sang out of her mouth in a golden stream, and yet, somehow, she made them ordinary words and Rosalind a real girl. And so it was when she played Maid Marian. Miranda always played the best parts, she never thought that she would not play them, and it seemed to be the rule that she picked what she liked and the rest of the class shared what was left over.

Both Miss Jay and Madame Moulin treated Miranda as somebody special when she was acting. When she was not acting, they treated her as the rather conceited schoolgirl that she was. It was all very muddling. In what little time Sorrel had to think about anything except her work, she thought about Miranda. Miranda was full of talent, she had inherited all the family gifts, everybody said so. To Madame Moulin and Miss Jay it was something wonderful to be descended from the Warrens. Sorrel respected Madame Moulin and Miss Jay, and so what they thought mattered to her. And she still thought of herself as a Forbes. But just now and again, when she was watching Miranda act, something stirred in her, and she felt excited. Then a part of her mind would say, "You're a Warren too. You're a Warren too."

Chapter VIII

An Audience

One morning the Academy bell clanged and all the students were summoned to the big main hall, for Madame wanted to speak to them. The big main hall ran through all three houses. At one end there was a platform with a table in the center. The students filed in, the small ones in front and the big ones at the back. As each class arrived its teacher left her pupils and went up onto the platform. When everybody was ready and after a little pause, Madame came to the middle of the stage. At once all the teachers and the girls swept big curtsies to the ground and the boys bowed. Everybody said "Madame." Madame smiled.

"Sit down, my dears," she said.

All the pupils sat on the floor with their legs crossed and their backs perfectly straight in the way they were taught to do in their classes. Madame waited until the last rustle had died down, then she addressed them.

"I want to talk to you about the performances we are going to give in hospitals and for the troops. First of all I want to talk to you about transport. As of course everyone here realizes, gasoline must not be wasted and neither must rubber. Each of you will in time appear at these concerts but we shall not be able, as is our custom, to send you all in taxis. A car will be hired, or two cars if need be, to carry the costumes, and as many of you as can be accommodated in the cars will travel in them. The rest of you will go in charge of your teachers by the usual means of transport, whatever that may be—buses, trams, trains, or the underground. It is not easy for your teachers to escort so many of you by these means and I shall expect perfect obedience from even the smallest. Owing to the possibility of air raids and the fact that most of you live at a distance, these concerts will take place in the afternoon, usually on a Saturday, so that you may get home well before black-out.

"Now I want to speak to you about the concerts themselves. We have in this country men of practically every nationality in the world, including the Asiatic races, who don't perhaps speak or understand our language. But every one of them has, of course, been a child and most of them think of their own boys and girls of your age whom they've left behind in their homes. We shall, of course, give of our very best to these entertainments. But each one of you will know that you're not very skillful and that you've got a great deal to learn. In spite of these defects, you will perhaps get a great deal of applause from your audiences. It's about that applause I want to speak to you. I want you to remember that when you've done a little dance or song or sketch, the applause which you get is not only because you yourself have done your best, but because each of those men is seeing in you someone he loves at home, and because of you is able to forget for a little while the unhappiness of not being in his home, and in some cases the great tragedy of not knowing what has happened to the children in his family.

"I am taking you all into my confidence about this because we, as a school, are gaining a great deal by these performances. Each one of you will have an opportunity of experiencing how it is to work before an audience, and it is, therefore, of the utmost importance that none of you should get conceited. Everyone in this room is a beginner, and whether you're going to be an actor or actress or a dancer, or perhaps a musical performer, you've a great deal to learn. All your life on the stage you will go on learning, and it would be a very sad thing if a great deal of applause just now made any one of you think that you knew more than you do."

Madame paused and smiled. "There, I've made you all look very serious! What I want from each of you is the best that you can give and a secret knowledge in each of your hearts of how many are your faults and how much better you will do next time. That's all."

The pupils all got up and curtsied or bowed, saying "Madame," and went off in neat lines back to their classes.

To Sorrel, Mark and Holly, Madame's speech was rather puzzling. In the few school and village performances in which they had taken part there was, of course, applause at the end, but they had never thought that it meant anything more than that people had enjoyed themselves. What sort of applause did Madame mean that was likely to make them think they knew a whole lot more than they did?

Sorrel was the first to find out. The upper middle concert for which they had rehearsed so long was taken down to South London to a seamen's hospital on a Saturday afternoon. Inside herself, Sorrel was scornful of the fuss that went on beforehand.

"You never saw such a to-do," she confided to Mark and Holly. "I know every skip of that horrid lamb backwards. I've known it for weeks and weeks and weeks, and yet we never seem to have finished. There's an awful thing called a lay-out. That means the order in which everything comes, and giving everybody time to change. It's all written out in a prop book with music cues. What on earth would it matter if there was a little pause? I bet the seamen wouldn't mind."

When it came to the Saturday afternoon, she had her first glimpse of the professional's angle of mind. Two cars took the costumes down to the hospital.

Five of the students and Miss Jay went in one and five more and Winifred in another. Miss Sykes, the English literature mistress, who was stage managing, sat in the front of one car and Mrs. Blondin, the fat woman who played the piano, sat in the front of the other. There were seven pupils over, of which Sorrel was one, and they were to be taken down by Miss Jones, the mathematics teacher.

The seven waited in the students' entrance and it was then that Sorrel first felt nervous. Nobody could possibly be nervous about dancing a lamb with a lot of other people, but it was a catching kind of nervousness for everybody. Would everybody get there all right? Were the clothes all right? Would all the music be there? Would anybody make a mistake? Would the Academy be disgraced?

Miss Jones was just as much puzzled about this performance in a seamen's hospital as was Sorrel. In Miss Jones's reckoning, if you could add and subtract and understood decimals then you did understand them and that was that. Surely, in exactly the same way, if you learned a dance or a song or a sketch you could do it and that, too, ought to be that. Then what was this nervous, keyed-up feeling? The only thing she could compare it to was an examination. She knew from experience how the things that you knew perfectly well could fade from your mind in an examination, and she guessed that giving a performance was the same thing. So it was that as she collected her seven students in the hall, she gave them the sympathetic smile that she gave to examination pupils, and said in the same encouraging tone:

"All ready? Now, off we go."

The merchant seamen had all walked or been wheeled into one big ward of the hospital. At the far end was a space meant to represent a stage, with a piano at one side. It made rather a good kind of stage because there was a door at either side and at the back there was a nurses' sitting room which the pupils used as a dressing room. The two cars had got there before the seven who had come with Miss Jones arrived. Everybody was talking in whispers and fussing about and trying not to look excited. Winifred and Miss Jay had rouge and some lipstick and were helping the young cast with their make-up.

The program was to open with a speech made by Miranda. For it she wore her school black overall. The clock struck three and Winifred looked around and beckoned to Miranda and Mrs. Blondin.

Miss Jay cautioned the others. "Absolute silence, all of you."

As Miss Jay said those words and the doors shut behind Mrs. Blondin and Miranda, Sorrel felt not herself, but part of everybody left behind in the dressing room. She felt her breath coming in little short gasps, she felt she could hear her heart beating, and she felt her fingers grow sticky. Miranda's voice, in a muffled way, came through the closed door. She was speaking beautifully, telling the seamen how proud the Academy students were to be allowed the chance to amuse them, how they would please remember that they were still young but were going to do their best, and how immensely grateful they were to the seamen because they knew, but for the men who were the audience and men like them, they would have starved. And then, in quite a different voice, she began to recite Kipling's "Big Steamers."

As Miranda finished, the heads of all the Academy pupils turned towards the doors and Miss Jay and Winifred exchanged glances. Everybody was waiting, and then it came—the applause. Because it was her first performance with the Academy, Sorrel did not understand why that clapping with its roaring, pleased sound meant anything to her. Of course, Miranda was her cousin, but why should she care so much how Miranda was doing? Why did she feel that what Miranda did was part of what she did? Winifred was shepherding through one of the doors the pupils who were dancing in a little ballet which was to come next, and as they went on Miranda came back through the other door. Miss Jay gave her a pleased nod and Miranda ran to the corner where she was changing and pulled off her overall. Winifred closed the door behind the last of the ballet and came across to Sorrel. She picked up a brush and began brushing Sorrel's hair.

"They're warming up nicely."

Sorrel liked Winifred and ventured a question. "Does it make a great difference if a thing starts well? I mean, if Miranda had forgotten her words, which of course she wouldn't, it couldn't have spoiled the ballet, could it?"

There was a very little bit of curl at the bottom of Sorrel's hair. Winifred made the best of this, twisting it around her fingers.

"It always matters. This sort of show has to be

built up. If anything goes badly and the men don't like it, then you've lost something, the interest and so on of the seamen, and you've got to start again to get it back."

Winifred went away after that and Sorrel, who was in her black crêpe-de-chine lamb's tunic and had nothing further to do for the moment, leaned against the wall and thought. If in a performance like this everything mattered so much, what on earth could it be like when you were a real actress such as her mother had been? If you were bad in your part for even a moment, if you became yourself and slipped out of the play for a second or, most awful of all, if you forgot your words, how fearful it must be, with everybody else who acted with you having to work doubly hard to get the audience back to the mood of believing in you.

The lambs' turn came in the last half of the performance. Sorrel was the third lamb from the end and she stood in a queue by the door fiddling with her tunic and seeing that her shoes, which she had just taken off, were where she could find them again, and looking at Winifred with an anxious eye. Then the shepherdesses' song was over, the door opened and Mrs. Blondin started to play one of Schubert's "Moments Musical." Sorrel held out her arms and raised her right leg.

While she was being a lamb, it was impossible for Sorrel to think about the audience. Even simple work such as the lambs did took all of her mind. Toes had to be pointed just right, hops had to happen exactly on a beat and she had to make her exit on exactly the right bar. But at the end, when she ran on to curtsy with the rest, she had a chance to look around. In the front of the ward were the beds, behind them the wheelchairs and behind those the walking cases.

It was then that Sorrel saw what Madame had meant about all nationalities. There were black faces and yellow faces and white faces. There were bandaged heads, limbs in plaster of Paris, there were some men so covered with bandages that you could hardly see them at all. She was certain that a whole lot of them could not understand anything that was said in English, and yet everybody was smiling and looking pleased. Because of Madame's speech she could see why, and what she had meant about conceit.

When Sorrel ran back the second time to curtsy with the rest of the lambs, she gave an especial smile to one of the three Chinese. He had an arm in plaster of Paris and, as far as she could see, the rest of him was in plaster of Paris, too. Anyway he was lying very stiff and flat in his bed, and in spite of it all he was managing to smile.

It was hard, having got her lamb off her chest, not to burst into excited talk with all the others, but Miss Jay and Winifred were strong on discipline and at the first sound of a raised voice they flew to the culprit with an angry face. Those of the lambs who were not taking part in any other act huddled together by the window.

"Seemed to go all right, didn't it?"

"I nearly tripped as I came on, there was an awful rough bit on the floor just there. Did you see?"

"Nancy's got her shepherdess dress on wrong. Those panniers ought to stick out."

"She sang all right, though."

"Did you feel nervous, Sorrel? Didn't make any mistakes, did you?"

The entertainment finished with another short speech from Miranda and then all the pupils came on in the dresses in which they had last appeared and sang "There'll Always Be an England" and "God Save the King."

It was while they were changing to go home that the exciting thing happened. The matron of the hospital came in and spoke to Winifred and Miss Jay. Winifred and Miss Jay had a puzzled conversation and then Winifred called out, "Will all the lambs come here a minute?" Surprised, the lambs stopped dressing and came over to her. Matron looked at them all and then laid her hand on Sorrel's arm.

"I think this is the girl."

Winifred finished fastening Sorrel's frock and tidied her hair.

"We'll bring her out and see." She turned to Sorrel. "There's a sick Chinese who wants to speak to one of you."

Matron took Sorrel by the hand and led her over to the bed of the Chinese in plaster of Paris. There was no doubt that it was Sorrel he wished to see, for he nodded. He was too weak to say very much but he smiled and whispered.

"Makee plesent." He then fumbled under his pillow and brought out a queer little china fish on the end of a string.

"It's a present for you, dear," said Matron. "Speak slowly if you want to thank him."

Sorrel went around to the left-hand side of the bed because that hand was free from the plaster of Paris. She laid her hand in his.

"Thank you, so very much," she said, speaking every word slowly. "I will keep it always."

The man smiled. "Makee mluch luck."

Back in the nurses' sitting room the others crowded around Sorrel.

"What was it? Who wanted you?"

Sorrel told them, then she held out the little fish. "He gave me that."

"Why you? What on earth for?" asked Miranda.

Sorrel was so frightfully pleased at having been given the little fish that she scarcely noticed the rude way in which Miranda spoke.

"Just for luck."

Miranda opened her mouth as if to say something and then she shut it again. It was as if words were tumbling into her head and she was swallowing them. Then finally she blurted out, not in the lovely voice in which she spoke on the stage, but in the voice of a jealous schoolgirl:

"Well, I hope it does you good. If you're going to be an actress, I should think it would take a row of fishes to make you a success."

Chapter IX

News

It was lucky in a way that Sorrel and Mark and Holly had to work so hard, for really it was very peculiar living with Grandmother. A lot went on in her drawing room—people came to call, telephones rang—but none of it concerned the Forbeses. Their world was upstairs with Hannah, and with Alice when she could make time.

Next to Hannah and Alice the nicest thing about Ponsonby Square was the garden. Before the war when there were railings around it, it had been beautifully kept up at the expense of the people who lived in the Square. Even in wartime you could see somebody was trying to do something about it. The grass was cut, there were Michaelmas daisies of all colors in the beds, crabapple trees with crabapples hanging all over them, and endless shrubs with gay leaves and berries. At one end of the garden vegetables were being grown, but right down the center of the vegetable beds were some incredibly old mulberry trees, fairly dripping with mulberries. Two aged gardeners looked after the garden and they became great friends with Sorrel and Mark and Holly. The head gardener told them that before the war dozens of boys and girls had belonged to the garden and played there regularly, but they were all evacuated now. He said he missed them very much and hoped that now that this there 'itler had stopped making a nuisance of himself they would come back.

"A garden ain't rightly a garden," he would say, shaking his head, "without young 'uns in it."

There was a shrubbery path all around the garden, which was very good for hide-and-seek when the three felt energetic, and there was a low overhanging branch which made a bar for practicing their dancing exercises.

In the house, Alice and Hannah had done everything that could be done to make their rooms look nice. They had bought some gay green paint and painted both Mark's room and the nursery. Alice had found some old curtains which she and Hannah washed and cut up and hung in Mark's room, and a red tablecloth out of which curtains were made for the nursery. Sorrel had been given a latch key which was hung on a piece of string round her neck so that they could always let themselves in and save, as Alice said, "Somebody's understandings on the old apples and pears." But in spite of a latch key either Hannah or Alice always managed to be about, looking pleased to see them when they came in.

Hannah, after a lot of searching, had found a church that she approved of in the neighborhood. And from the moment she found it and had gotten used to the times of the services, she began to feel at home. She considered that her charges ought to go to a young people's service in the afternoon on Sundays, but as there were so few boys and girls in London there did not seem to be any special services to go to. Instead, she took them to a morning service and managed to keep for each of them what she called "Sunday clothes."

"You may laugh, Alice," she said when Alice was amused at these efforts, "but I know what's right and proper for Mr. Bill's young ones and I'm going to see it carried out."

From the moment that Hannah found her own church and got the others' church-going settled, she became much more herself. All day long the sound of hymn singing was heard on the top floor:

> "The rich man in his castle,
> The poor man at his gate.
> What have I done with my thimble?
> And ordered their estate."

And when Harvest Festival time arrived:
> "We plough the fields and scatter
> The good seed on the land,
> What an awful hole Mark's made
> In thi—is sock."

Every day or two, one or all of the Forbeses were

sent for to visit Grandmother. It was a queer kind of visiting, they thought, because it was like going out to pay a call. A message would come to say that they were to be received, and then there would be a lot of tidying and brushing up by Hannah before they were passed over to Alice, who escorted them downstairs just as if they did not know their way and announced them like proper visitors.

"Here's Sorrel, Miss Shaw dear," or "Here's your grandchildren to see you, Miss Shaw dear."

Thanks to Miriam, Sorrel and Mark and Holly were beginning to learn about their family. Miriam's mother, their Aunt Lindsey, was the eldest of Grandmother's daughters and she had not married very young. And before she married, Grandmother had come to depend on her being about the house to see to things and to talk to. Then one day she had brought home Moses Cohen, the comedian, and said she was going to marry him. Grandmother had not been able properly to disapprove of Moses Cohen because he was a very great star in the music halls, but she was rather jealous of him because he had taken away her Lindsey. And so, because she was not always very polite, the Cohens got out of the way of calling on Grandmother and came only when they had a formal invitation. Sometimes, Miriam said, Grandmother forgot she was angry with her father and then they were around seeing her every day or so, but just at present they were not on very good terms.

"It's like that with Aunt Marguerite, too," Miriam

explained, "only it's worse for Aunt Marguerite because she thinks Uncle Francis the most marvelous actor in the world and Grandmother doesn't think he can act at all, and always says so. You wait till Grandmother imitates Uncle Francis and then you'll see. As a matter of fact I expect Grandmother will see more of them soon because of Miranda. Everybody, even Uncle Henry Warren in Hollywood, is pretty excited about Miranda. Somebody to carry on the tradition, you know."

Mark had puzzled about this. "But when Miranda goes on the stage she'll be Miranda Brain, so I shouldn't think anyone would know or care about that old tradition."

Miriam was amazed at his stupidity.

"Of course everybody knows. Who married who and what happened to everybody. When Sorrel's old enough to make her appearance, you'll see. It doesn't matter that she's called Sorrel Forbes, all the critics and most of the public will know she is Aunt Addie's daughter. Just like me—when I'm old enough they'll know, of course, that I'm Mose Cohen's daughter, but they'll know at the same time that my mother was a Warren."

Everybody talked to Miriam as though she were a great deal older than she was. She was an only child who had been brought up mostly with grown-up people, and everything to do with the theater was in her blood. Masses of theatrical people came to her parents' flat and talked business in front of her, so that on that particular subject she was much older than her age. Whenever Sorrel wanted to know anything about the theater she always asked Miriam's advice.

"If," she said anxiously, "everybody knows we're great-grandchildren of Sir Joshua, doesn't it mean that people will expect us to be fairly good?"

Miriam nodded soberly.

"You bet it does. As a matter of fact, we won't be allowed to go on with it if we aren't. My mother didn't do much. She started off with a bang when she was about eighteen and then she got some bad notices and then she got smaller parts, and then she gave it up. Mum says it was simply awful, she knew she couldn't do it. There were just two that were any good in the family—Uncle Henry, of course, and your mother."

"What about Aunt Marguerite?" Sorrel asked. "Didn't she act?"

Miriam lowered her voice.

"Well, that is one of the things that makes Grandmother angry. Grandmother never thought she could act, nor did Grandfather when he was alive. But she went on the stage and she didn't do so badly. Then she married Uncle Francis. Well, he made her his leading lady, mostly in Shakespeare. Sometimes Grandmother goes to see them act, and then on Christmas Day, and times like that, she shows Aunt Marguerite how she looked when she was being Lady Macbeth, or whatever it is." She giggled. "It's awfully funny. Dad adores it and leads Grandmother on to do it, though Mum always tells him not to. But then Dad's in a special position. Grandmother can't imitate Dad, and though she'd die rather than say it, she thinks he's awfully funny. I've sat in boxes with her and I've seen her laugh so much that all the paint came off her eyelashes."

Ever since she had been living with Grandmother, Sorrel had puzzled why, with one son who was a film star and a son-in-law who was a very successful comedian and another son-in-law who was Sir Francis Brain, the well-known Shakespearean actor, Grandmother should be so poor.

Again it was Miriam who explained. "Grandmother simply doesn't understand money and she never has, Mum says. Of course it's better now because there aren't so many things she can buy. But even now she spends all the money that she has, mostly on things she doesn't want. I don't exactly know but I think that now Mum and Aunt Marguerite give money for Grandmother to Alice, but Uncle Henry still sends it to her. Mum says he's just like her and spends every penny he has himself so he never has much to give away however much he earns. But I think it's Aunt Marguerite and Mum who see that Grandmother's all right."

Sorrel, Mark and Holly heard this in silence. It was evident from the way Miriam was dressed and all the things she had, that there was lots of money in her home. And it was equally clear that Miranda was so used to money that she took it for granted she could, as far as the war allowed, have everything she wanted. So it seemed a bit odd, if Aunt Lindsey and Aunt Marguerite were really giving Alice money for Grandmother, that they gave her so little. Alice had been quite right when she said bees and honey were words they would often hear her say. It was clear there was very little bees and honey in the house but, of course, they did not say this to Miriam. They could hardly suggest her own mother was mean.

Grandmother's favorite of the three children was Mark. She saw him at least twice to Sorrel's and Holly's once.

"Give me boys," she said. "I always preferred them." She would talk to Mark about his Uncle Henry. "I should like you to meet your uncle. There's a man! Can say more with his little finger than that ham actor, your Uncle Francis, can say with all the breath in his body. We must turn you into an actor like your Uncle Henry."

Mark was not at all afraid of Grandmother.

"I've told you hundreds of times I'm not going to be an actor. I'm going to be a sailor. In fact, I'm going to be an admiral."

Grandmother swept him to one side, leaped off her chaise longue, scattering her shawl and cushions all over the floor and, putting on a deep voice like a boatswain, quoted from *The Tempest*:

"Down with the topmast! yare! lower, lower. Bring her to try with main course. A plague upon this howling! They are louder than the weather or our office."

Mark hated Shakespeare and he particularly hated having Grandmother recite it.

"They don't say things like that in the Navy now,

whatever they did in that old *Tempest*." He picked up the cushions and said hopefully, "Can I tuck you up again, Grandmother?"

Grandmother saw why Mark was being so polite and it made her laugh. "Getting your own way? Come on, then. You shall amuse me. Tell me how Miriam's getting on."

Mark lay on his face on the floor and dug little holes in the carpet with his finger.

"Miriam can dance. Winifred thinks that Madame's going to teach her next term."

"Doesn't she teach all of you?" said Grandmother, surprised. "I thought that was what she started the school for, because she wanted to teach dancing."

Mark had been a pupil at the Academy sufficiently long to be appalled at such ignorance. "Of course she doesn't. Scarcely anyone. You've got to be absolutely outstanding for her to teach you by herself."

"Stupid waste of time, too much dancing; but good for deportment. I always said to Fidolia that she'd end by having a school for the theater, that it's all-round training we want, and I was right. Hope she doesn't waste too much of Miriam's time. Dancing's all very well in its proper place but I've hopes for Miriam. We don't want anyone making a dancer of her."

Mark dug into the wool of the carpet with his fingernail. "If Miriam can dance and can't act, wouldn't it be a good thing if she was a dancer?"

Grandmother sat up. That day she had on a gray dress with blue trimming on the sleeves. She took a deep breath and, throwing out an arm, said in a very grand voice:

"A Warren and not act! Never!"

Mark hurriedly got up off the floor and tucked Grandmother in again lest she get right up and recite some more Shakespeare. Having tucked her in, he was not going to relinquish his point.

"But just supposing, I said," he went on. "After all, just because your grandfather and your great-grandfather and all the rest of it were actors, you needn't be one. Somebody must start somewhere being something else."

Grandmother smiled. "Are you arguing with me?"

Mark was annoyed and scowled back at her. "If an interesting discussion has to be called an argument just because I'm young and you're grown-up, then I am."

Grandmother looked as though she were going to shake him. Then all of a sudden she laughed.

"Run away, my dear grandson. I'm glad that you're not a manager whom I have to see about a salary, for I feel you'd be a very hard nut to crack. Be off, now."

On Sorrel's visits, Grandmother usually asked a lot of questions about Miranda.

"How did my eldest granddaughter do today?"

Sorrel was nothing like as unafraid of Grandmother as Mark was. Grandmother's polish and finish made her feel all elbows and hands and she was awed by Grandmother's quick, vivid way of talking. She always had a feeling that Grandmother was wondering how on earth, in a brilliant family like the Warrens, they had managed to produce so dull a person as herself.

"We did *As You Like It* after tea. Miranda was Rosalind today, she was lovely. I was just being a forester."

Grandmother was looking at her hands.

"How do you mean, lovely? Like a girl who had fallen in love, or like a schoolgirl reciting?"

Sorrel glanced up to catch Grandmother's twinkling eyes fixed on her. "Well, I've not been in love much myself, and, of course, Orlando's only one of the girls, but I think she's like Rosalind. She certainly isn't a bit like anybody reciting."

Grandmother chuckled.

"And a very good thing, too. You've not met your Uncle Francis. Now, there's a real actor!" She giggled as she said this. "All wind and roar. One of the few sensible things they ever did was to send that child to Fidolia. She won't be allowed any of those tricks in her school."

Sorrel felt for words. "I don't think Miranda wants to do any tricks. Miss Jay never teaches her much and she generally does things right all by herself."

Grandmother gave her shawl an angry shake. "It maddens me to think that when that girl appears, her father will say she has inherited his talent. His talent indeed! He doesn't know the meaning of the word. If he had even a grain of understanding he would never allow your poor aunt to play the parts that she does. You've not met your Aunt Marguerite, Sorrel. She never had much talent but the poor girl deserved a better fate than to be Lady Brain.

"Your Uncle Francis was a young man when we

first met him, playing in our company. It was a costume piece and he was very good-looking, though just as much of a ham actor as he is today. Your Aunt Marguerite had a little part and the poor girl could hardly get through it for goggling at Francis. She thought him a genius and still does, if it comes to that. There they go, round and round the provinces with occasional trips to South Africa or Australia. There's scarcely a corner of the British Empire that has not had to endure your Aunt Marguerite in such parts as Lady Macbeth, for which she's totally unfitted. How upset your poor grandfather would be if he could see her!"

"What happens to Miranda when they're away?" Sorrel asked.

Grandmother waved a hand as if these domestic problems were of no importance. "A governess, a good soul. And her doting parents come home practically every weekend."

"But they couldn't from Africa or Australia, could they?" pursued Sorrel.

"Naturally, with the war on, they remain in England. When they went overseas, they took Miranda with them. They dote on her." Grandmother stroked the shawl and pleated it over her fingers. "Let them. That child is pure Warren. The Warren voice. The moment she sets a foot upon the stage, the critics will all say so. I would give a fortune to see your Uncle Francis's face when he reads that sort of notice." She suddenly remembered that Sorrel, too, was training. "And how are you doing, my dear?"

Sorrel was so afraid of being asked to recite that

she purposely made very little of her parts. "Well, of course, it's my first term. I'll have bigger parts later on."

"I must see Fidolia and inquire after you all. Mark, now, I'm sure there's talent there."

This pulled Sorrel out of her shyness. "Oh no, I'm sure there isn't. There wouldn't be likely to be. You see, he's going to be a sailor."

Grandmother would allow Mark to argue, but not Sorrel. Her eyes flashed.

"Mark will do what he's told. I've only one grandson and I pin great hopes on him. Great. Run along, now. Run along."

Holly looked forward to coming to see Grandmother because of the things there were to play with in the drawing room. The green jade horse was still her favorite but there were other things as well — ivory fans, and a silver cart, and a case full of bangles. It was an understood thing that if she put everything back, she could play with what she liked while she was in the drawing room. Holly amused Grandmother.

Because visiting Grandmother was an event and because they lived so much more in the world of the Academy than the world of home, the three never felt that there was excitement in the house. They knew Grandmother was out a lot but they never thought of asking why. Then one night when Hannah was giving them their supper, Alice came in looking important.

"I'll bet you a lord of the manor none of you three'll guess my bit of news." Mark was trying very hard to think what a lord of the manor might be. Alice ruffled his hair. "A tanner. A sixpence." They were all looking at her and she could not keep her secret any longer. "We're working again. We've got a new part, a very good part, and we start rehearsing the week after next. Our play opens in January."

Although of course they knew Grandmother was an actress, they had somehow never thought of her as working any more.

"Do you mean Grandmother's got a part?" Mark asked, obviously amazed. "She must be acting somebody very old, mustn't she?"

Alice laughed.

"'Tisn't only young nippers like you that people see in plays. All ages, all types, they are." She lowered her voice. "If you'll all swear not to repeat it I'll tell you something else. Come on, touch your loaves of bread." Sorrel and Mark and Holly all put their hands on their heads. Alice took a deep breath. "There's a little girl in the play and your grandmother wants young Miranda to play her."

"What, in a real play?" said Sorrel. "She told me she wasn't going on the stage until she was eighteen."

"That's what she thinks, but we think differently and we're seeing Sir Francis about it—and we generally get our own way. So you can take it from me that in the next few days you'll see young Miranda setting off to apply for a license."

Chapter XI

Mostly About Mark

Grandmother got her way. Miranda was to act in the play with her. And Miriam told her cousins bits of the excitement that had gone on about it.

"Aunt Marguerite telephoned to Mum about every twenty minutes all last night and all the night before. Uncle Francis thinks it would be better if Miranda waited to make her first appearance under his management. When Mum heard that, she just threw her telephone down and left it hanging from the wall without even putting it back on its rest. I heard it growling and sighing and went and put it back for her. Mum said to Dad, 'That's all this awful jealousy. He thinks nobody in the world can teach anybody to act but himself.' Anyway, in the end, Grandmother got her way. I knew she would, she always does."

Miranda's engagement caused a certain amount of stir in the Academy. It would have caused more only it was the autumn term and a number of the other girls who were old enough for a license had gotten engagements too. True, they were mostly for pantomime, though two of the students were going into *Peter Pan.* Of course, Miranda's acting part was something rather grand and special. Nevertheless, an engagement was an engagement and just because Miranda's was for acting and most of the others were for dancing, that was no reason for her to think she was of more importance than anyone else.

All the pupils at the Academy, as they neared their twelfth birthday, had prepared what they called "m'audition," which was their way of saying "my audition." It meant that they had learned a speech or a recitation which suited them, and that they had a song ready, or special music to which they could do a little dance. This was the full audition. If a pupil was working on a singing part or a dancing part or an acting part only, naturally he or she only sang or danced or acted, but for a pantomime they usually did all three. Nearly forty of the students were over twelve and every day one or two were standing in the hall in the best frock or suit they had, waiting to be inspected by Miss Jay or Winifred before they went to their audition. The rest of the school, passing them, would call out "Good luck, John," or "Good luck, Mary."

Sorrel had studied the twelve-year-olds waiting in the hall pretty carefully. Although she was nearly thirteen, she still had plenty to learn before she could expect to have an audition, and she wanted to get a good idea of what ought to be worn, and the right sort of face to put on. It was not at all a good thing to look cocky, because if you did and then came back without the engagement you had gone after, you looked a fool. On the other hand, it was not a good thing to look nervous and miserable because then the school said, "Gosh, I shouldn't think anyone would ever give her a job; she looked as if it had been raining for a week."

Miranda's rehearsals were not starting for ten days and she was to continue with her ordinary training until they did, and as far as possible while rehearsals were in progress. Until the Christmas holidays began, she had to get in five hours of lessons a day by law, and in the meantime the management was trying not to call her to rehearsals until the late afternoons and on Saturday mornings. Miranda resented having to come to the Academy at all. To Sorrel's great surprise, she chose her to confide in.

"It's a long and difficult part," Miranda told her. "I ought to be at home studying it. It's ridiculous to waste my time here."

"Couldn't you arrange with Madame to do only dancing, singing and lessons, and drop the acting classes? I shouldn't think anyone would mind if you did."

Miranda looked at Sorrel as if she were a worm.

"So that's what you think, do you? I suppose it has never struck you to wonder what would happen to these troop concerts if they didn't have me to keep them together?"

Sorrel had no wish to quarrel with Miranda, but she did wonder how anybody could be so conceited, and she could not help her voice showing a bit of what she was thinking.

"I suppose somebody else could do your part. I mean they'd have to if you weren't there, wouldn't they?"

"I'd like to know who," said Miranda, and stalked away.

As it happened, a concert for the troops was at that very moment being discussed by Madame and her staff.

"They want us to give a matinée for the forces in the Princess Theater, or rather they want us to take over one half of it. The rest will be music hall turns. It's to take place just before Christmas. I had said yes, intending to use Miranda, but now I don't know what we are going to do if we can't have her. I don't think we've any other student competent to act as mistress of ceremonies. However, I've written to her management to ask if they will release her from rehearsal for that one afternoon, and we must wait to see what they say. For the rest we'll use the best of the items in the various other programs that we have given this term, and I think, as it's a Christmas entertainment, we should put in a Christmas ballet and perhaps a carol or something like that. Has anyone any ideas?"

The result of that conference began to filter through the Academy. And Winifred started some strenuous rehearsals on the new ballet. Miriam was, of course, too young to be allowed to work on her pointes, but she was so very much the most promising dancer in the school that the ballet was to center around her. To the Forbeses' surprise, Miriam was not at all pleased at what the rest of the Academy thought her good fortune. She tried to explain to them why.

"It's very important at my age that I shouldn't be brought forward in any way," she said. "I should now be getting my technique firm so that in a year's time when I begin to work on my pointes I can take my training seriously."

Sorrel had to laugh. "You can't say you don't take it seriously now, Miriam. You never think about anything else."

"That's perfectly true," Miriam admitted. "But it isn't making me do too advanced work that I'm so worried about—I know neither Winifred nor Madame would allow that. But if I dance in public there's almost sure to be notice taken of me and then Dad'll hear and probably there'll be a row. Not, mind you, that a row is going to make any difference at all. I'm going to be a dancer whatever anybody says. But it could be tiresome, and I don't want it to be."

Sorrel, in her free moments, thought a lot about these conversations with Miranda and Miriam. How confident they were! And how different about it. Miranda was conceited somehow and spoiled, but

Miriam was like a person following a path through a wood. There might be a lot of other interesting paths branching off at the side, but Miriam saw only the path that her feet were on, and nothing could distract her from it.

Miriam was not the only person who came into prominence over the forces matinée. The juniors were dancing and miming some of their nursery rhymes, and four of the rhymes were to be sung as a solo. Dr. Lente was asked to pick a child for these solos. To everybody's surprise, because he had never said anything about him before, he at once mentioned Mark. Dr. Lente was a refugee who did not speak English very well.

"The little Mark, when he is trying, which is by no means always, has the voice of much charm, true and clear."

At the next nursery rhyme rehearsal Mark was placed beside the piano and Mrs. Blondin and told to sing "I Had a Little Nut Tree." Miss Jay knew Mark liked to find something that he personally thought was interesting about what he was asked to do, or it was very difficult for him to attend properly. Since Dr. Lente had said that Mark could sing like a bird, Miss Jay built on that idea.

"I want you to think of yourself as rather an important kind of bird singing on a bough."

Mark considered this. "What sort of bird?"

Ornithology was not Miss Jay's subject, but she knew that Mark would want to picture himself in feathers.

"A special bird. A foreign bird. I think his feathers

are blue and green and he has a scarlet crest."

Mark visualized such a bird and then his eye fell on Mrs. Blondin. She was in her red blouse. That day, she also had on a small green felt hat with a little feather in it.

"What's she doing in the wood with me?" he asked in a confidential tone. "Is she a bird, too?"

Miss Jay was not going to risk offending a good accompanist, so she moved away, saying with that sort of dismissing smile people use when they do not want a child to go on with a conversation:

"Of course, dear, a lovely bird."

Then she turned her head towards the piano and barked in the only tone that was known to penetrate Mrs. Blondin's daydreams:

"Begin."

Mrs. Blondin played the opening bars and Mark, proudly swaying on his branch, began to sing.

"I had a little nut tree and nothing would it bear," then he stopped. He turned a pleased face to Miss Jay. "Not a bird at all, one of those monkeys that's got no fur behind but blue and pink instead, and its fingers are moving all the time because it's looking for fleas."

The children laughed, though nobody except Miss Jay knew what Mark was talking about. Mrs. Blondin certainly had not heard. She was still playing, for Miss Jay had not said "Stop." Miss Jay looked severe.

"I'm not interested in anyone in this particular forest except a bird that I'm waiting to hear sing." Then she changed her voice to a bark. "Stop." Mrs.

Blondin's fingers shot off the piano and fell in her lap. Miss Jay went over to her and tapped her shoulder. "We're doing that all over again. Begin."

Mark's singing really was a lovely noise. He had an absolutely true voice, and now that he had placed Mrs. Blondin as a mandrill in his mind, he was able to dismiss her from his thoughts and sing with the unforced ease of the bird he was certain he was.

Then came discussion about what Mark should wear. An old student of the Academy, who was visiting, made an offer. Her little boy had been a page at a wedding at the beginning of the war. He had worn a Kate Greenaway suit with a very frilly white shirt, blue satin trousers, white silk socks and blue satin shoes. Everybody was enchanted, and from Madame Fidolia down they all said so.

They had all reckoned without Mark. The box with his clothes arrived one morning and Mark was sent for to try them on. After gazing at them in an almost trancelike way, he pulled himself together.

"Who is going to wear this?" he asked.

Winifred opened her mouth to say "You" when Miss Jay gave her a little nudge. She had caught a look in Mark's eye she did not like.

"Kate Greenaway designed clothes very suitable for singing nursery rhymes," she said briskly. "When she was alive, boys of all ages were dressed like this."

Mark looked at the socks and shoes and dismissed what Miss Jay was saying as sheer foolishness. And indeed the argument about that set of clothes was not worrying him for he had no intention of wearing them. But he was furious with Miss Jay. He considered her a friend and thought she had let him down.

"You promised me I'd be dressed in blue and green feathers with a scarlet crest."

Miss Jay wished with all her heart she had never invented his bird. It had never crossed her mind that Mark thought he was going to be dressed in feathers. She was a scrupulously fair woman and would never pretend that something was going to happen that was not in order to bribe a child to work well. She decided that she must have time to think of the right approach to Mark before she forced the clothes on him. She put the lid on the box and put her arm around him.

"Sorry, I had never planned you should be dressed as a bird. I had only imagined you singing like one. But we'll see what can be done."

It was no surprise to Miss Jay that at the next rehearsal Mark sang very badly. She was sorry but she would have been sorrier still if she could have known how violently angry and hurt he was.

He confided just how he felt to Sorrel. "It isn't only that they thought they could dress me like a girl in blue satin," he said. "I'm used to all that sort of thing. But I just hate the way older people make promises and then break them. She says she didn't, but she absolutely did. I was being a bird on a branch, and the only person near me was that Mrs. Blondin, and she was a mandrill looking for fleas."

Sorrel had known, from Mark, that he was going to be dressed as a bird and that he was pleased about it. But this was the first time she had known to what lengths his imagination had carried him.

"But, Mark," she said, "Mrs. Blondin's going to be sitting at the piano in the orchestra, where all the audience can see her. You couldn't really have thought she was going to be dressed as a mandrill." She thought a little more on the subject and then added: "Especially a mandrill, seeing what they look like in back."

Mark's imagination, when in full flood, was quite incapable of being checked by material difficulties. He could only repeat in a voice suffocated with anger:

"It's what she said and what she promised."

Miss Jay went to see Madame and told her the whole story. All her life Madame had worked with imaginative people and she had known what it was, when she was Mark's age, to build a completely imaginary world from fragments of conversation overheard, or things invented by herself.

"Send Winifred along here, will you?" she said now.

When Winifred came dashing in Madame pointed to a chair for her to sit on and then told her about he dilemma she and Miss Jay were in, adding:

"I think, since we can't dress him as a bird, that we'll have to suggest a compromise. Could we put a polar bear into the winter ballet? We could alter that white cat's skin we've got in the wardrobe, and I expect we can hire or contrive a white bear's head. And we must make a stumpy tail. Anyway, it would be near enough."

Winifred got up and hummed the ballet music, now and again doing half a step demi-pointe. Then she turned to Madame.

"Why shouldn't the child, when she wakes up in the land of winter, find herself lying with her head on a polar bear? As a matter of fact, I wanted to think of something that would add to the fairy-tale atmosphere of that scene. Mark can't dance much, of course, but he can manage a few simple steps and he'll certainly add to the charm of the scene."

Winifred was sent to fetch Mark. He came in to Madame's sitting room, bowed nicely, and said "Madame," but his eyes were not the friendly eyes that Madame usually saw. They were hard and angry. She smiled at him.

"Well, my son, I hear we've disappointed you."

Mark was fair enough not to blame Madame for what had happened. "It was an absolute promise, blue and green feathers and a red crest."

Madame spoke quietly. "No, Mark. It was not an absolute promise. You thought it was a promise, but it was a misunderstanding." Mark moved forward to speak. Madame lifted her hand and checked him. "And what is more, my child, you cannot be dressed as a bird because we have not got anything at all in the way of a costume for a bird. And, as you know, we cannot waste coupons on materials for these things. Before we go any further with this discussion I want you to apologize to Miss Jay. You should have known her too well to think that she would make you a promise and not keep it."

"But she did promise. And Mrs. Blondin was a mandrill."

This was too much for Madame. She laughed.

"Nonsense, Mark! I do not care how vivid your imagination may be, you cannot seriously, even at your age, have thought Miss Jay was going to dress Mrs. Blondin as a mandrill." She changed her tone. "But I do think you thought there was a promise and, because you thought that, when you have apologized to Miss Jay I shall tell you what I propose to do to make it up to you."

Mark wrestled with himself, and at last he managed to say:

"Well, I'm sorry if I said you broke a promise when you didn't."

Miss Jay accepted this. "Thank you, Mark."

Madame beckoned him to her and held out a hand. "Now hear what we have planned for you instead. How would you like to be a bear?"

Mark's world reeled. He flew off his branch, cast aside his feathers and dressed himself in fur. "What sort of bear?"

"Polar," said Madame.

Mark turned to Miss Jay. "All the songs will have to be set very low to be sung in a growl."

Miss Jay had a horrifying vision of what Mark as a bear might do to her nursery rhymes. She spoke slowly and rather severely, so that there might be no mistake this time.

"The nursery rhymes come first, and for those you wear the Kate Greenaway suit that you saw in the box. You will sing the nursery rhymes just the same as you did when you were a bird, but you will be dressed as a boy."

Madame took up the conversation.

"You know all about the ballet in the second half, Mark. We want a polar bear in that. If you sing the nursery rhymes well you shall be that bear, but one of the other children will understudy you, and if you don't sing well then you won't be the bear."

Mark took most of the day to get his ideas sorted out. But after tea there was a rehearsal of the winter ballet, and he was given two or three steps to learn, including some pas de chats, which, in his opinion, were just right for the movements of a bear. Coming home on the underground he was in the wildest spirits and told Sorrel and Holly all about it.

Holly was looking forward to the matinée. She was small and pretty and what the staff called "dressable." She was given three little parts and for each she had something very nice to wear.

Sorrel was the only one of the family to stay in the background. She still had nothing to do but dance as a black lamb. She tried to pretend she did not mind. She told herself she never had wanted to be an actress anyway, so what did she care. But actually she did mind very much indeed. She had been getting on well in her acting classes—both Madame Moulin and Miss Jay said so—and as soon as she had heard of the matinée she had secretly hoped that she would be given a little part in a sketch. Not a big or showy part, just something quite small. It had been a blow and made her feel discouraged when the parts were handed out and she had nothing. To make things worse, because she had so little to do she was made to take Miranda's parts while Miranda was at her play rehearsals. Miranda, of course, heard about this.

"You'll have to stand-in for me again today, Sorrel. They need me at the theater."

Sorrel tried not to be rude but it was difficult. "I'm not standing-in. If it's anything, it's understudying."

"Call it what you like. You ought to be pleased. It's admirable experience for you."

When a notice was put on the board to say there would be a dress rehearsal at the Princess Theater on the morning before the matinée, Sorrel was delighted.

"They can't get that awful old matinée over quick enough for me," she confided to a fellow lamb. "I'm so bored with it, it makes my mouth yawn every time it's mentioned."

Chapter XII

A Swollen Head

Alice took Sorrel and Mark and Holly to their dress rehearsal. Hannah did not exactly refuse to go but she said, looking very stubborn, that she couldn't seem to fancy it. Alice was glad of the opportunity to get inside any theater.

"We've gone to our rehearsal," she said, "and we can manage by ourselves for one morning. What's more, I know my way about behind the scenes, so you can trust old Alice to see the three young ones through."

Sorrel found, as she had when she went to the performance for the seamen, that she felt wormy inside—at least, that was how she described her feelings to herself. She was not really worried about being a lamb; it was a mixture of things. Worrying whether Mark would sing all right, wondering if all Holly's dresses were there, if the girls would turn up in time, and how it would feel to be on a real stage in a real theater.

The dress rehearsal was supposed to start at half-past ten, but like most dress rehearsals it did not start punctually. The stage was hung with curtains of a pale gray shade; colored lighting was to be used to give different effects to different scenes. Miss Jay and Winifred had written out what lighting they wanted for the various items, but that did not seem to satisfy the electrician and for some time there was a great deal of "Put in your ambers, Bill," "Might try a frost on that," "Would you like it all frost, Miss? You get a colder look that way, if that's what you're after."

Miranda, in her black overall, and the pupils who were taking part in the small ballet which followed the prologue, stood on the edge of the stage watching and whispering and trying to keep quiet, but not succeeding very well because they were all rather excited and it is difficult to behave quietly when you feel like that. Miranda was very quiet but that was because she was very annoyed. She considered herself a star now, and was furious at being kept waiting.

"It's disgraceful, keeping me hanging about like this," she declared. "If I had known, I'd have come much later. My management didn't let me off my rehearsal for this sort of thing."

The others got bored with Miranda for making such a fuss. And one of them said so. "Why don't you go and tell Miss Jay about it? Tell her that with a person as important as you in the cast we've simply got to begin."

The girl was, of course, trying to be funny. To everybody's surprise Miranda took her quite seriously. She tossed her head and said "I think I will" and marched down to Miss Jay, who was standing by the footlights. The other girls, their eyes round with horror, watched her, holding their breaths for the explosion which was bound to follow. Miranda spoke to Miss Jay quite quietly. Miss Jay, busy talking to the electrician, did not hear what she said.

"Thank you very much," she called to the electrician. "That's exactly the effect I want." She turned to Miranda. "What is it, dear? You can see I'm busy."

Miranda lost her temper. "I was asking if we could begin. It's really ludicrous to bring me here at this hour of the morning to hang about."

Miss Jay, a very steely glint in her eye, was turning to answer, when a voice came from the dress circle. Nobody had seen Madame arrive, for she had come in quietly and sat down, and there was very little light in the theater. The group of dancers, quite cold with fright for Miranda, hurriedly curtsied and said "Madame," but Madame was not attending to them.

"Miranda, would you please repeat clearly the words you have just used to Miss Jay?"

Miranda had the grace to look a little frightened. She dropped a beautiful curtsy and said "Madame" before she answered.

"I was just asking if we couldn't begin."

"And why, pray, did you take it upon yourself to dictate to Miss Jay about when the curtain should go up?"

"Well, I've got a morning off from my rehearsal to come here and it seems a most awful waste of time. I mean, it isn't as though it was a real performance or anything like that. I mean..."

"I see quite clearly what you mean, but I see no point in your argument. I have here a letter from your management saying that you may have the morning off and that they would not have needed you in any case, as they are not taking your scenes. I'm most distressed, Miranda, that a pupil of mine should behave as you've just behaved. Because you have been engaged for a part in a production is no reason for you to behave in a spoiled and vulgar manner."

Miranda felt the girls behind her were enjoying the row, and that the electricians were looking on, and that Miss Jay must be delighted because Madame was telling her off. She lost her head.

"I do think it's inconsiderate. It's an important part and naturally I'm nervous. I think it was a bit too much to expect me to do this matinée as well."

There was an awful pause. Then Madame's voice at its coldest was heard across the theater. "Miss Jay, Sorrel Forbes knows Miranda's lines, I think."

Miss Jay was in a quandary. Sorrel did know the

lines, but she had only just rattled them through, and in any case she could hardly be as good as Miranda. But Miss Jay knew Madame. Madame would far rather have a part less well played than have one of her pupils go unpunished for bad behavior such as Miranda had just shown. So she nodded.

"Yes, she knows the lines. There was no thought of her playing, as you know, so I've not rehearsed her in them."

"Then please send someone to tell Sorrel that she will be taking over Miranda's parts and, as soon as she's changed and you're ready, the rehearsal can begin."

Miranda was like a pricked balloon. All the arrogance had blown out of her. "But, Madame, I didn't mean it, truthfully I didn't. I'm awfully sorry. I want to take my parts in the matinée."

"You should have thought of that before," Madame retorted. "If you will change, I will see that some arrangement is made for sending you home."

Sorrel was talking to Alice in the passage outside the dressing rooms.

"The call boy comes along when they're ready to start," Alice was saying, "and raps on each door and says 'Overture and beginners, please.' That means that the overture is about to start, and everybody who's concerned in the beginning of the act goes down on the stage. When it's a proper play, like the one your grandmother is rehearsing now, he calls people by their names. He'll rap and he'll say, 'Overture and beginners, Miss Shaw, please.' When the play's been on a bit of time I'll take you around to one matinée. You won't be allowed to come into our dressing room—anybody about gets us in a fidget—but I'll see if I can get the stage manager to let you stand down in the prompt corner."

One of the children had been selected by Miss Jay to find Sorrel. Now she came tearing up the passage. Her words tumbled out in a jumble.

"Sorrel, there's been the most fearful row. Miranda's sauced Madame, and Madame told her off good and proper, and she isn't to take part in the matinée, and Miss Jay says you're to take all her parts, and will you go to number three dressing room where the clothes are."

Alice was the one who grasped all this. An understudy thrown on in a hurry was the breath of life to her. She snorted like a hunter who hears hounds.

"Come on, ducks, here's your chance. Fancy, the very first time, too! The numbers of understudies I've known who have waited from one end of the run to the other for something like this to happen. Even got so far as to grease the old apples and pears, hoping for a sprained ankle or something, and here you're going on the very first time."

Sorrel clutched at Alice, as if Alice were the only piece of wood and she a drowning mariner in a large sea.

"Alice, I can't, I don't know it. I mean, I've never acted them properly or anything."

Alice took her firmly by the arm. "Nonsense, come on now. You show young Miranda she's not the only member of the family who's inherited the Warren talent." She pulled Sorrel into dressing room number three. "Sit down, ducks, while I comb out your hair, and give you a bit of make-up." She turned to the girl who had come to fetch Sorrel. "Nip along to the room we were in, number nine it is, and get Sorrel's socks and sandals."

Sorrel thought that morning the most awful she had ever lived through. Miranda, besides being mistress of ceremonies, took part in two little sketches in which she had the leading parts. Miranda was bigger than Sorrel, and none of the clothes fitted properly. Because she was nervous, Sorrel stammered over some of her words. In the little sketch in which she wore a crinoline, she tripped over her frock. She felt in such a rush and tear there was never time to be sure what she was doing with anything. Now and again she cast anxious glances at Miss Jay and she saw that Miss Jay looked harassed and she did not blame her. Poor Miss Jay! How sickening for her to have the show ruined like this!

At the end of the performance, Miss Jay asked to have the curtain raised. She called the cast onto the stage to receive notes from Madame. Madame came down to the front of the stalls. She had a page of notes in her hand. First of all, because it was the subject she liked best, she spoke to the dancers. She had been, she said, exceedingly pleased with the winter ballet. The fairies had kept their line very well, but the glissades were not clean cut, and the line was untidy during the pirouettes. Then she turned to Miriam. She spoke in a warm voice, which all the Academy pupils knew meant she was pleased.

"You seemed to be having a very happy time."

Then she nodded to Mark. "And as for Mark, you were really a most energetic and sprightly bear. A most realistic study, I thought."

When she had finished with the dancers Madame turned to the singing numbers. "I was pleased with the nursery rhymes but, Holly, I thought you were a very restless buttercup. What was happening to you?"

Holly came down to the footlights. "I thought there was a little wind blowing through the garden."

Madame laughed. "Well, I don't think we'll have any wind blowing, Holly. I want a very grand, proud buttercup who stands still and shows off her petals. Now all the dancers and singers can go; I only want those concerned with the sketches to remain."

Sorrel wriggled her way to the back of the waiting children. "Oh, gosh!" she thought. "Now it's coming. She's going to tell me I was terrible and I know it's perfectly true."

Madame waited until the last of the dancers and singers had gone through the pass door.

"The two sketches were, understandably, a little ragged," she said. "You're used to playing with Miranda so that is only natural, but on the whole I am very pleased with you all. When we get back to the Academy Miss Jay will, of course, take you through them again, and give Sorrel a chance to feel easy in her parts. Now where is Sorrel? Come here, my dear. I'm really delighted with you. It's your first term and your clothes don't fit. They will, of course, be altered today. You have in no sense been the official understudy, so really it was a splendid effort.

Now don't feel anxious or worried. I'm sure we are all going to be very proud of you tomorrow."

Sorrel went back to her dressing room hardly knowing that she was walking. She had been so certain that Madame was going to say she was going to send for Miranda after all, that she had hardly taken in what had been said to her. As she changed she told Alice all about it.

"I'm going to do it tomorrow, all of it—the two long speeches at the beginning and the end, and the three little ones explaining about the nursery rhymes, the winter ballet, and the songs. I don't mind them so much—it's the sketches, particularly that awful one where I am a picture come to life. Of course the thing I step out of may look like a picture on an easel to the audience, but I feel that I'm twitching all over and that everyone knows from the beginning that I'm not a painting. Then, in the scene where I'm a schoolgirl who dreams that she's in a Victorian schoolroom, I feel all legs. The awful part is I'm meant to be funny. Of course I know there was only Madame in the theater this morning, so of course nobody could laugh, but won't it be awful if nobody laughed tomorrow? The seamen laughed and laughed when Miranda did the part."

Alice brushed out Sorrel's hair. "Now don't go working yourself up into a state, my dear," she said. "All you have to do is go on and do your best and nobody can't ask for more."

Sorrel stood beside Miss Jay. They peered at the audience through a little hole in the curtain. It was a special performance for forces on leave and there were all sorts of uniforms—the khaki of the girls' coats and skirts, the navy blue of the sailors and of the W.R.N.S., and the light blue of the Air Force and the W.A.A.F.'s. Because everybody was on leave and therefore in good spirits, there was an absolute roar of conversation and laughter, and the theater was gray with cigarette smoke.

Sorrel looked up at Miss Jay. "They don't look as if they needed amusing very much, which is a good thing, isn't it?"

Miss Jay laughed. "We shall soon know if we don't amuse them. They won't mean to but they'll shuffle their feet and cough when they aren't amused. Even the nicest audience can be turned very easily into a nasty one." She was holding Sorrel's hand and she gave it a squeeze. "Not that I'm worrying about you. I'm sure you're going to be a great success."

"If only something didn't seem to be turning round and round in my front," groaned Sorrel.

"Everybody's got to be nervous," said Miss Jay, "but there are some things you can do to help it. Try taking very deep breaths."

Sorrel tried. But somehow the breath got stopped halfway. "I can't. It's coming out in little pants like a dog in the summer."

"Try again," Miss Jay encouraged, "and I'll try too."

Miss Jay breathed and Sorrel breathed, and all of a sudden Sorrel found it was quite true—the deeper her breaths the less disturbed her front felt.

Winifred came over to them. "I've got a message for you from Madame. What do you think is waiting for you at the Academy when we go back after the matinée?" She saw that Sorrel was not going to guess and she was bursting to tell her news. "It's a letter from Pauline Fossil, and there's one for Holly from Posy."

Miss Jay beamed and then looked anxious. "I'm afraid we can't spare another minute. It must be about time we were ringing up. Come along, Sorrel dear."

Sorrel followed Miss Jay back to the prompt corner. And suddenly the orchestra stopped playing popular songs and began Roger Quilter's "Children's Overture." It was their own music. She clutched at her front.

"Oh goodness, that means we are going to begin, doesn't it?"

Miss Jay kissed her. "It does. As you are down already and won't be called, I shall say to you 'Overture and beginners, Sorrel, please.'"

The curtain was up. Sorrel had to come through the front cloth to speak the prologue. She looked small against it, standing there all by herself, but her dark hair and black tunic stood out clearly against the light lemon color of the cloth, and the effect was nice. For this reason, or perhaps just because the forces were on leave and in a very good temper, before she could speak at all they began to clap. Sorrel tried to speak through it. The audience saw her mouth moving and, while half the people were still clapping, the other half were saying "shush." Then from the prompt corner, in just as ordinary a voice as she used in the classroom, Miss Jay said:

"Make a nice curtsy, Sorrel, and begin all over again."

It seemed queer to Sorrel to hear her voice in that big place, and the first few words that left her mouth sounded very weak. Then all of a sudden the audience's friendliness came to her like a hug, and she spoke directly to it as if it were an old friend. When she finished with a curtsy, there was a roar of applause. She slipped back through the curtain and joined Miss Jay on the side of the stage. Her first entrance was over.

The ballet was not Miss Jay's business. It was Winifred's. Winifred watched it from the wings, muttering, "Look at Angela's posture! That's a queer sort of jeté. Oh, what a shocking pirouette!"

Miss Jay drew Sorrel against the wall. "Very nice, dear."

"I'm sorry about the muddle at the beginning but I never expected them to clap."

They were, of course, speaking in whispers. Miss Jay leaned down. "Never mind, you've learned a very valuable lesson about speaking through applause."

Sorrel's next entrance was to announce the nursery rhymes and then she had to change for her first sketch. Mark came through the pass door and strolled down to her. He looked absolutely unconcerned and he also, though Sorrel would not have dreamed of telling him so, looked very nice indeed in his Kate Greenaway suit.

"Alice has gone in front. Hannah won't sit in the dressing room. She said when Holly's face was painted that Holly was like Jezebel—you know, the one the dogs ate."

Nothing could be encored on the program because there was only an hour and a half allowed for the Academy, and they had a program lasting exactly that long. But if it had been possible to encore, then Mark's singing would have been.

The other big success of the matinée was Miriam. Her dancing absolutely charmed the audience, who shouted for her when the ballet finished.

Winifred watched her and there were tears in her eyes. "What extraordinary fortune! You would think that a school that had produced Posy Fossil would not get the same luck twice."

It was most disheartening how ordinary everything became the second the matinée was over. The dressing rooms were inspected to see they were perfectly tidy for the real actors who would use them that night, and then Sorrel and Mark and Holly were walking to the underground with Hannah and Alice.

Sorrel said, "Nobody would believe, looking at us, what an exciting afternoon we've had."

Hannah had been rather proud really, but she was not going to say so. "I should hope not. You look as though you might be going to tea at a vicarage, and very proper too."

"But the afternoon's not over yet, Sorrel," Alice said. "You and me are going round by the Academy to fetch some letters."

In a minute the world stopped looking gray, flat

and dull and was as gay as a chalk butterfly. Sorrel skipped with excitement.

"My letter from Pauline Fossil! Isn't it super it turned up just this afternoon!"

Sorrel could not wait to get home to read her letter. She and Alice read it in the underground.

Dear Sorrel,

This is difficult to write because it's odd writing to somebody you've never seen. I shall find it much easier when I've had an answer from you. I am very glad that Madame has given you my scholarship, and I hope it will be useful to you.

Madame has told me about Mark and I have written by this mail to Petrova and told her about him, as I think she would like to give him a scholarship in the way that Posy and I have to you and Holly. I expect Mark will be hearing from her. Tell him not to mind if she doesn't say much. She's very busy and anyway she never was a person who expressed herself much. She lives in a cottage near where she flies, with our Great-Uncle Matthew.

When you answer this will you tell me exactly how Madame looks and how the school is run now? I hear you do lessons there as well as stage training. We never did in my day and I can't imagine it somehow. I hope they've changed the design of rompers for tap—we always hated those. I am sending over some money for you to buy yourself a Christmas present. We were always wanting things so dreadfully when we were your ages, and we never had the money to buy them, and I daresay you're the same.

Please give Winifred the most enormous hug and tell her not to go and see my newest film called *Look Up and Laugh*. It's all about entertaining soldiers, and I was made to do a song and a dance, and it so reminded me of the first audition I ever went to, and how she said to me, "You were out of tune in the song, and your ankle shook awfully in the arabesque." Please remember me affectionately (and respectfully) to Miss Jay and Madame Moulin. I have written to Madame by this post. Please write soon.

    Yours affectionately,
    Pauline.

Posy's letter was in such a sprawling, difficult handwriting that Alice read it to Holly.

My dear Holly,
    I've heard from Madame that she's given you my scholarship. She says she is not sure whether you are going to dance in the way I meant, so I have written to her and said to give you a scholarship anyway, and find another dancer for me, as that is what I really want. I am not liking it here. Ballet is most unsatisfactory on the screen. It is all right

during the shooting and much of the choreography is lovely, especially as in my last picture, which Manoff directed. But when you see it it goes too fast—the space is too small and much of the footwork gets blurred. Garnie (my guardian) and Pauline say it's a good thing I have a contract because it means I will have money for afterwards when Manoff starts his ballet. I am to be one of his prima ballerinas. We've planned to do some beautiful things, and he will collect many of his old company. I think it's bound to be a success, but Pauline, Garnie and Nana say they think it will be the kind of success that means it is a very good thing to have money behind you.

I have sent over two pounds for you to have a Christmas present. Nana says you'd better spend it on woollies because she always thought the Academy cold. But of course you won't. I'm only telling you because she asked me to. Please give all my love to everybody in the Academy that I know, and tell Madame that every day, no matter what happens, I do her six special exercises, and I have worked out a message which my feet say to her every day.

With love,
Posy. XXXXXXX

Chapter XIII

Christmas Day

Christmas Day in every family is built up on little bits of custom. Something happens one year and it is amusing and gay and Christmasy, and so it becomes part of all future Christmases. Christmas Day in Guernsey had been full of things like that. The Forbeses' father had come into the nursery for the opening of their stockings. There were always band instruments in each stocking, and when the stocking opening was finished they played "Good King Wenceslas" with their father singing the solo part of the King and Mark singing the page, and a lot of repeat verses for the band only. There had been visits to friends after morning church and a lovely party with a Christmas tree in somebody else's house in the afternoon.

When Sorrel and Mark and Holly went to live with Grandfather, Hannah did the best she could with Christmas. She managed the band instruments in the stockings and she tried to sing "Good King Wenceslas." This was lucky because that first wartime Christmas had been a bit queer and miserable, with their father away. But Hannah singing the King's part in "Good King Wenceslas" had been so funny that they had all laughed until they felt sick. As Hannah could not sing "Good King Wenceslas" they had made her sing "The First Noël" as a solo, with the three of them helping in the Noël bits, and this having happened for three Christmases, it was now an established custom.

This year Christmas was obviously going to be quite different from anything they had known before. They were keeping, of course, a few of their own customs, but mostly they were going to be part of Grandmother's. Christmas Day was the day when she received her family. She had them all to dinner in the evening. It made the day exciting, in a way, to be going to meet Aunt Lindsey and Uncle Mose and Uncle Francis and Aunt Marguerite, and to be going to see Miranda and Miriam away from the Academy.

"Proper set-up it is," said Alice. "I'm worn to a shred by the time I've laid the Cain and Abel. And when it comes to dishing up I never know how to drag my plates of meat up the apples and pears. This year it won't half be a set-up. We're receiving in style. We've got a part. We're on top of the world. We shan't half see that we're number one at our own party."

Because of the Fossil scholarships, Sorrel and Holly had a shilling pocket money every week. This, divided into three, made eightpence each. They spent some of their eightpences on their month's sweet ration, and they each gave a penny a week to the Red Cross, and there was, of course, a penny for the collection on Sundays. But what was left over they had saved for Christmas presents.

They could not, of course, buy much because there was scarcely anything that was cheap enough to buy, but they managed parcels all around. Sorrel had bought a party hair bow for Holly, and some pencils for Mark. For Alice and Hannah there were calendars. Mark gave Sorrel and Holly drawing pins, which seemed a funny present but was one of the few things he could afford to buy that was useful. For Hannah there was a little wooden ruler, and for Alice some thumbtacks. Holly had never been able to grasp how coupons worked. Up till almost Christmas Day she hoped to buy soap for everybody, because she liked to smell it. When at last she realized that no matter what shop you went into they would all want soap coupons, it was Christmas Eve and the shops were nearly empty. So in desperation she bought buns—not even nice buns, but the sort you would expect to get when you stand in line for them on Christmas Eve. For Grandmother, the three of them had put their money together. They bought a white heath in a little pot. It was really a tiny plant and it cost a fearful lot, but it was the best they could manage, so that was that.

Christmas Day started in a proper way. There were the stockings and there was Hannah. And Alice too came in to hear the carol singing. Then she said:

"Christmas carols always make me cry and that's a fact." She laid four little parcels on the bed. "You pay your money and you take your choice."

How Alice had managed to save the sugar and get the highly rationed treacle nobody knew and nobody asked, but there were four packets of toffee, home-made, brown and stiff. So the hat was, as it were, put on the day when they all had a piece of Alice's toffee in their mouths.

Hannah's church was very nicely decorated. "Just what we might have had at home," she said. "I can't praise higher."

In the afternoon it was not a bad day so they went over to the Square garden, and there they saw two boys and a girl kicking a football about. Evidently what the head gardener had said was true. Now that the chance of bombing was less, the boys and girls were beginning to come back. Holly and the smaller boy, whose name was Robert, went off to ride on the tricycle that he had been given that morning, and Sorrel and Mark played football with the other two. They got very hot and the time passed extraordinarily quickly; they were amazed when the nurse belonging to the other children came along and said it was nearly time for tea.

Sorrel did wish she had something nice to wear for Grandmother's party. She had her school velvet, but it had been outgrown before Grandfather died and she had been meant to have another as soon as there were enough coupons. Although she did not seem to have grown very much, the frock seemed to fit her a great deal worse than when she last wore it. And as well as fitting badly, it was shabby looking. It was meant to be green, but Sorrel noticed as she put it on that in a lot of spots it was much nearer gray.

"If only this weren't the first time that the uncles and aunts were seeing me!" Sorrel thought. "They're bound to expect rather a lot from Mother's child, and really, I do look pretty drab. I hope Holly and Mark will make a better impression. It wouldn't be so awful if only I could put my bad clothes down to the war. But Miranda and Miriam live in the war too, and I bet they look quite nice."

She hoped, when she came along for Alice to inspect her, that perhaps she did not look as bad as she thought she did. But what Alice said was:

"Well, there's a war on and you're at least covered, and I suppose we mustn't expect more."

Which, the more you thought about it, became the less encouraging.

To save heating and trouble, dinner was being served in one end of Grandmother's drawing room. Sorrel and Mark and Holly thought they would go down when they were dressed, but Alice had given her instructions.

"Nobody takes a step till I fetches them. We are more fussy about Christmas Day than anybody would believe. All kinds of goings on we have. You'll see."

When they were called down Alice did not an-

159

nounce them, as she usually did, but led them into the drawing room, which they found entirely empty. By the fire was an armchair with Grandmother's green cushion on it. The sliding doors were closed. Alice, who was rushed because of cooking the dinner, gave Sorrel her instructions.

"You stand around your grandmother's chair until your uncles and aunts arrive, and then do what the rest of the family do. You can't go wrong if you keep your eyes open."

They longed to ask, "Wrong about what?" But Alice had dashed out, shouting to Hannah to come and lend her a hand.

Sorrel looked at Mark and Mark looked at Holly and all of a sudden it seemed so silly to be standing solemnly in a row around an empty armchair that they began to giggle. Mark giggled so much that he had to lie down on the floor. Then they heard the front doorbell. Sorrel pulled him to his feet.

"Oh, goodness! There are our uncles and aunts! Do get up. It's most terribly important that we shouldn't be a disgrace. We don't want them to despise the Forbeses."

A perfectly strange man dressed as a butler threw open the drawing-room door and roared out, "Mr. Moses Cohen, Mrs. Cohen, Miss Cohen."

The first person to come in was Miriam. She stood just inside the door, and in a very affected way that was not a bit like her, said:

"This is my Daddy, and this is my Mummy."

As Sorrel knew quite well that she called her parents Mum and Dad, and as Miriam was never affected, she stared at her in amazement. Miriam saw her face and added, in a hoarse whisper, "We always work up everybody's entrance on Christmas Day."

Aunt Lindsey came in. She was dark and rather severe looking and very smart. She stood in the doorway with both hands outstretched, and said in an acting sort of voice:

"Little Addie's children!"

She then stood to one side. There was a moment's pause and then there was Uncle Mose with a tiny cardboard hat on the side of his head, rubbing his hands in front of him.

"Vell! Vell! Vell!"

Evidently saying "Vell! Vell! Vell!" like that was something for which he was famous, because as soon as he had finished saying it Aunt Lindsey and Miriam laughed.

Once the laugh was over and the Cohen family safely in the room, everybody began to behave in an ordinary way. Miriam raced across and, hugging her three cousins, said "Happy Christmas" and told them about her presents. Aunt Lindsey kissed them and was very nice. Uncle Mose told them to feel in his pockets and when they did out came three envelopes marked Sorrel, Mark and Holly. In each one was a ten-shilling note. He kissed Sorrel and Holly and rubbed Mark's hair the wrong way, and said that what he would like them to do would be to buy books, but that the money was their own and they could spend it on anything they liked. They took a great fancy to Uncle Mose.

Then the Brains arrived. The strange man dressed

as a butler said: "Sir Francis and Lady Brain. Miss Miranda Brain." This time Miranda came in first. She stood in the doorway and said in her lovely voice:

"A merry Christmas, everybody!" Then she turned and, holding out both hands, added in a surprised voice as if she had not known her mother was there, "Mummy!"

Aunt Marguerite was shorter than Aunt Lindsey and thinner. She had an anxious, strained expression. She put one arm around Miranda as she said:

"A happy Christmas!" And then, holding out her free hand toward the passage, "Look who's here! Come to say merry Christmas to everybody."

Uncle Francis was a large man with a big, booming, deep voice, which sounded as though he kept it mellow by giving it caramels. He looked around the drawing room as if he were surprised to find himself there. He stood between Aunt Marguerite and Miranda, an arm around each.

"My dear wife, my little daughter, this is an occasion." And then, with a big smile for everybody in the room, "A merry Christmas to you all from the Brain family."

The moment this introduction was over Aunt Marguerite ran across the drawing room to hug Aunt Lindsey, but her eyes were on Sorrel and Mark and Holly.

"Oh, isn't this fun! I have so wanted to meet you, but we've been touring." She kissed each of them in turn. "I didn't know what to bring you, dears, it's so hard these days to find anything nice." She turned to

Miranda. "Run and get the parcels out of the hall."

Miranda and Miriam were both looking as well dressed as Sorrel was afraid they would. Miranda had on a party dress of green taffeta, and Miriam was in white with an orange ribbon around the waist. Sorrel felt at her worst, as if she were sticking out in all the wrong places.

Miranda, who had gone into the passage to fetch the parcels, came back with her arms full. Aunt Marguerite selected three of the parcels and handed them out.

"Don't undo them until Grandmother comes. We keep the presents until then."

Grandmother's arrival was announced. The butler threw open the drawing-room door and said:

"Miss Margaret Shaw."

Grandmother stood in the open doorway. She was wearing a dress of black trailing chiffon, and fox furs, and her hair was held up on the top of her head with a diamond comb. There was not very much light in the hall and as she stood there she did not look like an old lady, but like somebody out of a fairy story. She stretched out both arms.

"My children! Now this is really Christmas."

The children to whom she referred were, of course, Aunt Lindsey and Aunt Marguerite, and they hurried forward and kissed their mother.

"Darling Mother."

"Mother dearest."

Then Uncle Francis came across the room and kissed Grandmother's hand. "Wonderful, wonderful woman!"

Uncle Mose followed Uncle Francis. He kissed Grandmother's hand too. All this time Sorrel, Mark and Holly had been waiting to do something, and now they had their cue. Miranda and Miriam danced across the room.

"Granny, Granny!"

Uncle Mose winked at Sorrel and jerked his head in Grandmother's direction. Sorrel caught hold of Mark and Holly and they hurried forward. After kissing Grandmother, the right thing to do seemed to be to lead her to her chair. She sat down, shook out her skirts, rested her back comfortably against her cushion and twinkled up at Aunt Lindsey.

"Well, what is it this year?"

Aunt Lindsey looked positively nervous as she produced her parcel.

"I do hope it's something you'll like, darling, but you know how difficult things are."

Aunt Lindsey's being obviously so nervous seemed to affect everybody else, and they all leaned forward while Grandmother opened the box. Inside was a beautiful handbag.

"Of course," Sorrel thought, "one shouldn't criticize one's grandmother," but she did seem to take presents in a funny way. She turned the bag upside down, she smelled the leather, and she looked at the lining. When she had examined the latter carefully she said to Aunt Lindsey in a shocked way:

"Artificial."

"I know, dear," Aunt Lindsey agreed, "but there is so little real silk about these days."

Uncle Mose gave Grandmother an affectionate tap on the shoulder.

"You've fooled her as usual, Mother. I know you're not looking at the lining; you're hoping to find the price ticket."

Grandmother twinkled up at him. "Quite right. I love knowing what things cost."

Aunt Marguerite laid her present on Grandmother's knee. This time it was a thin parcel. Inside was an umbrella.

"I know, dear," Aunt Marguerite said, "that you never have used an umbrella, and that you never walk anywhere, but now that you're going into this show I do think you ought to be prepared in case you have to—there are so very few taxis."

Grandmother turned over the umbrella as if it were some curiosity from a foreign country.

"Interesting. I remember I carried one just like this in the first act of *Aunt Celia*. You remember, that was the play when I had to try and look dowdy."

Uncle Francis cleared his throat. "Good umbrellas are scarce today, Mother."

Grandmother answered him in a very good imitation of his own voice. "Then it was very kind of the Brains to give it to me." Then all of a sudden her manner changed and she swung around in her chair and looked at the children. "Now, what about the children's parcels? Where are they? Bring them out."

Aunt Marguerite's parcels were opened. In Sorrel's and Holly's were very pretty strings of beads, and in Mark's a penknife. Then there was a parcel each from Aunt Lindsey: a book for Sorrel, a flashlight for Mark and a game for Holly. They took a very good view of their aunts' ideas of presents.

Sorrel and Mark and Holly had made Grandmother's plant look better by putting a bow around the pot. They had given it to Alice to put on the table. Now Sorrel began rather to wish they had not. Evidently this was the right time to give presents, and anyway it looked pretty shabby of them not to have given something to Miranda and Miriam. But even with the presents they had given they were cleaned out.

They need not have worried; their present was a great success. Grandmother said she should put it on her dressing table at the theater to bring her luck.

Dinner was tremendous fun. Grandmother and Uncle Mose were both terribly funny and said the most amusing things about everybody. It seemed to be the kind of party where nobody minds how excited you get or how noisy you are. They had turkey, and for dessert there were some mince pies and plum pudding. The Forbes family all chose the plum pudding because as Alice laid it down she said:

"There's a thimble, a china baby, a horseshoe and a sixpence in there, and I want everything except the sixpence back for next year, so mind you don't swallow them."

The thimble and the china baby were found by Holly, the horseshoe by Miranda, and Uncle Mose got the sixpence. Uncle Francis had brought with him a bottle of port wine from his club, and when dinner was over there were the toasts. There seemed to be a custom about this. First of all Grandmother's health was drunk, and Uncle Francis made a speech about it. Then Aunt Lindsey fetched an enormous photograph of Uncle Henry and put it down by Grandmother's side, and Grandmother made a speech about "my eldest boy" and everybody drank to Uncle Henry. Then Grandmother made a speech about the Cohens and another about the Brains. And at the last, Grandmother suddenly held up her hand for silence.

"There's someone we specially want to drink to tonight," she said. "These children's father. May he be home with them by next Christmas."

It was quite awful, but somehow, thinking of its being Christmas and even imagining Father home by next Christmas was so absolutely gorgeous it made Sorrel want to cry. She looked at Mark and saw he was going to cry too, and then she looked at Holly and saw that she was, too. Fortunately Sorrel was not the only one who knew what was going to happen. Uncle Mose was quicker than she was. Before more than two tears had flopped down Sorrel's cheeks and Mark was only at the making faces stage, and Holly just puckering up, Uncle Mose had got off his chair and was walking around the table on his hands.

None of the Forbeses had ever seen a person do that before, and they were so interested watching him that the crying moment passed, and they were back feeling Christmasy again.

After dinner they played charades, and the man dressed as a butler and Alice and Hannah came in as audience. The charades started like ordinary party charades, only of rather a grand kind. Uncle Mose, Grandmother, Miranda, Holly and Aunt Lindsey were on one team, and they acted "manifold." The second charade was acted by the rest of the family. This was more serious because Uncle Francis seemed to play only serious parts, and so that charade was not very funny.

After that Uncle Mose, pretending to be Aunt Marguerite, and Grandmother, pretending to be Uncle Francis, did a scene from *Macbeth*. Sorrel, who had learned *Macbeth*, knew that neither of them was using the real words but making them up. Some of the things that Uncle Mose did were really funny but otherwise the people who enjoyed themselves most were Grandmother and Uncle Mose. Uncle Francis was not amused at all.

When the charades were over, Grandmother went back to her chair. Aunt Lindsey looked at her watch and said, "I think it's time we started the carols."

They sang "The First Noël" and "Good King Wenceslas," and then Grandmother held out a hand to Mark.

"Come here, Grandson. I hear from Madame Fidolia that you can sing. What carol will you sing for us?"

Mark did not want to sing at all. He felt more in the mood to stand on his head than to sing a carol, but Grandmother was holding him firmly and she obviously meant to have her way.

"If I sing one you won't say 'sing another,' will you?"

Grandmother looked around at her daughters.

"See how he bullies me? You'd never have dared to do that. Very well, Mark, just one carol and I won't ask for another."

At the Academy they had learned "I Saw Three Ships." It was easy to sing without a piano and Mark liked it. He leaned against Grandmother and sang it all through.

There was complete silence when he had finished. Sorrel did not wonder for, really, Mark's singing was a very nice noise. She looked at him with pride. It was a good thing that one of them could shine in this clever family. Uncle Francis was the first to speak, and he used his most caramel voice.

"Beautiful, beautiful."

Aunt Lindsey kissed her mother.

"I think that's the right ending to a lovely evening. We've hired a car, you know, and it ought to be here any minute."

Grandmother was kissing everybody.

"Good night, dears. Good night, Francis. Good night, Marguerite. We must hope for peace in 1943."

Chapter XIV

First Night

Holly woke very early one morning and thought about the two pounds Posy had sent her. Holly was not exactly vain but she liked nice things, and all through the term she had had to look at Miriam, who was given the best of everything by Aunt Lindsey. But the most impressive thing of all, in Holly's opinion, was her brief case. Not having a brief case mattered much more to Holly than it did to Sorrel or to Mark. Holly was forgetful and could easily drop a thing and not notice it, and she was not very good at tying up a parcel. Almost every day she dropped a sandal or a tap shoe or a sock somewhere in the Academy, and though at first people had been kind and helpful about it, now everybody groaned, "Oh, Holly!"

It was still dark and it was very cold, but as soon as Holly had thought of the brief case, she was so thrilled about it she simply had to tell Sorrel. She got out of bed very quietly, for the iron beds that she and Hannah slept on creaked horribly if anyone moved quickly. Her dressing gown was lying over the end of the bed, but she could not find her slippers, so she ran up the passage without them.

Sorrel was asleep. Miles and miles down in sleep, dreaming one of those nice dreams where you keep meeting people all together who in actual life could never meet at all. Her father was having a talk with Madame, who pulled forward a little girl and said, "This is my best pupil." One moment the little girl was Sorrel and the next it was her mother at the same age. And then Hannah came running in with an enormous tray of ice cream, singing, "Pease porridge hot." Sorrel had just taken a dish of strawberry ice cream with real strawberries in it and whipped cream on top, the sort of thing that even in peacetime would have been something to remember, when Holly woke her. She tried very hard to be pleasant but really, what with missing the ice cream and just waking up, she was not in the best of humor. Holly sat on the edge of the bed.

"I simply had to come. Do you think I could buy a real leather brief case, the grand sort like Miriam has, with the ten shillings Uncle Mose gave me, as well as Posy's two pounds?"

Sorrel thought about it. She remembered the shops they had been to and the brief cases they had seen.

"I am awfully afraid we couldn't. The nice ones we saw were five pounds, I think."

Holly was wriggling her toes to keep them warm.

"May I get into bed with you? My toes are awfully cold. Well, that's what I thought. So I wondered if we could buy just one and take turns with it—you one week, me one week and Mark one week."

Sorrel shuddered as Holly's feet touched her.

"Oh, goodness, Holly, your feet are cold! Whatever will Hannah say!" She made room for Holly and pulled the eiderdown around her. "It's a very good idea about the brief case, but I don't know whether having one for just one week out of every three wouldn't be worse than not having one at all. And then, who's going to look after it? I mean, it's bound to get scratched and marked—they all do—and who's going to be to blame?"

Holly looked up at the felt doll which was on her side of the headboard. Reaching up to stroke it, she said:

"I wouldn't mind having something like this if I can't have a brief case. Do you think you can buy them now? Or I'd like a white cat like yours to put my pajamas in. When we first came here and you let me have that white cat to sleep with me, the nursery was quite different. I've wanted a cat like that ever since."

Sorrel always laid the white cat on a chair for the night. Now she leaned out of bed and pulled it to her by its tail. It was a nice-looking beast and she had grown fond of it.

"Do you think I'm awfully mean not to give it to you?"

Holly had no idea what she was talking about. "Why should you give it to me? I wouldn't give it to you if it were mine."

Sorrel looked around at her blue chintz curtains and her pretty dressing table with the silver dressing-table fittings, at her white furniture, and her carpet with pink flowers, her bedside lamp and the green frog, the picture of the cornfield and her books.

"It doesn't seem quite fair—it never has since we've been here—that I should have everything and you and Mark nothing."

Holly, without knowing it, had been harboring a grievance and now you could feel it was a grievance from the way she spoke.

"I don't see how you can say Mark hasn't anything when you've given him your fourteen bears."

Sorrel wrestled with herself. It was not so much for herself that she wanted the things in her room; it was because of the way they somehow made a picture of her mother. In the months they had been in the house, she had felt that she knew her mother better every day. She had felt that her mother had told her on the night before the matinée not to be a fool, that of course she could do it. She had thought that her mother had told her to worry and fuss less about the ordinary things that went on every day. If she had a bad day at the Academy and got into trouble, or was rude and cross to Hannah, or snapped at Mark or Holly, she had begun to feel, when she got into her bedroom and shut the door, that somebody laughed and said, "Who's got a black dog on her shoulder?" And then she felt quite different, and stopped wanting to be angry. Because of all these things that she would not tell anybody, she dreaded seeing anything leave the bedroom. On the other hand, it did seem pretty sickening for Holly. The one thing she really wanted was a brief case and she could not have that, and her next choice was to have something from her mother's room. She gave the cat an affectionate stroke.

"You needn't buy a cat, you may have this one."

Holly gazed at her, speechless for a moment, and then she flung her arms around Sorrel's neck.

"Darling Sorrel! I think this is the most beautiful thing that has ever happened to me."

Sorrel pleated the eiderdown. "I've got ideas about my money. I want to buy a frock. You know what mine looked like on Christmas Day."

Holly stroked the cat. "Pretty awful. It doesn't look as though it could possibly button. It's surprising that it does. And where it buttons it kind of pleats, and that makes your vest show. The velvet looks as if it had been left outside all night in the rain. Otherwise it's all right."

"What I'm afraid of is this first night of Grandmother's. Did you notice when we were down last night seeing her that she said something about our coming to the first night?"

Holly bounced with pleasure. "Oh, goodness, I hope she meant it!"

"It's all very well for you, Holly, you've got all my party frocks passed down to you. And it's all right for Mark. But it's absolutely awful for me. I know what's going to happen. Grandmother will go pushing us about and saying we're her grandchildren and there I'll be, looking a disgrace to any family, especially to the Warrens."

"If you can't get a frock for your money you can have mine, and I expect Mark would give you most of his ten shillings if we had the coupons."

"If we had the coupons I don't think I should need any extra money," declared Sorrel. "I could buy a utility frock. That dress that Mary had for her audition was utility and I thought it looked awfully nice."

Holly recalled Mary standing in the hall in something green and tailored. "It did. Much nicer than I thought Mary ever could look. How much was it?"

"Less than two pounds."

Holly was giving her whole attention to Sorrel's clothes.

"I don't think you wear things like that for first nights. When Alice told me about them she said all the ladies wore satin and velvet and diamonds and foxes, and all the gentlemen had top hats and black tails. Why do you suppose men wear tails at a first night?"

"They're not the sort of tails you mean, silly," and Sorrel laughed. "They're two black pieces that hang down at the back of their coats. Men wore them at parties before the war. Daddy had them, I remember quite well. What you said about satins and velvets is what's worrying me. I don't believe we've got many coupons left, and I don't think Hannah will let me spend them on a real party frock."

"Couldn't you get another velvet?" Holly suggested. "Only get one that fits."

"I thought of that, and I could if they're cheap enough. But I think Hannah will think it ought to be in a serviceable color—a dark red or navy blue or something like that—and what I think I need is a party frock, something that rustles and sticks out."

The door opened and Hannah's face, with her nose red with cold, appeared. "I'll 'rustle and stick out' you, Holly. What are you doing here without your slippers?"

Sorrel held out a hand to her. "Hannah, darling, come and sit here a minute. Holly and I will do without my eiderdown so it can all go over you and keep you warm. I wanted to ask you something."

Hannah sat down on the bed. It was a well-made, well-sprung bed but it sagged under Hannah. She could not really have been any heavier when she was not wearing her corset. But in her red dressing gown, without a corset, she looked twice as big as usual.

"Well, what is it?" she said.

Sorrel explained about her money and the first night.

"You see, Hannah, I'd have to have a new dress anyway, wouldn't I? I mean, that velvet's finished, even if it would let out, which it wouldn't."

Hannah nodded. "Shocking, it is. If we can get you something new I'll put it aside or maybe cut it up for a pair of knickers or something later on. You haven't enough coupons in your book, but you can have a few from young Holly and a few from mine. You'll have to buy something big, though, with room for turnings—nice, solid, dark stuff that'll last."

Sorrel leaned against Hannah and looked up at her feelingly.

"Oh, Hannah, I knew you were going to say that, but it's a party dress I want. That's what I was saying when you came in—something that would rustle and stick out. Don't you think we could possibly spare the coupons for that? After all, it wouldn't be wasted. I could wear it to church on Sundays in the summer."

"There's enough funny goings-on in this house," said Hannah, "without my taking a dressed-up monkey along to church of a Sunday." But she did not say it with any conviction. She was obviously worried and after a moment she added: "You ought to have something pretty in white, with a sash, like the ones you've passed on to Holly."

"I'd like something a little more grown-up," Sorrel pleaded. "Just think, Hannah! Suppose it could be yellow. Crêpe-de-chine or silk net over taffeta."

Hannah got up. Her voice was cross in the way it was when she had to hurt and disappoint one of her darlings.

"It's no good talking like that, Sorrel dear, and well you know it. What with things you've got to have, like shoes and socks and warm clothes, and you all growing, I don't know which way to turn for coupons as it is. Yellow silk indeed! You know we couldn't manage it so what's the good of talking. Come on, Holly."

Sorrel did not give up the party frock easily. And Hannah, who was really very sorry about it, patiently went with her from one big store to another. They must have seen hundreds of dresses, but not one that met even halfway between Hannah's idea of sensibleness and usefulness and Sorrel's of what she should wear at a party.

A fortnight before Grandmother's first night the three of them were officially told they were all going and that they were to sit in the stalls. Alice had told Sorrel that she thought they would sit in a box, and "If you do, dear," she said, "there's no one behind to see if your frock's too tight." There was no comfort like that about sitting in the stalls, and it was the very day when Sorrel heard it was to be stalls that she gave up the search for the frock.

"Don't let's try any more, Hannah. I'll wear the old velvet. It's silly to spend the coupons or the money on something dark and sensible, because I don't want that kind of frock for anything. I'll keep the money and buy something with it later on."

She said this so nicely that neither Hannah nor Alice grasped how despairing she was inside, though they watched her carefully to see.

The week before the first night, Sorrel and Mark and Holly were asked to spend the day with Miriam. Uncle Mose was going on tour for the Department of National Service Entertainment, and he had a week's rest beforehand. So the moment he knew his holiday was fixed he told Aunt Lindsey to arrange with the Forbeses for a day's visit. They chose to go on Holly's birthday.

It was a lovely day with a nip of frost in the air, and the sun caught the silver of the barrage balloons and turned them into gigantic pink and gold fish. Most of the things Sorrel and Mark and Holly had thought they would do in London, and had been hoping were going to happen, happened that day. They went to the zoo. They went to Madame Tussaud's. Uncle Mose said that he would have taken them to the Tower of London, only you could not see it in wartime. And then he laughed and said that much though he would have liked to have shown them The Tower, in his opinion the zoo and Madame Tussaud's were enough for one day, and it was an ill war that did nobody any good.

After tea, at which there was a cake with nine candles, they sat around the fire and roasted chestnuts. The Cohens had a lovely flat, all white paint and very shiny. The Forbeses had liked Uncle Mose from the beginning and they had always been fond of Miriam, but now they discovered how nice Aunt Lindsey could be. She talked in a friendly way as if she had known them always. She asked a little about Guernsey and a great deal about the vicarage. She and Uncle Mose laughed and laughed when they heard about Grandfather and the Bible animals, and then she began asking about living with Grandmother. Were they comfortable? Mark was busy with the chestnuts.

"Sorrel is, she's got our mother's room," he said.

"And you?" Aunt Lindsey asked.

Sorrel managed to kick Mark to remind him that Grandmother was Aunt Lindsey's mother. Mark looked over his shoulder and made a face at her to show that he had not forgotten.

"Quite, thank you," he said politely.

Aunt Lindsey looked down at Holly. "Which room have you got?"

Holly wriggled up to her aunt and leaned against her knees. "I think it was your nursery. Mark's in the room next to me."

Aunt Lindsey turned to Uncle Mose. "He must be in the little room that the kitchen maid had. I suppose Mother's put them on that floor because that's where Addie's room was. Henry and Marguerite and I slept on the floor below."

"I daresay you did," said Mark. "Those rooms haven't any furniture in them now."

Aunt Lindsey laughed. "How can you say that, Mark, after having lived in that house all these months? You know there's hardly room to turn around for all the furniture Mother's collected."

Sorrel was so afraid that Holly's face, gazing up into Aunt Lindsey's, would give her away that she pulled her arm, saying, "I think your chestnut's burning."

Miriam, by accident, led the conversation away from Grandmother's house.

"Do you know that Mum's written to ask whether, as Dad will be away for Grandmother's first night, you may all sit in the box with Mum and me? What are you going to wear, Holly? I've got a blue silk frock. Mum's let it out and altered it, and it looks very nice now."

"I've only got white," Holly explained. "But I've got the coral beads Aunt Marguerite gave me and I'll be wearing a coral bow."

"And what's Sorrel wearing?" Aunt Lindsey asked kindly.

There was an awful pause while Mark and Holly looked at Sorrel to see what she would say.

Uncle Mose had his eyes on Sorrel. He caught hold of her arm and pulled her to him, and made her sit on the arm of his chair.

"Come on, what are they dressing you in? Something you don't like?"

The most awful thing happened to Sorrel. Because she really was so worried about the frock and the shame of wearing it, and because Uncle Mose was so nice, she suddenly found herself crying. Uncle Mose did not seem in the least upset by this. He pulled her off the arm of his chair and onto his knee, found his pocket handkerchief and mopped her face, and then said he would like to hear all about it.

Sorrel had reached the cry and hiccup stage, but somehow she managed the entire story, reminding him what the velvet frock was like, telling him about the shopping expeditions and what Hannah wanted and what she wanted, and the dreadful story of the coupons.

When she had finished Uncle Mose looked at Aunt Lindsey.

Aunt Lindsey got up. "You come with me, Sorrel.

If there was one thing I was extravagant about before the war it was evening dresses, and I'm a very good dressmaker. Let's see what we can find."

They did not find yellow, but there was a white evening dress made of stiff rustling silk, with bunches of yellow flowers embroidered all over it. Aunt Lindsey had piles of magazines lying on the table in her bedroom. She kept turning these over until at last she came to a picture on the cover of one. It was colored and showed a girl of about Sorrel's age in a party frock with puffed sleeves. Underneath it was written, "It may be wartime but Miss Adolescent wants her fun."

"There!" said Aunt Lindsey. "How would you like that frock?"

Sorrel could not believe it was true. She kept fingering the stuff. "Do you mean honestly made of this?"

Aunt Lindsey had whipped up a yard measure from somewhere and was measuring Sorrel. She stopped measuring for a moment and held Sorrel's chin between her fingers and looked into her eyes.

"Of course I mean it, goose. It'll be fun and you'll look a darling in it. But never let me hear of your crying and worrying about anything like this again. You come straight along to us, that's what uncles and aunts are for. There's no dressing-up at first nights these days, so I shall make you the smartest person in the theater. You'll see."

Sorrel and Mark and Holly had heard about first nights from Alice and from Miriam. Fortunately Miriam's theater-going had been mostly during the war. If they had relied on Alice's story of what happened they would have been bitterly disappointed at the real thing.

Alice, through long years of dressing Grandmother, had seen the splendid sort of first nights that there were in peacetime, when the whole road was blocked with cars driving to the front of the house, when the foyer was full of lovely clothes, and all the smart people stood packed together talking to each other while the more important of them were photographed.

A first night in January 1943 was not a bit like that. Nobody came in a car, but a few lucky ones, including the Forbeses, came in taxis. In the days of first nights that Alice talked about plays had begun quite late in the evening, eight or half-past; but now, because of the black-out, no play began later than half-past six. Grandmother's was to begin at six-fifteen.

For fear of getting messed up, the three did not change until after tea. Hannah had laid Sorrel's frock out on her bed. It looked, Sorrel thought, quite lovely against the blue eiderdown, and she stroked it a long time before she began to undress. Aunt Lindsey had made it beautifully. Moreover, she had not only made the frock but she had also sent some yellow ribbon which matched the flowers for Sorrel to tie on her hair. Hannah, coming in to see how Sorrel was getting on, found her just standing there stroking and she had to tell her to hurry.

"Come along now, I've had Holly dressed this last ten minutes."

Sorrel looked at her with shining eyes. "I shouldn't think there was ever a prettier dress in this room, would you? I mean, even when my mother lived here."

Hannah privately thought the dress rather too grand, but not for worlds would she have told Sorrel. Sorrel had got as far as her knickers and socks and shoes, so Hannah lifted the frock off the bed and put it over her head.

Sorrel really did look very nice. Hannah felt a swelling inside, she was so proud of her. She did not, of course, say anything, as she thought flattery was a sin.

Mark and Holly also were immensely impressed by Sorrel's appearance. Holly said that she looked as if she had come out of a fairy story, and then added:

"It isn't a taxi that is going to take us to the theater, it's a beautiful coach, sent by Sorrel's fairy godmother. And I'm a lady-in-waiting and Mark's a lord-in-waiting."

Mark had been staring at Sorrel in silence, for he found it very hard to believe that something odd had not happened to her. Now Holly's suggestion that she was a princess made everything fit into place. He glowed.

"Every time Sorrel wants anything, you and I, Holly, will have to run and fetch it and I shall bow and you will curtsy."

Sorrel saw in a second what was going to happen to this evening unless she was careful. She spoke to Mark very severely.

"I'm not going to have you make a fool of me. I'm

not a princess. I'm Sorrel Forbes, going to my grandmother's first night in a frock made out of an old evening dress of Aunt Lindsey's." She tried to think of something that would bring Mark to his senses. "And I'll tell you one thing which will show how ordinary I am. If you make even one little bow or behave like anybody but Mark Forbes, the moment we get back here tonight I'll take away those fourteen bears I lent you. I always told you they were only a loan."

Mark felt the excitement die out of him. He was back in London. It was a dark, cold night in January, and they were three ordinary people going to the theater in a taxi. It was a pity.

There was only a little cloakroom at the theater, and with the three of them and Hannah in it, there was not room for anybody else. Sorrel could see that the attendant was as glad as they were when Hannah finally said, "There, you'll do. Now come outside and find your aunt."

They stood by the fireplace in the foyer. There was very dim lighting for fear of its showing in the street, and they were terribly afraid of missing Aunt Lindsey. They need not have worried, because Miriam had eyes like a cat. She was no sooner inside the door than she shrieked, "There they are," came burrowing her way through the people, and flung herself at Sorrel, who happened to be the first of her cousins whom she found.

Miriam could never look pretty because she just did not have that sort of face, but she could and did look very smart. She had on a white ermine coat, a blue crêpe-de-chine frock, and white socks and silver shoes. Holly and Mark began stroking her the moment they saw her.

"White fur," said Holly. "Oh, Miriam, how lovely to be dressed all in white fur!"

Aunt Lindsey, who had forced her way to them, stooped and kissed Holly.

"It looks all right in this dim light, Holly, but it's not so good in the daylight. She's outgrown it, for one thing, and the fur is getting very yellow-looking. But it's got to last for the duration, because we've no coupons for another."

"She's exactly like I was as a polar bear," said Mark, "only I was fur all over, including my legs."

Aunt Lindsey had her arm around Sorrel. "Well, let's come into the box, and examine each other. I can't wait to see how Sorrel looks in my frock."

Aunt Lindsey was a very thoughtful person. She had guessed that Hannah would leave their coats in the cloakroom and she knew how badly heated theaters were in wartime. But she knew too that however badly heated they were, neither Sorrel nor Holly would want to wear school coats over their best frocks; so under her arm she had brought a white angora rabbit jersey of Miriam's for Holly to wear, and for Sorrel there was a white jersey of her own. Holly, of course, could not wait to put on the angora rabbit, it looked so lovely. But Sorrel did not think very much of the plain white cardigan that she was offered. Aunt Lindsey quite understood.

"You won't wear it during intermission, of course, darling," she said, "but you can put it on while the curtain's up, and I expect you'll be rather glad of it."

The theater was a blaze of light and Aunt Lindsey seemed to know dozens of people. First one waved and then another, and she was always waving back and getting Miriam to wave too.

"Look, darling, there's old Sir Richard smiling at us. Look, darling, there's Aunt Meg and Uncle Sam." Everybody seemed to be an uncle or an aunt to Miriam.

Mark and Holly found all this waving entrancing. They leaned on the edge of the box and peered at the people, and every time anyone waved they drew their aunt's attention to it.

"There are two ladies waving." "Look over there, three ladies and a man."

Sorrel felt shy. It seemed as if everybody in the theater was looking at them, and she wished they would not. Her cheeks burned. Why didn't the curtain go up and the lights go down? The audience was exactly as Miriam had said it would be, and not a bit as Alice had described it. The women were in uniform or dark overcoats, and most of them had big boots with fur linings. The men were in uniform or exactly as they had come on from work. Nobody was dressed up. Aunt Lindsey was looking very nice in a black frock and fur coat, but only nice in the way that anybody might look in the afternoon. One thing that Alice had promised was there, and it evidently had nothing to do with clothes. The excitement. From far up in the gallery, down to the upper circle, down through the dress circle, through the pit and up to the front row of the stalls, everybody was keyed up, just chattering to fill in the time until the moment when the curtain would rise.

Sorrel turned to Aunt Lindsey. "I wonder how they're all feeling behind scenes."

Aunt Lindsey laughed. "I can easily tell you that. Sick as dogs." And then she said, "S-ssh," and leaned forward. Sorrel could see she was clutching the front of the box so hard that her knuckles shone white. The lights dimmed, the orchestra's music faded away. The curtain rose.

The play was about a family in the reign of Queen Victoria, and everybody in it was in costume. It must have been funny because the audience laughed a great deal, but most of the time Sorrel and Mark and Holly could not see anything to laugh at. About halfway through the first act Miranda came on stage, wearing a funny little hat and holding a muff. She played the part of the youngest child, Sylvia, and she seemed to be a different person from the Miranda the Forbeses knew every day. All through the act it was known that the grandmama of the father in the play was expected. At the end of the act the sound of horses' hoofs was heard offstage, then the door was flung open and there was Grandmama. The grand-mama of the play was, of course, Grandmother, and she was just as big a surprise to the family on the stage as Grandmother in real life had been to the Forbes family. She was a mass of feathers and bows and colors, and had a manner about her and a twinkle in her eye which made the family on the stage gasp and the audience clap and clap and rock with laughter. She said something that Sorrel could not quite grasp, but the audience found it very amusing and the curtain came down in a storm of applause.

During the intermission all kinds of people came to the box. Some of them were critics and some of them were actors, but to all of them Aunt Lindsey would say:

"These are Addie's children."

Everybody in turn would look puzzled and as if they were searching in their memories, and then Aunt Lindsey would add:

"She married a man in the Navy called Forbes."

And then the people would nod as if they were re-membering. Each time it happened, Sorrel couldn't help thinking that they were remembering her mother's elopement. Several people commented on Addie's children's looks. Some said they had Warren noses, some said they had Warren eyes, and every-one said they had the Warren hair.

In the next act Grandmama was ruling the house-hold, and Miranda had her big scene when she planned an elopement for two lovers. It was this elopement which finished the act, for just as it was taking place, Grandmama discovered it.

This act did not get quite so much applause as the first act, which made Aunt Lindsey worried and rest-less, and she said she was going out into the foyer for a little fresh air. The others went with her. There they met one of the critics who had come to the box in the first act. He talked about Miranda.

"Quite a part for your little niece," he said. "It's very difficult at that age to distinguish precocity from talent."

189

Aunt Lindsey frowned. "It was Mother's doing. Francis was against it."

The critic cleared his throat. "Of course there's plenty of precedent for it. Ellen Terry was a very small child when she started, but the theater was a different place in those days. I don't imagine that much spoiling went on."

Aunt Lindsey laughed. "You don't know Miranda. She's a very mature young lady. I don't fancy that anything you critics say will affect her opinion of herself, and don't think by that I mean conceit. I think she's just got it in her, and she's got confidence."

He was moving off to speak to somebody else but he changed his mind. "You tell Marguerite from me that if she must stick the child's press cuttings into a book not to let her know that she's doing it. How old is she?"

"Fourteen."

He turned to Sorrel. "What about you? Are we going to see you soon?"

Sorrel nodded. "Yes, if I can get a part."

The critic was looking at Mark. "What about you? Are you going to follow in your Uncle Henry's steps?"

Sorrel answered for Mark. "No, Mark isn't going to be an actor. He's going to be a sailor."

Aunt Lindsey was looking amused. She shook her head at the critic. "I don't know what all this sailor talk's about. He's following in the usual family footsteps so far as I know."

The critic moved away and as he went Sorrel suddenly stopped enjoying the evening and felt worried and depressed. Alice had promised that Mark should be properly educated in the autumn, but could Alice really see to it? Could anybody? What happened if your uncles and your aunts and your grandmother were all against you? How was she going to get things done all by herself? It was not even as though she could absolutely rely on Mark. In theory Mark wanted to be an admiral but little things could change his mind. It was certain that if he were given a part which meant dressing up as a dragon or something like that he would forget all about the Navy.

Aunt Lindsey was leading the way back to the box. She drew Sorrel's hand through her arm. "Tired, darling?"

"No. I was thinking of what you were saying about Mark."

Aunt Lindsey was not quite herself that evening because her mind was so wrapped up in the play. She badly wanted her mother to have a success. If she had not been thinking so much about the play she would probably have probed further into what Sorrel was saying. Instead, she just squeezed her hand.

"I don't think we need worry about Mark yet, darling. He's only a little boy, really, and there will be plenty of time to worry when the time comes."

The last act Sorrel thought lovely. Things began to come right just as in a fairy tale. The act opened where the last one had ended, and there was Grandmama searching through the house, unable to believe that a granddaughter of hers had had the spunk to plan an elopement. And sure enough she presently found that another granddaughter (Miranda) was the culprit.

"That child," said Grandmama, "must be spanked."

Mark, who was hanging over the edge of his box, bounced on his seat.

"Goody, goody, goody, I bet she hates that!"

Aunt Lindsey told him to be quiet, but Mark gave Sorrel a nudge to show that although he was going to be quiet he still thought that Miranda's being spanked was a very good idea.

Grandmama held Miranda's hand when they took the final curtain. All the ladies in the cast curtsied to the ground and the men bowed and the audience clapped and clapped. The author, who was dressed as an officer in the Air Force, came on and bowed and made a speech, and then the play was over. Aunt Lindsey took her charges through the pass door across the stage to see Grandmother. Visiting Grandmother in the theater was very much like visiting her in the drawing room. After Aunt Lindsey had knocked on the door, Alice looked out and then went back into the dressing room.

"Mrs. Cohen and the children to see you, dear."

When Aunt Lindsey got inside, she behaved not at all like herself, but as she had on Christmas Day. She held one of Grandmother's hands in both of hers and said, "Wonderful, Mother! Wonderful!"

Grandmother had taken off her stage dress and was in a dressing gown. She pretended to be seeing to the frills on it but really you could see she was attending entirely to Aunt Lindsey.

"How do you think it went? Was I really all right? They seemed to like it, didn't they?"

"Ate it," said Alice. "I told you from the beginning it was just the sort of sentimental stuff they would eat."

Grandmother turned to her grandchildren. "And how did you like it?"

"It was super," said Sorrel.

Miriam leaned against her grandmother's chair. "I thought it was a lovely play."

Grandmother looked at Mark. "What about you, Grandson?"

"I liked every single moment of it. But best of all I liked the bit where Miranda was spanked. But I thought it a pity that it happened upstairs."

"You had such lovely dresses," Holly broke in. "I would like to have a little hat and muff like Miranda wore."

Grandmother was looking severely at Mark. "You're a bad boy." Then she turned to Aunt Lindsey. "Miranda's done very well. The children might go up and see her. She's on the next floor."

A lot of people came in to see Grandmother, and Alice was busy showing them in, so Sorrel, Mark, Holly and Miriam went alone to see Miranda. Miriam was quite used to being backstage, and so it was she who led the way along the passage and up some gray stone steps. When they came to a room marked number nine, which had a card under it reading "Miss Miranda Brain," Miriam thumped on the door.

"It's us, Miranda. May we come in?"

Aunt Marguerite and Uncle Francis were on tour so Miranda's governess had brought her to the theater. None of the visitors had met the governess before, and she looked, they thought, rather nice. She had pretty gray hair and a smiling face. Miranda was sitting at her dressing table taking off her make-up.

"Hullo! Did you like it?" she greeted them.

Miriam was prowling around examining Miranda's clothes, which were hanging on pegs on the walls. "You were awfully good, everybody thought so."

Miranda seemed much easier to talk to than usual. She swung around in her chair.

"I was dreadfully nervous at the beginning. Did it show? Do you like my clothes? Grandmother said she was pleased. Did she say anything about me to you? Did…"

Miranda's governess gently patted her shoulder.

"Come along, dear, get your make-up off. The car will be here and I want to get you home for your supper." She turned to the cousins. "Her father has hired a car for tonight as it's her first night, and I don't want her to be late because we've got two shows tomorrow."

Sorrel wanted very much to have a real look at Miranda's clothes, and to read all the telegrams that were pinned up on the wall, but she could see the governess did not really want them in the room.

"Well, we just came to tell you how good you were, Miranda," she said, "and anyway I think we ought to be going. We left our coats in the cloakroom when we came in." Then Sorrel hesitated. It seemed rude just to walk out, and yet Miranda was not the sort of person you kissed.

Miranda surprised them all. She jumped up and kissed each of them. "Good night. I'm glad you came around. Hold your thumbs for me, I am so terribly fussed over what the papers will say tomorrow. It's sickening that Daddy and Mummy can't be here. It's so flat just going home."

Grandmother was being taken out to supper so Alice took the Forbeses home. It took ages to get a taxi, and when they finally did get into one safely, what with the excitement and one thing and another, they were all half asleep. Alice put Holly on her knee and Mark leaned against her on one side, while Sorrel did the same on the other.

"That's right," said Alice, "you make yourselves at home. That's what shoulders are for. Make very comfortable weeping willows."

Chapter XV

Miranda had had an immense success. The notices said such things as, "The evening really belonged to little Miss Brain." And, "This latest shoot from the Warren tree seems to hold promise of bearing a crop of talent unusual even from a branch from this parent stem." The other type of paper, which did not write in that grand way, said, "Miranda romps home" and, "Child star born in a night." One paper was tactless enough to say that Miranda acted everybody, including her grandmother, off the stage. Sorrel and Mark and Holly did not see these notices themselves, but they heard Alice telling Hannah about them at meals.

"We've taken it very well, I must say that. No one can say that we begrudge the child her success, but we're afraid of early success and quite right, too. A child star born in a night indeed! Let one cloud no bigger than an acorn appear and that star will be out. We know, we've seen it."

"But if Miranda acts her part so nicely," said Hannah, "that's not to say she couldn't do another, is it?"

Alice spoke with the weight of one who knew. "It isn't that they mean any harm, these critics, nor the public either. But they rocket somebody into the sky and let them sit there sparkling and twinkling with no more to keep them up than one of these tracer bullets. Then everybody's surprised when they drop. You see, the next part may be more difficult or wrong for their personality, and they haven't the technique to put it over. Then what happens? Scream from the papers. 'Mr. or Miss So-and-so doesn't fulfill early promise.' 'I was disappointed in the performance of Miss So-and-so.' No, there's just one way for sure success and that's building up your knowledge and your reputation together, and when you do that you can't topple off. It's like having a concrete house under you."

Sorrel broke into the conversation. "Don't you think that perhaps Miranda's different, that she just has to be good?"

Alice nodded. "Shouldn't wonder at all, clever as a cartload of monkeys. But that won't stop her from having her ups and downs like the rest. The higher she climbs the harder the bump when she falls. From what I've seen there's no such thing as an easy road to success."

Oddly enough, success did not seem to have done Miranda any harm, but neither had it done her any good. She went on being very much herself. Because of her theater work, she no longer came to the Academy for lessons, but did them at home with her governess. She was at the Academy only for special dancing—two ballet classes a week and two tap—and all in the mornings. Sorrel met her at only one of these classes. The work was really too advanced for her, but during the parts that were too difficult for her Sorrel sat down and watched a lot of it, and this brought her in contact with Miranda's governess, Miss Smith. Miss Smith had, in a long career of governessing, been used to houses in which, at suitable intervals, cousins came to stay, and it worried her that the Forbes children or Miriam never visited Miranda.

"You see, all the autumn your uncle and aunt were rehearsing as well as working," she apologized, "and now they're away on tour and, of course, Miranda and I live very simply. You've no idea how hard it is, now the term has begun, to fit in her lessons and her dancing classes as well as eight performances a week. She gets very tired, poor child."

Sorrel looked at Miss Smith's nice face and thought that it looked tired. And she was not surprised, for she could imagine that a tired Miranda would make anybody who had to look after her very tired indeed.

"Some Saturday afternoon," said Sorrel, "Alice is

going to take me backstage during matinée. She's going to get Grandmother to ask the stage manager if I may stand in the wings. Perhaps that day I could come up and see Miranda."

Miss Smith looked pleased. "Of course. You'll come and have tea in the dressing room. I'll ask Alice to let me know in plenty of time that you're coming, and I'll run out in the morning and see if I can get something nice."

"Please don't bother to get anything extra," Sorrel said. "We scarcely ever do have cake, so I wouldn't miss it."

Miss Smith looked at her with fondness.

"That's sweet of you." She lowered her voice. "But as a matter of fact it will be nice for Mary. She's the understudy, such a dear little girl. She sits in our room because, as of course you know, somebody has to be with her and I can save her poor mother having to do it. There are four other children at home and her father's in the Army, so I'm glad to help. It isn't much fun understudying, I'm afraid, and all in all she has a hard time."

Sorrel thought about Mary. Understudying Miranda must be a very nasty job. She could just imagine how it would be—Miranda very much owning the dressing room and expecting you to sit in the corner and be humble.

Miss Smith was looking at Sorrel's shoes. "How worn your dancing sandals are getting! Miranda had to have some new shoes lately. She's still wearing her old sandals and tap shoes, but I was thinking the other day she ought not to, they're pinching her toes.

And she's got a lot of pairs of socks that have shrunk in the wash. You're so much smaller than she is they will either fit you right away or you can grow into them. I'll bring the things to her class tomorrow and put them in her locker, and you can fetch them from there. We've got an old brief case I'll put them in. It'll make it easy for you to carry them home."

The next evening Mark and Holly saw the brief case in Sorrel's hand. They asked questions about it until they ran out of breath.

"Whose is it?"

"How did you get it?"

"Is it your very own?"

"Could I, oh, could I carry it?"

Sorrel explained the sad truth — that it was Miranda's — but she was very fair about it. She agreed that each of them in turn should carry it — Holly as far as the station, Mark on the tube, and she from Knightsbridge home, and that the next morning the system would be reversed.

Then Sorrel turned to Mark. "But at the bottom of the Academy steps you're to hand it to me, for I've got to put it back in Miranda's locker." She passed the brief case to Holly. "There you are. Make the best of it — you'll only be carrying it as far as Russell Square."

They walked along in silence for a bit, eyeing the case, and then Mark said what was in all their minds.

"To think there could be a person in the world with a brief case like that which was only her second best."

For Mark, Miranda's brief case was eclipsed the

next day by a letter from Petrova. Pauline had said she would not write much, and she did not.

Dear Mark,

I've heard from Pauline about you and I have written to Madame to say that I will give you the same as Pauline gives Sorrel and Posy gives Holly. This will, of course, include a shilling pocket money. I have also sent two pounds for your Christmas present. I would have written before but I have been posted to a different place for a week or two, and Gum (my great-uncle Matthew) never can remember to forward letters.

I hope you like the Academy. I simply hated it myself, but then I had no talent.

Yours,

Petrova.

P.S. Let me know if you want anything special, a spanner or anything like that.

Madame sent for Mark and told him she had received his two pounds and that he could have it whenever he liked. She also said she would give him his shilling every week, as she did Sorrel and Holly. Then she added that she was going to make a formal announcement about the scholarships and had only been waiting for this letter from Petrova to do it, and would Mark please find Holly and send her to her.

Holly was devoted to Madame. She came skipping along the corridor and only collected herself at the door of the study. In answer to Madame's "Come in," she opened the door and made a really beautiful curtsy before saying, "Madame."

Madame was sitting at her desk. She held out her hand.

"Come here, my child." When Holly came to her she put an arm around her. Holly wanted to play with the fringe of Madame's cerise shawl but Madame took hold of her hands and held them. "I want to talk to you about Posy's scholarship. As you've heard from Posy, she's making another scholarship especially for you. What she means by that is that she would like to pay for the training of somebody at the Academy, but that her scholarship and all her interests and her letters are to go to a dancer if I can find one. And now I think I have. You know who that is, don't you?"

Holly nodded. All the children in the Academy knew that.

"Miriam."

Madame held her tight.

"Yes, Miriam. Would you mind very much? If all you receive is the money? You'll get your pocket money every week, and birthday and Christmas presents, but it is only fair to tell you that when it comes to writing letters, at which Posy was always very bad, I think they'll go to Miriam."

Holly could not, at the moment, see why Madame should suppose she would mind. It was nice to get a letter, of course, because everybody at the Academy wanted to see it and read it, but it was the presents and pocket money that were really important. She looked up at Madame.

"No, I wouldn't mind."

Madame gave her a pleased squeeze.

"I'm very glad, Holly. You have worked very hard and I shouldn't like your feelings to be hurt, and your dancing's coming on very well indeed. But we can't pretend you're the same sort of dancer as Miriam, can we?" She gave Holly a kiss. "Run along now, back to your class."

That afternoon the students were summoned to the big hall. After they had greeted Madame, they were seated in the usual rows across the floor. Madame addressed them from the platform. She told them about the scholarships.

"All of you know, I think, that last term I was given scholarships from Pauline and Posy Fossil in Hollywood. I granted them temporarily to Sorrel and Holly Forbes. After Sorrel's performance at the matinée, I made up my mind that she was exactly the right person for a scholarship, and, therefore, she will hold the Pauline Fossil scholarship for the rest of her time here." She searched the rows of children. "Congratulations, Sorrel." Everybody clapped. Madame waited for them to finish clapping and then she went on, "Posy's scholarship was for a dancer and I granted it to Holly because last term there was nobody else who in my opinion was entirely worthy of it, and when she came to an audition here she certainly was promising. Well, since then, somebody else has come along who is the sort of dancer Posy wants to help. Miriam." Everybody clapped again. "Now we come to a third scholarship, which is not for any particular talent, but is presented by the third Fossil sister, Petrova. Petrova is giving her scholarship because the Fossil sisters always stuck together and did the same things, and so, because I know that's what she would like, I'm giving it to Mark." Everybody clapped again. "Thank you, my dears."

It was when Holly was back in the classroom that she realized she had lost something very important. Everybody thumped Miriam on the back and most people said, "Bad luck, Holly."

Miss Jones, who was taking the class for arithmetic, said to Holly in what was meant to be a kind way:

"Well, dancing isn't everything, is it, Holly?"

Holly, sitting at her desk, and trying to look as though she was attending to the arithmetic lesson, felt as if all of a sudden she had grown older. Nobody was being deliberately unkind, of course. It was just that they had made her see herself as she was, and it hurt. She suddenly saw how inferior she was to the other children. To begin with, everybody else had a mother and, because of these mothers, they were always a bit better dressed than she was. And the house still looked awful. It was not a lovely flat like Miriam's where you would be proud to ask anyone to tea. Then, of course, there were the brief cases. This term she was absolutely the only child in the class who was carrying her things about in a brown paper parcel. The more she thought about things the worse she felt, and suddenly she knew that she was going to cry. She could not cry, she simply could not. Everybody would think she was crying because she was jealous of Miriam. So she asked to be excused, and ran downstairs to the cloakroom, where nobody would see her, and cried and cried.

Of course the awful thing about crying is that even when it is over, it leaves your eyes all swollen and red-looking. Holly, after one horrified glance in the mirror, felt she simply could not go back to her class looking like that, so she decided to stay where she was until dancing class began and then go and apologize to Miss Jones. It was while she was filling up the time that she noticed Miranda's locker was ajar and, idly opening the door, saw the brief case lying in the locker looking very abandoned because there was nothing else in the locker at all.

Holly looked at the brief case. What a difference it would make if it were hers! How little it would matter to Miranda! Quite likely it would lie there all term without Miranda's every noticing it. How lovely if Miranda would just lend it! In all likelihood Miranda *would* lend it if she were asked. If that were so, could there be any harm in borrowing it without asking? When Holly had reached this point in her reasoning, the brief case was in her hands.

Holly's eyes were still a little swollen, but her face was flushed with pride when she walked back to her arithmetic class.

"You've been a long time, dear," said Miss Jones. "I was just about to send someone to look for you."

Holly looked around the class to be certain that everybody was listening. It was going to be a lovely moment when they all started envying her instead of thinking her inferior.

"I was talking to my cousin Miranda," she explained. "She came around to see me specially. 'Dear Holly,' she said, 'I don't like to see you carrying a nasty paper parcel when everybody else has a brief case. Do let me lend you this one of mine.'"

That evening Holly put the brief case in her locker. Though by now she had almost persuaded herself that Miranda had lent it to her, she had not convinced herself to the point of thinking that Sorrel and Mark would believe such a story. It was sad to think of that lovely brief case having to be put away in a locker all night, but there was no doubt it was safer there.

The case was not missed for a week. Then Miss Smith asked for it and when Sorrel went to fetch it she found it was gone. Anything missing in the Academy had to be reported. So the loss was reported to Winifred who, having examined the locker and found it empty, reported what had happened to Madame.

Madame was puzzled.

"Brief case? Empty, you say? I expect one of the students borrowed it. Have you asked everybody in Miranda's class?"

"Everybody," repeated Winifred.

"Oh, well," said Madame. "I'll keep the whole school back after lunch and inquire about it. I don't suppose it will be far off."

The students had finished lunch and were pushing back their chairs when Madame came in. When she had been greeted she walked to the top of one of the tables where everybody could hear her.

"One moment, my dears. I'm sorry to keep you from your recreation time but there is a little muddle that needs to be cleared up. Last week Miranda's governess, Miss Smith, brought a brief case to the Academy with things in it for Sorrel, and asked Sorrel to put the case in Miranda's locker when she was through with it. This Sorrel did and Miranda saw it there the next day. Since then it seems to have disappeared. Has anybody seen it, moved it or borrowed it?"

All the children, except those in Holly's class, shook their heads and looked as uninterested as they felt. Holly's class was sitting around the junior dining table with Miss Sykes in charge. The children were bobbing around like corks in a rough sea, and a storm of whispers ran around the table, with one name predominating—"Holly." And the more the children thought about Holly the more full of expression this whisper became. "Hol-lee. Ooh! Hol-lee."

Madame's attention was caught by this bobbing and whispering. She came over to the junior table.

"You all seem very excited. Do you know anything about the brief case?" There was a pause. The children sat still but their eyes swiveled around to Holly. Madame looked smilingly at Holly. "Everybody seems to think that you know something, Holly. Have you seen Miranda's brief case?"

In the last few days Holly had thought of the brief case as being almost her own. When Madame first mentioned the case, so convinced was she that it had been a real loan she did not even feel uncomfortable.

But when the whispers had started they began to penetrate the wall of imagination which she had built, and suddenly the wall fell down, and there was nothing left but the awful fact that she had taken something that did not belong to her, and told everybody it was a loan. The horror of the situation was beyond tears, it just made her feel as if she were full of hot coals. She shut her lips tightly together and stared with a very red face at Madame.

Madame, who had come to ask a simple question, saw that something had happened which was not going to be so simple after all. She looked around at the other students.

"Holly doesn't seem to be going to answer me. Who else knows about this case?"

Once more the whole class began bobbing about like corks and whispering, and this time the name that came to the top was "Miss Jones."

Madame hated whisperings and nudges. She felt convinced that a lot of fuss was being made about nothing. She looked around the room with some impatience, and caught Miss Jones's eye.

"Would you come here a moment, Miss Jones?"

Poor Miss Jones was feeling miserable. She hated telling tales and had hoped most passionately that Holly would spare her by explaining what had happened. However, where Madame beckoned the staff went. She came over to the table. Madame still had a slightly impatient note in her voice.

"Do you know anything about Miranda's brief case?"

Miss Jones had an accurate mind. She said that of course she did not know if the brief case Holly had brought in was the one that was missing. But she reported how Holly had appeared with a brief case and then repeated, word for word, what Holly had said about Miranda's having lent her the case.

Miss Jones's words fell on a breathless hush. Every face looked shocked except Sorrel's and Mark's. Sorrel and Mark were looking at the floor, not knowing where else so shamed a family could look. Madame faced Holly.

"Is the brief case you have the one that's missing, Holly?" Holly nodded. Madame held out her hand. "Come along, dear, I think this is a matter that you and I should talk over alone."

In her study Madame sat down in an armchair by the fire. Holly, as the door shut, felt trapped and frightened and all her self-control gave way. She lay down on the floor and sobbed so that her whole body shook. Madame let her cry for a little while, and then she patted her shoulder.

"Be quiet, Holly, that's quite enough crying. Suppose, instead of lying on the floor there, you come and sit on my knee and tell me all about it."

Even after Holly was on Madame's knee, it took her a long time to stop crying, but when she did the whole story came out. For a while, after she had finished, Madame was silent. She went on stroking Holly's curls and gazing into the fire. Then she said: "I do see what happened, Holly, and I can understand how your mind was working. But all the same

209

it mustn't go on working like that, must it? It's most important that you should know clearly what you make up and what you don't. Do Sorrel and Mark want brief cases too?"

"Dreadfully."

Madame rang a bell.

It was the duty in wartime when staff was scarce for one of the students to answer Madame's bell. The senior class took turns and were known as the messengers. When the day's messenger appeared Madame sent her to fetch Sorrel and Mark.

Sorrel and Mark were appalled at that summons. To both of them came the idea that because they were the brother and sister of a child who was almost a thief they were going to be expelled. Outside Madame's door they met and looked at each other with scared eyes. Sorrel gave Mark's tie a nervous twitch and pulled up her socks. Then she knocked.

Madame greeted Sorrel and Mark with a radiant smile.

"Come in, my dears. Mark, open that top left-hand drawer. I've got a new box of candy sent me by Pauline from America." When they had all chosen a sweet she told Sorrel and Mark to sit on the floor. "Well, Holly and I have got to the bottom of this brief case business. It seems that Holly and Mark suffer from the same complaint of letting their imaginations run away with them. But even though it's not a very bad fault, it is a fault and it's got to be got rid of. Now, what I suggest is this. I'm going to buy three brief cases. They'll cost a lot, as you know, and they'll take more money than we've probably got, but we can add to that because presently the Fossils will send you money for your birthdays. On each brief case I shall have your names stamped so that there'll be no chance of your losing them. Sorrel and Mark will have their brief cases right away, but Holly will only be shown hers once and then it will be locked up in a cupboard until the beginning of the summer term."

She turned Holly's face towards her. "You can see then how vivid your imagination is, Holly. You can see whether you can imagine you are carrying your new brief case when you are not, and whether you can turn your brown paper parcel into a brief case. That'll be a very good way of learning where imagination ends and real things begin. Now, take one more sweet, each of you, and then, Sorrel, I want you to take the family home. I think an afternoon off will do you all good. You have had enough excitement for one day."

When the door had shut on them, Madame got up and fetched her book of telephone numbers. She opened the page at "C" and laid her finger on the name Cohen.

In spite of Madame's being so nice, Sorrel and Mark and Holly felt pretty wormy inside when they arrived at the Academy next morning. And they felt no better when they got a message to say Winifred wanted to see Sorrel at once.

Winifred was working at the bar. She was in the middle of some frappés when Sorrel came in. She stopped with one foot against the calf of the other leg.

"Oh, Sorrel, your Aunt Lindsey has rung up to say that she wants to take you three and Miriam to lunch in a restaurant. And Madame says that's all right and it won't matter if you are half an hour late coming back."

The school were just finishing lunch in the Academy dining room when Madame came in. This time a kind of shudder ran around. Madame making a speech two days running! Something pretty awful must be going to happen. Probably the Forbeses hadn't really gone out to lunch with their aunt, they'd probably been expelled. Madame waited until the students had greeted her and then she beckoned to them all to come and stand around her.

"I'm going to take you into my confidence, and I trust, without asking for a promise, that you will not repeat a word I have said to the Forbeses. The brief case that was missing has, as you know, been found. Holly had it. I need hardly tell you that of course it was no great crime she committed. She's a child with a vivid imagination and she persuaded herself that it had been lent. However, that is a fault and it has been dealt with. How, concerns none of you.

"The reason I wanted to talk to you is that I discovered from talking to Holly something in which I think you can all help. The Forbes children have, as you know, no mother, and their father is missing. They live with their grandmother but, of course, even the best grandmother isn't the same as a mother. The result is that Holly certainly, and probably the other two as well, feel that the rest of you look down on them." There was a gasp from the

212

school. "I know you'll all say to me, 'Of course we don't.' But are you sure?" Madame smiled. "Now, I don't want anything silly. I don't want anyone racing out to buy Holly a brief case or all of you children making a pet of her. But I think it would be nice if you kept it firmly in your minds that the Forbes children, in some ways, are less fortunate than you are, and see that when you have any special piece of luck, like being allowed to give a party, or having a few sweets to hand around, you share with them."

While this talk was going on, Sorrel and Mark and Holly were having a superb and uproarious lunch with Aunt Lindsey and Miriam. Aunt Lindsey took them to a grand restaurant where a band was playing and there was goose upon the menu. Not being used to goose, they felt a mixture of pride in having eaten it and rather doubtful in the middle because it was not their usual form of food. It was with dismay they saw Aunt Lindsey look at her watch, and heard her say that the best of everything must come to an end and they were already half an hour late for the Academy.

Climbing the Academy steps, each of them except, of course, Miriam, felt a sinking inside. Would people look at them differently after yesterday?

Half the school were down in the changing room when Sorrel and Holly walked in. One of Sorrel's class ran up to her.

"Hullo, there you are! We thought you'd gone off for another afternoon. You wouldn't think it but we miss your old mug when you're away."

One of the juniors came up to Holly.

"My mother bought me a Mars bar out of my ration this month. I meant to save you half but I didn't quite manage that." She fumbled in her brief case and brought out a dusty, bitten little end of chocolate. "There you are! I won't watch you while you eat it and then I won't miss it."

Chapter XVI

Audition at the B.B.C.

Sorrel's thirteenth birthday came at the beginning of the summer term. She woke up to find the sun streaming in and a parcel on the end of her bed. The parcel had been smuggled from the Academy in Mark's brief case. It was from Pauline. Inside was a big box marked "Candies" and a card.

The card said, "I hope this arrives in time for your birthday. I have sent some money for you to buy something, but I think birthdays ought to have parcels."

The candies were tied up in the loveliest way. Being used to seeing the sweet ration in a paper bag that was inclined to burst, or a flimsy cardboard container, Sorrel found pleasure even in unpacking Pauline's parcel. And the candies themselves were breathtaking, large and squashy, many of them covered with nuts. Sorrel put one in her mouth and then hurriedly put the lid on the box to keep away temptation. It would be so easy to eat the lot and then she would feel sick. That would be disastrous on this day of all days.

Lying back in bed chewing, Sorrel thought about Pauline. She had seen her now, for Alice had taken them to the cinema so they would get to know the faces of Pauline, Posy, and, especially, Uncle Henry. Pauline was so lovely in the films that the first time she saw her Sorrel felt as though she were a stranger, somebody grand and remote. But then had come Pauline's second letter, just as friendly as the first. There did not seem to be the smallest thing about the Academy in which she was not interested, and nothing was the slightest bit grand about the way she wrote. What fun it must be to be Pauline! All the same she, Sorrel, was going to an audition today. She wished she could tell Pauline about it.

Miss Jay had said, "Let's pity the poor Story Hour staff and try to find something new for your audition. How awful it must be for those who have to listen to hear the same thing over and over and over again."

In the end Miss Jay, assisted by Sorrel, wrote a short version of *The Princess and the Pea*. It was nearly all conversation.

"One ought to have some stuff in dialect," Miss

Jay had said, "but you're not very good at dialect. I think, for the second item, you'd better recite some Shakespeare. You shall learn Titania's speech from *A Midsummer Night's Dream.* You'll be able to have the script in your hands, because people do when they're broadcasting, but no pupil from this Academy has ever gone to an audition without being entirely word perfect, and they never will."

Sorrel sat up in bed. In a much bigger and heartier voice than her own she said, "Sounds a wild night," and then she spoke in a deep gruff voice: "Aye, there's a rare storm. The yard's a-swim with water and the river's running down." Then she went back to the hearty voice but this time it sounded anxious. "You'll not go out again tonight?" Then the man's voice, "No, I have locked the gates, none will wish to go through now till morning."

Suddenly Holly and Mark and Hannah came bursting in at Sorrel's door.

"Happy birthday, Sorrel," they chorused.

"I've brought you the most lovely present," said Holly. "Will you undo mine first?"

Sorrel made room for Holly to get into bed with her. Mark and Hannah sat on the sides. Before she undid her parcels Sorrel opened her box of candy. Hannah made clucking noises.

"Oh, you shouldn't go eating all that rich stuff before breakfast, bound to turn your stomachs."

Nobody paid any attention to Hannah because they knew that she knew that one sweet before breakfast was permissible on a birthday or Christmas or Easter Day. Sorrel looked at the three parcels on her knee. She undid Holly's first. Inside was a pincushion, made not very well but with immense pain and toil out of a piece of one of Grandmother's old stage dresses.

"It's to be put away until you have a part," Holly explained, bouncing with excitement. "Now you're thirteen and going to an audition, you're sure to have a part soon."

In Mark's parcel there was a ruler, a hammer and a small bottle of glue.

"That's so you can mend anything yourself that wants mending," he explained. "Or at any rate you can get me to come and mend it and then you've got the things you need."

From Hannah there was a big, black bow. "As you're going to wear your black tunic up at the B.B.C. I thought you might like a new ribbon."

Alice came in with her present wrapped in a tiny bit of tissue paper. "It's a little chain to hang that little fish the sailor gave you around your neck when you go to your audition. He said it was for luck, so that's the time to wear it."

Mark sprawled across the bed and looked longingly at Sorrel's box of candies. "Of course I know it's Sorrel's birthday, but anyone would think that she was the only one who was going to an audition. Nobody seems to remember that I'm going to sing."

Alice gave him an affectionate slap. "Nobody's under any illusion that you're going to be nervous about it. All I hope is that you don't break the microphone. As a matter of fact, you've not been forgotten, has he, Hannah? Old Hannah here has sat up night after night knitting you some new almond rocks."

Mark recognized almond rocks as socks. He looked suspiciously at Hannah. "What sort?" he asked.

"Gray wool," said Hannah. "Two pairs of lightweight for the summer."

Alice moved to the door. "Well, I can't stay here gossiping, I've got our breakfast to take up yet. When you're dressed, Sorrel, your grandmother would like to give you a kiss."

Mark waited until the door had closed behind Alice and then he lowered his voice.

"Of course one shouldn't criticize one's grandmother, but ever since I've been in this house I've thought it pretty mean that there's never been a present—not at Christmas, not at Easter, not on Holly's and my birthdays, and now not on Sorrel's birthday."

"That's enough, come and get dressed," said Hannah. "There are some people who don't need to give presents to show their affection."

Mark followed Hannah obediently to the door, but before he reached it he looked back at Sorrel. "I don't think our grandmother's one of those people, do you?"

The auditioning was to go on all afternoon. Sorrel and Mark had an appointment at half-past three. They were taken by Miss Jay and Dr. Lente. As a rule only one teacher went to an audition however many pupils were going, and for two to go caused rather a sensation in the Academy, especially as one of them was Dr. Lente, who never went to auditions. However, a talent once accepted acquired squatter's rights, as it were, and so the pupils looked wise and said to each other, "That's because of Mark."

The B.B.C. looked very imposing with its sand-bagged entrance and police outside, and when they got inside and Miss Jay and Dr. Lente were at the reception desk getting passes, even Mark was reduced to respectful silence.

There were several other boys and girls in the Story Hour waiting room: Three boys who had obviously come to sing, a very smartly dressed girl of about fourteen, who had a mother who kept pulling her curls over her shoulders, and a small boy in spectacles with a violin case on his knee. The door into the studio opened and somebody ushered a girl out and said that he would be writing to her. Then the first of the boy singers was called in. His voice came to them faintly through the door singing, "I'll Walk Beside You." The girl with ringlets was sitting beside Sorrel. She gave her a nudge.

"I got here much too early. That's the eighth time someone has sung that song. It must be pretty awful for them up there," jerking her thumb at the ceiling.

"What is up there?" Sorrel asked.

"The judges. They sit in a room with a glass window looking into the studio. All our voices come to them up there. You can see them peering down at you. I always wonder what they're saying."

"Have you been to an audition before, then?"

"Twice. Once before the war, and once in Bristol. Each time I was going to be used, my family moved and I couldn't."

"What do you do?" Sorrel asked.

"Well, I think it's a mistake not to give them an all-round view of your work, don't you? I'm doing a speech from Bernard Shaw's *St. Joan*—that's just for diction—and then I'm doing a speech of Edelgard's out of *Children in Uniform*. It's two separate speeches, really, but I'm putting them together. And then I'm doing a little short funny thing in Scotch, and a rather pathetic bit about a child waiting for its father who's down the mine—that's with a Welsh accent. I finish up with a bit of good old North country, which is where I come from. What are you doing?"

Sorrel was appalled. How clever everybody else in the world was! And how idiotic everybody in the B.B.C. would think it that she had prepared only a little bit of *The Princess and the Pea* and one speech of Titania's!

"I'm just doing some Shakespeare," she answered, "and a version of one of Hans Andersen's fairy stories. It doesn't seem much, does it?"

"Well, it's no good doing what you can't, is it? It will only put them..." the ringleted girl jerked her finger at the roof again, "off."

The door opened, the boy singer came out and the second one went in. Once more there were muffled sounds of "I'll Walk Beside You."

The girl sighed. "You'd think it was catching, like measles or something."

Dr. Lente rolled anguished eyes at the roof. "It is not suitable as a song for little boys, and that child has a voice that overtrained is."

It was after the third boy had sung "I'll Walk Beside You" that Sorrel was called. Miss Jay gave her a smile and sounded as matter-of-fact as she did in the classroom.

"Come along, dear."

In the studio there were seats all around the room, a piano on the left-hand side, and in the center, of course, the most important thing there, the microphone. A pleasant-looking girl came up to Sorrel and asked her what she was going to do, and whether she would announce herself or would like to be announced. Sorrel looked desperately at Miss Jay, but Miss Jay was nodding and smiling at what appeared to be the roof. Sorrel, turning around, saw behind her the glass window and the faces looking through that the girl had told her about. She touched Miss Jay on the arm.

"They want to know if I want to announce myself."

"Certainly," said Miss Jay, "and you'll start with the Shakespeare as arranged."

It was a queer feeling to stand by yourself in the middle of the room and speak to an inanimate thing like a microphone. It was a queer feeling to think that in the room behind the glass window people were not hearing your voice as it sounded in the studio, but as it sounded brought to them over the air. It was altogether so odd that just at first the queerness of everything overawed Sorrel and she could not bring Titania to life.

"I'm reciting Titania's speech from *A Midsummer Night's Dream* by William Shakespeare," she said. The lines came out of her mouth, just nicely rehearsed words, but meaning nothing. Then suddenly the studio was not there. She was in a wood. She was Titania.

When she had finished, the leaves and silver birches were gone and she was back in the studio. Then quite suddenly a voice came out of nowhere, a friendly, cheerful woman's voice.

"Thank you very much, Sorrel. That was nice. Now what else are you going to do for us?"

Sorrel felt silly talking to someone whom you could not see, but she answered as politely as possible.

"Please, I was going to tell you about *The Princess and the Pea.*"

"We shall enjoy that," said the voice, "it's one of my favorite stories."

Sorrel folded her hands. "*The Princess and the Pea,* freely adapted from the story by Hans Christian Andersen."

She had finished. She had been the princess, she had been the peasants. In her mind it had all been real.

The voice spoke again. It was laughing.

"Delightful. We all enjoyed that. Are you doing anything else for us?"

Sorrel looked at Miss Jay. Miss Jay was talking to the girl who had shown them in, and the girl spoke into the microphone for her.

"No, that's all."

Then the voice said, "Thank you very much, Sorrel. Good-bye."

Sorrel was not asked to leave the room, so she and Miss Jay sat in a corner and listened while Mark sang "Where the Bee Sucks, There Suck I." He sang it beautifully. Evidently the people behind the glass window thought so too. The same voice that had talked to Sorrel said, with obvious enthusiasm:

"Thank you so much, Mark. That was lovely. Will you sing something else?"

Mark was charmed. "I'm going to sing you 'Matthew, Mark, Luke and John,' and then something whose name I absolutely never remember."

"It seems to be a little folk song translated from the Russian," said the girl. "Go on, Mark."

When Mark had finished the voice said, "Thank you very much indeed." And then, "Wait a minute." And then, after a pause, "I'd like to see Dr. Lente before he goes about fixing Mark into a program."

Sorrel did not mean to feel jealous and it was not exactly jealousy that she did feel. But it is hard when your young brother is engaged and you are not. Pulling on her coat, she felt flat and sad. There were Dr. Lente and Miss Jay and Mark and the B.B.C. people in the passage all talking together about Mark broadcasting. And there was she, just one other person who had been to an audition and in whom nobody was particularly interested. It was not even as if singing on the radio would do Mark any good. In fact it might be very bad for him. It would be a terrible thing if he got to like it, for it would take his mind off his education to be a sailor.

Leaving the B.B.C. seemed very different to Sorrel from coming into it. Coming in, it had seemed a grand, gray building but full of excitement. Going out, it was just a place where you had done your best but somehow it had not come off.

They walked down the road, Mark skipping along in an unconcerned way, and Dr. Lente and Miss Jay talking about his singing on the radio program. Sorrel trudged along beside them trying not to look disgruntled but feeling in the mood to drag her feet and kick at something. Then suddenly Miss Jay turned to her.

"They were pleased with you, Sorrel. There's a new serial starting in a few weeks' time and they are planning to give you the part of one of the girls."

Sorrel was so surprised her breath was taken away.

"Me!"

Miss Jay laughed. "Yes, you. You did your stuff very well indeed. I gather it's a very exciting thriller, all about catching a spy. You'll enjoy that." She caught hold of Sorrel's arm. "Won't you?"

Sorrel beamed at her, marveling that a world which a few minutes before had seemed so dismal and gray could so quickly be sparkling and colorful.

"You bet I will, it will be simply super."

Chapter XVII

News for Sorrel

Quite suddenly, perhaps because it was nearly summer or perhaps because Sorrel and Mark were going to broadcast, or perhaps because they began to take an interest in their work, the Forbes family settled down and found they were quite liking living with Grandmother. Of course it was a funny life. Now that Grandmother was earning money, Alice was trying to improve the appearance of the rooms. But when she had sold the carpets and furniture she had not known there was a 1943 coming when, however much bees and honey you might have, there were no carpets or furniture to buy.

"It's not," she would say, looking at the bare

boards in Mark's bedroom, "that we aren't willing to put our hands in our skyrocket, but we're not going to give, even if we had it, a hundred pounds for a bit of carpet that would be expensive at five."

Mark heard what Alice said but naturally he knew nothing about prices and conditions, and he supposed that Alice was trying to put Grandmother in a good light. Her explanation did not satisfy him.

"Even," he said to Hannah, Sorrel and Holly, "if Grandmother had to spend a million pounds, I wouldn't think it too much. I'd rather spend a million pounds than make my grandchild sleep in a room that's much too shabby to give to a dog that's had distemper."

Mark, having got something into his head, was not the sort of boy to let it go again, and he would, as long as he lived in the house, and quite likely always, be angry with Grandmother about his room. All the same he did not dislike Grandmother. All of them had grown, in a way, fond of her. It was not the sort of fondness that anyone would expect to have for a grandmother. Not that kind of fondness which means that you feel you can tell her things because she is tolerant and gentle, as well, of course, as being admirable about Christmas and birthdays. Instead they had found their grandmother exciting, which is the last thing you expect to feel about a grandmother. Grandmother, with her moods and fusses, made such a difference in the house even when you never saw her.

Now that Grandmother was working she was not

in a great deal. She acted every night, of course, and Sorrel and Mark and Holly were out all day, so the only possible meeting days were Sundays, for on Saturday afternoons she played a matinée. On Sundays she often had people in to see her and she usually sent for her grandchildren. Even on the Sundays when she was alone, she sent for them. And though she was sometimes difficult to understand, she was always entertaining. They discovered too that though she never seemed to take much interest in what was happening to them, she obviously was in constant touch with Madame on the telephone, because she apparently knew exactly how they were getting on.

Another thing which made a change for the better in their lives was the Square garden. In the spring it was beautiful. And what the gardener had said was true: the boys and girls had come back. The houses in the Square began to be lived in again; not properly lived in, of course, because there was no one to look after them, but one or two floors were opened and in these families settled down. The three youngsters Sorrel and Mark and Holly had met on Christmas Day became their friends. There was a little fair-haired child whom Holly played with and mothered. She was called Penny and Holly treated her like a doll. There were babies in perambulators and babies toddling, and lots of the families had dogs and were willing to let other people know their dogs well. When the spring flowers disappeared summer ones began to come out—roses and lupins and delphiniums—and more and more chairs were set out on the lawns on Saturday afternoons and Sundays, and a very friendly atmosphere sprang up.

At the Academy, life had been quite different ever since the day Holly took the brief case. Very few of the pupils lived in central London, and so there was no possibility of the Forbeses being asked out to tea or anything like that. But Madame's words had taken root and everybody did his best to be extra nice. It was not that they would not have been friendly before, because all three were quite popular, only nobody had thought them in need of extra consideration. The pupils had been used to Miranda and had learned from her that a granddaughter of the Warren family was so grand a thing to be, that it put all of the family in a world apart. When the Forbes children and Miriam arrived, they had had quite a lot to live down. After the brief case affair and what Madame had said, Sorrel and Mark and Holly made, as it were, a fresh start. All the other pupils let their natural feelings of friendship for them have free play without any intervening wonder as to whether they were putting on "side" or getting unfair advantages because they were Warrens.

For Sorrel life had looked up very much since she was engaged to broadcast. Mark's broadcasting was taken as a matter of course. He was too young to have a license and, therefore, not competing for parts, but Sorrel was engaged for one of the older parts in the new serial after being heard at an audition, and she was given it because she had the right voice for it, and was chosen from among hundreds of applicants. There was a very decided barrier among the over-twelves between those who were working and those who were not. There were, of course, a number of pupils who were not supposed to be working, and who had been sent to the Academy with a view to their being dancers or going on the stage when they grew up. But among those who wanted work, to be engaged for a part, whether in a film or on the stage or on the air, meant a great deal. It gave one a cachet.

Sorrel knew nothing about the negotiations for her part in the serial because those were conducted for her by the school. As a matter of fact, she did not know she had been given the part until she got the first instalment of her script, and was called for rehearsal. The script was given to her by Miss Jay.

"You won't find the whole story here, Sorrel. This is the first week's instalment. It seems most exciting as far as it goes. You're to play Nancy."

Sorrel knew that if she were going to broadcast she was probably going to be paid. She had always kept Alice's conversation about bees and honey very much in mind. Alice had said she had sold things because tradespeople had to be paid. Of course now that Sorrel had met all the family she could see that nobody would ever let Grandmother starve. But equally it would not be fair to expect her to support them all. And above all, it would not be fair to let her pay for Mark's schooling. Not that as things were at present Grandmother would dream of paying for it. She did not even know that Alice had promised to see that he went to a proper school when he was eleven. Of course, by then all those things that Alice had talked about concerning probate and lawyers might have been settled, and the question of Mark's school fees would not arise. But it was certain that in case there was any lack of bees and honey when the time came, it would be a great help if she had some money to offer, at least for the first term. She felt terribly shy about talking to Miss Jay about it, but she felt she must.

"What happens to money that I earn?"

Miss Jay looked amused. "What do you want to happen to it?"

Sorrel liked and trusted Miss Jay and she decided suddenly to explain about Mark. Miss Jay listened in attentive silence until she had finished.

"I think I can help about that," she said then. "I can arrange to have your money deposited to your account in the post office. As for Mark, I don't know what to say. If it is your father's wish that he should be trained as a sailor, I think you should get your uncles and aunts to help. Don't you think they would?"

Sorrel fidgeted with her hair.

"Well, I don't believe Aunt Lindsey and Aunt Marguerite would, because they're like Grandmother. They just can't believe there could be anybody in the world who wanted to do anything but act. Of course there's Uncle Francis. I suppose he might help, but he's rather a distant kind of uncle. Even when you seem to be talking to him you never feel absolutely sure he's listening." Then her face lit up as a thought struck her. "But I tell you who I'm certain would help, and that's Uncle Mose."

"Mose Cohen! Now, of all your family I should

have thought that he'd be the one who thought the stage was the only career."

Sorrel shook her head violently.

"No, he isn't. Uncle Mose, in a way, is a little like Daddy. Daddy always said, about anything I asked him, 'Well, let's thrash it out, old lady, and see if we can manage it.' Uncle Mose is like that." She looked at Miss Jay with great conviction. "Yes, that's what I'll do if the worst comes to the worst. I'll ask Uncle Mose to help."

The rehearsals for the broadcast were held in the same studio where Sorrel had been for the audition, only this time there were a lot of people present. She noticed some bits of furniture, too, and some cups which she was told would be used for clinking sounds when the actors were supposed to be drinking tea. There was a door in a wooden frame, which was to be shut when anybody was supposed to be going in or out of a door. There was a plank on which to make the sound of footsteps, and there was a doorbell. A young man called Henry in a jersey and gray slacks was producing the play. And of course there were the people in charge in that room upstairs with the glass window looking into the studio. From there came all the music, and green lights for cues and pauses, and a red light for when the cast was on the air, and from there too came all the other sound effects. At one end of the studio a little tent had been built, and in this sat the narrator.

Henry explained the tent to Sorrel. "We get the difference that way of pitch and tone. All of you are in the story, but he's the man who links it all together, and it mustn't sound as though you were all in the same room."

There were three of them in the story. A brother and sister called Robert and Nancy and a Cockney evacuee called Bill, and they all met at the beginning in a cove on a beach. The effects upstairs, Sorrel was told, did lovely things to make the beach come true—seagulls mewing and water lapping, and the crunch of steps on pebbles. Sorrel and a blond-haired boy called John and a little red-headed boy called Edward stood around the microphone, their scripts in one hand and their pencils in the other, reading their parts. Henry stopped them at intervals for different things. Sometimes they were not excited enough, and sometimes he wanted them to sound as though they were moving about. Whatever Henry said they wrote down next to their lines. By the time they had gone through their parts twice, Sorrel and Edward and John began to live them.

But Sorrel's broadcast of the first episode was completely eclipsed so far as home interest was concerned by a family storm. Uncle Francis was, as Alice had told them, putting on *The Tempest*. He was to play Prospero and he had engaged a splendid Caliban, about whom he was excited. Generally, when he did a London season, he put on two or three plays as a repertory. But this time he had decided to give all his attention to one production, which should be as beautiful as war conditions would allow. All Shakespearean actors have violent views on different plays and parts. Uncle Francis had always had ideas about *The Tempest*. One was that the ideal Ariel would be a child. Now suddenly he had an idea Miranda should play Ariel. Uncle Francis was the sort of man who expected everybody to do what he wanted. He simply could not believe that anyone would do anything to displease him. So he thought that when the time came he had only to ask for Miranda to be released from her part in her present play for his request to be granted.

Unfortunately, he did not wait to ask her management before he told Miranda. He told her what he meant to do and that she was to study the part, but she was not, for the moment, to speak about it. That had been three months ago, and in those three months Miranda had lived and dreamed Ariel. Miranda was Shakespeare mad. She was perfectly prepared to play in modern comedies, for she knew quite well that good Shakespeare productions are few and far between, but her ambition was to have the big, tragic parts. Most of all she longed some day to play Lady Macbeth. That she should have a chance at Ariel before she was fifteen was beyond her wildest dreams. She had often asked her father to give her a part and he had always said he did not care for precocious children. She must wait until she was eighteen, he had declared. When Grandmother had overpersuaded him and Miranda had been allowed to play Sylvia, he had seen her perform at a matinée on one occasion when he was appearing near London, and had been full of pride. That was how he came to think of trusting her with Ariel.

Uncle Francis did not even write a very pleading letter to Miranda's management. He simply stated that he was putting on *The Tempest* at the end of June and he would like them to release his daughter for the part of Ariel. The management wrote back courteously but very firmly and said they would not consider it under any circumstances whatsoever. It was then the fur began to fly. Uncle Francis saw Grandmother, Grandmother saw Aunt Marguerite and Grandmother interviewed her management.

It took ten days, during which Uncle Francis fought passionately and tried everything including the use of lawyers, before it was finally accepted that Miranda was not going to be released. She was a success, her management wanted her, and they were keeping her. It was then that Grandmother had her brilliant idea.

"I quite realize that it's not at all the same thing to you, Francis, because naturally you wanted your daughter. But, fortunately, you have a niece who has Warren blood too and who also is very promising." She saw that Uncle Francis was going to argue, so she spoke in her firmest and most settled kind of voice. "Sorrel shall play Ariel."

Chapter XVIII

It was the day after Sorrel's first broadcast. When she came back from the Academy, Hannah told her that she was to sit up in her dressing gown to see Grandmother when she came back from the theater. Nothing like that had ever happened before and Mark and Holly as well as Sorrel were wild with curiosity to know what Grandmother could want to see Sorrel about.

"I expect she didn't like your broadcast," said Holly. "I expect she was sorry that she borrowed somebody's radio and had it in her dressing room. I can't think why she shouldn't like it because we thought you were awfully good, didn't we, Mark?"

The only radio in the house belonged to Alice and

was kept in the kitchen. Mark and Holly had been allowed to leave the Academy early and by arrangement with Hannah had been back in plenty of time to hear the broadcast. They had sat around the table in the kitchen expecting to be thrilled at hearing Sorrel's voice. Actually they found the story so exciting that they had clean forgotten Sorrel was Sorrel and thought she was Nancy.

Mark tried to explain this. "It wasn't till this morning that I remembered it had been you and that was odd because that girl, Nancy, rode a pony and you can't."

If the Forbes family must do stage work, then, from Hannah's point of view, let them appear in the Family Hour for the B.B.C. At the vicarage her favorite program had been the Family Hour. She approved of everything about it, especially the short services.

"Of course, what I'd fancy for you," she told Sorrel, "would be to take a part in one of those Bible stories, but that would mean acting on a Sunday and I couldn't think that right." Then she looked muddled. "Not but what it makes very suitable listening to, so maybe somebody ought to do it. But I don't think your grandmother wants to see you about anything of that sort, certainly not in a complaining way, for Alice told me on the quiet that it was a bit of good news."

Because she was sitting up to see Grandmother, Sorrel had a special supper with Hannah in the kitchen. There was a recipe that Hannah had heard on the radio for making a sort of scrambled egg with powdered egg and onion and cheese.

"A bit indigestible," said Hannah, "but it'll have time to settle before you're in bed."

Sorrel was sitting on the kitchen table. "I do wish I knew what Grandmother wanted. Even though you say it's going to be good news I can't help feeling as though I were waiting at the dentist's."

Hannah never seemed to know when she was telling something really important. Important things dropped out of her mouth in just the same tone of voice as when she said, "That was ever so nice a bit of meat I got from the butcher this week." Or, "I've been round to see that shoe-mender again and he's promised Mark's shoes by Thursday without fail."

Now she was at the stove stirring the scrambled egg. "I shouldn't wonder if it was something to do with your school. That Madame and Miss Jay came here this afternoon."

Sorrel shot off her chair and came over to the stove. "Hannah! And you've known that ever since we came in and you never told us!"

"I didn't know you'd be interested. That Madame looked ever so comic, I thought."

Sorrel paid no attention to Hannah's views on Madame. She caught her arm. "What did they come about? Didn't you hear anything?"

Hannah was puzzled at Sorrel's eagerness. "No. I've got more things to do than to wonder why your teachers come around. I've got ever such a lot of washing and mending. Holly's torn a great jagged piece right out of those rompers that she was given for her dancing."

Sorrel went back to the table. If only Alice were

in! Alice was never muddled about what was important and what was not. Rows of ideas rushed
through her mind. Alice had said it was good news.
Of course Alice was probably right, but just suppose
she were wrong. Nobody knew it, but Sorrel was not
quite clear in her conscience. She had felt that everybody was pleased with her about the broadcast, but
perhaps she had been rather overbearing this morning.

Miss Jones had said to her during arithmetic,
when she had answered a little rudely:

"I don't know what's the matter with you, Sorrel.
It's not like you to speak like that."

Later, when she had asked somebody to bring up
something for her from the cloakroom, one of the
girls had said: "You want a lot of waiting on today,
don't you? You know, you're not the only person
who ever broadcasted."

Neither what the girl had said nor what Miss
Jones had said had made much impression on Sorrel
until this minute, for she had felt important and
thought other people ought to think her important,
too. Now a fearful doubt crept into her mind. Had
Madame and Miss Jay come to see Grandmother in
order to say:

"If Sorrel gets cocky about everything she does,
perhaps we had better not let her take another part"?

Alice came down to fetch Sorrel.

"Run along up," she said, giving her an unex-
pected kiss. "You're to go straight in while I get our
supper."

Grandmother was in her drawing room. She came
home from the theater in a hired car and did not

bother to take off her make-up until she got back. So she was looking more like Grandmama on the stage than Grandmother in real life. She was sitting in an armchair. She held out a hand to Sorrel.

"Come here, Granddaughter. You have, of course, heard all about Miranda playing Ariel in her father's production. Well, the management won't release her, and so I have told your Uncle Francis that he's to try you in the part."

Sorrel felt as if the drawing room were turning upside down. "Me! But I couldn't!"

Grandmother thought a moment before she answered. "No actress should say that about any part, but possibly on this occasion you're right. Your Uncle Francis is, in my opinion, a pompous fool of an actor. But then I've always thought Prospero was a pompous fool of a man, therefore it's never been any surprise to me that your uncle's considered superb in the part. I, fortunately, have never had the misfortune to see him play it."

Her voice changed. "All the same, whatever my private opinion may be, your uncle is considered an extremely fine Prospero. You know the play, I suppose."

"No. I've heard about it lately, of course, because of Miranda, but we haven't done it yet at school."

"Well, Prospero, pompous fellow, lived on an island with his tiresome daughter. He had magic powers and made creatures his slaves. One of these was Caliban, a strange subhuman creation, and the other, Ariel, was what Shakespeare calls an airy sprite. Your Uncle Francis sees Ariel as neither a man nor a woman, but as a creature of light and air and spirit, and to get this effect he thinks he needs a very young girl. That's why he wanted Miranda, who speaks blank verse so exquisitely."

"But I don't," Sorrel exclaimed. "I'm getting on quite well, Miss Jay says. But it's only my third term and we didn't learn that kind of elocution at Ferntree School."

"Naturally, I know how far you've got," replied Grandmother. "I saw Madame Fidolia and your Miss Jay this afternoon. Miss Jay said that you have a natural gift for verse speaking, and that you have rhythm and a nice singing voice. The latter's important because Ariel has a song."

"Oh, goodness!" said Sorrel. "A song too! He—I mean she—I mean it—doesn't dance as well, does it?"

"Never still for a second," said Grandmother. "Every step a dance, every movement an inspiration. You'll see what your uncle wants when you get to rehearsals." She patted Sorrel's hand. "Don't look so scared, my dear. Exactly two things can happen to you, and neither would mean the end of the world. You will, of course, be rehearsing on approval and your uncle may refuse to let you play the part. Or you may be allowed to play the part and get quite appalling notices. Appalling notices are unfortunate for anyone, but at the age of thirteen they are unlikely to ruin your career. Now, run up to bed, child. You should be transported into the seventh heaven of happiness by what I've told you. What an opportunity!"

Sorrel went down to the kitchen where Alice was cooking Grandmother's supper. Alice grinned at her from the stove.

"That'll teach you, Miss Can't-do-it. I said to Hannah we should see you coming in looking like a wet week."

Sorrel had almost lost her voice. "But, Alice, you know I can't do it, don't you?"

Alice had no patience at all with faint hearts. "Oh, run along up to bed! You've got a chance that hundreds of girls would give their eye teeth to have and you stand there with eyes like a frightened cow, saying, 'Oo-er, Alice, I can't.' You make me sick. You've got Warren blood in you, haven't you? Well, run along up to bed and before you get into it say fifty times, 'I can do it if I try. I can, I can, I can.'"

Sorrel's rehearsals were to begin on the following Monday, and since it was term time and she had to continue with her schooling, it was arranged that Miss Smith was to teach her with Miranda. The lessons were to be taught in the wardrobe of the theater in which Sorrel was rehearsing. Sorrel dreaded the rehearsals. Bolstered up by Alice and conscious of Grandmother's scorn if she showed any fright, she was managing to pretend that she had some confidence. But she could not even pretend she looked forward to doing lessons with Miranda. To begin with, it was bad enough that Miranda, who had lived and dreamed of playing this part, was not going to play it. To have it given to her younger cousin must obviously be a great blow to her. Then, too, Miranda was not the sort of person who liked her life upset for other people. At the moment she and Miss Smith were doing lessons comfortably in her own schoolroom. And now, instead, she would be expected to go around to a theater after breakfast and do lessons in a wardrobe for the convenience of the cousin who had taken her part. Whichever way you looked at it the arrangement was a pretty mean one for anybody, and it would take an extraordinarily nice girl to be pleasant about it. Miranda might be a lot of things, but "nice" was not a word you would ever use about her. Sorrel shuddered whenever she thought of lessons on Monday.

Sorrel was not the only one who was shuddering. On Thursday Alice came back from the theater with a message from Miss Smith. Would Alice bring Sorrel to the Saturday matinée so that they could discuss what books and things she would need for Monday?

Miss Jay was taking an enormous interest in Sorrel's part. From the time Sorrel had been given it, less than a week remained until the first rehearsal. So there was no time, with everything else she had to do, to learn the whole part. But Miss Jay took her through as much of it as she could, explaining any word that she did not understand, but being careful not to teach her any inflections.

"I know your Uncle Francis is a great authority on this play and I don't want to let you get ideas before he starts in on you. All I want is to be certain that you're word perfect in each scene as you study it, and that you don't say any word like a parrot but know its meaning."

Sorrel confided in Miss Jay her fear of lessons with Miranda. She did not, of course, put it that way. She said:

"Do you think I must do lessons in the wardrobe? If I absolutely promised to come here every minute I could and worked before breakfast and when I got home at night, wouldn't that do?"

Miss Jay laughed. "I sympathize with you, but I can't help you. The law is the law and you've got to do lessons. It'd be a shocking thing if when you go down to the London County Council on Monday you're turned down because you're not having sufficient education. That's why Miss Smith's taking you. They've approved Miss Smith to teach Miranda, and they can trust her to see that your lessons are not neglected for your stage work."

"Well," said Sorrel, "I don't care what anybody says, I think it's going to be awful for everybody. If I were Miranda, I'd simply hate it—and *being* Miranda she'll hate it even more than I would."

Miss Jay reopened Sorrel's copy of *The Tempest*.

"I quite see your point, but really what you two girls like and don't like can't be considered. If you are to play the part it's the only solution and, as a matter of fact, it will be very good for you. If you're ever to be the actress that I hope you're going to be, you'll have to learn to assert yourself." She looked up from the Shakespeare. "You do want to be an actress, don't you?"

Sorrel was surprised at the fervor with which she

answered. She had not known until that moment how very much she did want to be one.

"More than anything in the world!"

"Good," said Miss Jay. "Because in my opinion, and, mind you, it's only an opinion, you've got as great a chance of becoming a good one as any pupil I've taught since Pauline Fossil." She turned back to the book. "Now then, we'll take that scene again. I'll give you the cue.

"'Come away, servant, come! I am ready now. Approach, my Ariel; come!'"

Because Sorrel was going to the matinée with Grandmother, Holly and Mark were allowed to invite Miriam to tea. Miriam came flying to Sorrel the moment her cousins reached the Academy on Saturday morning.

"I've had another letter from Posy. She says I don't tell her any of the things she really wants to know. And she's asked me rows and rows and rows of questions that I do most awfully want to answer. Could you possibly write to Posy for me if I told you what to say? You write beautifully and I write so terribly slowly."

Miriam was so full of hope that Sorrel simply had not the heart to say no.

Miriam practiced little steps while she dictated.

Dear Posy,
    I do a little center practice, but Madame says you forget that I'm not quite nine and

you didn't do her things nearly as young as that. I don't understand all that bit you have written about ballets in America, Britain and Russia. Would you please write in littler words next time? I take your letters to Madame and we read them together, but though Madame explains them they are still very difficult.

Now I will tell you about the ballets...

And Miriam dictated two long paragraphs full of technical details about the ballets she had seen. She ended with:

I shall be starting pointe work this autumn. Madame says that you always had precision, why haven't I?

Love,

Miriam. XXXXXXX

P.S. Holly sends her love and says she still hasn't got much beyond dancing a baby polka, so you wouldn't have wanted to give her your scholarship. Holly dances the baby polka as Dr. Lente would do it, and as Miss Jay would do it, and sometimes when she is very bad, as Madame would do it. She makes us laugh and laugh.

Sorrel, whose hand was getting tired, folded the letter and said:

"Well, I won't have any more P.S.'s. That's quite enough. It's lucky I've taken so many lessons on the history of the ballet or I would never have been able to spell those words and names. I never knew Holly did imitations."

Miriam was always immensely serious about people's work. "She does, but nobody's seen her yet. She does talking imitations, too. I told Mum and she said that your mother was a mimic and she was awfully funny, but that she was never allowed to do it properly because Grandmother and Grandfather wanted her to be a serious actress."

Sorrel handed the letter to Miriam. "You won't lose it, will you, after I've taken all the trouble to write it?"

Miriam looked surprised. "Of course not. I'm taking it this very second for Madame to read and she'll send it away."

Miriam dashed out the door and Sorrel looked after her. Miriam was always a puzzle to her. She was so purposeful, so unafraid of anybody, so certain where she was going. If Miriam could speak blank verse at all, which she would never try to do, she would not be afraid of acting Ariel. If she were going to play the part at all, she would know she could do it. Why, oh why, was she, Sorrel, not like that?

Sorrel arrived at the theater that afternoon well before the curtain was up. Alice sent her to Miranda's dressing room.

"It's no good your coming in with us, we get in a state if people hang around when we're making up. I've had a word with the stage manager and when Miss Smith's done with you, you can come down on the stage and watch the play. Wait till we're on the stage and then knock on our dressing-room door and call me. I'll take you down."

Miranda was making up when Sorrel went in. Miss Smith was sitting by the dressing table doing the *Times* crossword puzzle, and in a corner of the room sat a fair-haired girl knitting. Sorrel had wondered what on earth to say to Miranda. Miranda saved her the trouble of wondering.

In answer to Sorrel's knock Miss Smith said, "Come in."

And Miranda, smearing greasepaint on her face, muttered in a furious voice, "They can let you come into my dressing room if they want to, and they can make us do lessons together. But I won't speak to you, ever."

Miss Smith was in an armchair, and she now patted its arm. "Come and help me with my puzzle, Sorrel. Mary's trying very hard to get a vest finished for her baby brother. But we'll ask her to help us with words if we get stuck."

Miranda rubbed her greasepaint smooth. "Well, I hope you don't all chatter. If you do and I dry up on the stage, it'll be your fault."

It was terribly awkward. Miss Smith went on with the crossword puzzle as though nothing were wrong and tried to pretend that Sorrel was helping, which she was not. Occasionally she asked Mary to help but Mary obviously was not the sort of person who was good at crossword puzzles, because when she was asked for something with nine letters she suggested words with three or four. When the call boy came around and said, "Overture and beginners, please" Miss Smith got up and took Miranda's first

248

act dress off a coat hanger, and Miranda put it on. Then Miss Smith fetched her bonnet, muff and gloves and gave her those. Still Miranda said nothing. At last the call boy knocked on the door and said "Miss Brain, please" and Miranda, with her nose in the air, stalked out and slammed the door.

When the door was shut Miss Smith tidied Miranda's dressing table. "I don't have to go down with her for this entrance. Alice looks after her. I'm sorry she's being so difficult, Sorrel, it's not your fault."

Mary laid down her knitting. She was a round-faced girl with fair hair cut in a fringe and she looked the sort of young person who would never say anything but, "Yes, please." However, her voice was angry now.

"I think Miranda's being perfectly hateful."

Miss Smith went on calmly tidying the dressing table. "Miranda isn't really angry with Sorrel. She's so terribly disappointed, poor child, she doesn't know what she's doing."

"All the same, she needn't take it out on Sorrel," said Mary stubbornly.

Miss Smith smiled at Sorrel. "You mustn't let it make any difference to you. Just go on as if nothing had happened. Now, tell me about your lessons. You were in the same class as Miranda, weren't you? But she seems to be a little bit behind you, judging from the reports from the Academy, especially in mathematics and literature."

Sorrel, to the best of her ability, explained to Miss Smith exactly where they had gotten to that term. But she knew she was not sounding very intelligent. Miranda was being even worse than she had expected. How awful to have to rehearse with Uncle Francis, who would probably be angry with her because she was not as good as Miranda! And how dreadful it was going to be to go up to the wardrobe and do lessons with Miranda, who would not speak to her.

If Miss Smith thought Sorrel's answers were not very intelligent she showed no signs of it. Instead she unpacked a paper bag and held out a sponge cake, saying:

"Look, this is the sponge cake I said I'd get with a cream center, or what is supposed to be cream. We'll have tea after the act and then you can go down on the stage and watch the rest of the play, dear. I'll just pop along the passage and put on the kettle."

Mary waited until the door had shut behind Miss Smith. Then she winked at Sorrel. "I may be mean but I couldn't be more pleased, really. I know Miranda's your cousin and all that, but if you ask me, a disappointment won't do her any harm."

Sorrel rather liked the look of Mary. "I feel that too in a way. Only the awful thing is that she really would have been good as Ariel."

"Do you think you won't be?"

Sorrel fidgeted with a lock of her hair. "When somebody like Grandmother or Alice or Miss Jay at the Academy has just that minute been talking to me I know I will. But when I'm alone, like in my bed or my bath, then I'm not a bit sure."

Mary held out the vest to see how it was getting on. "I know just how you feel. It's the way I felt when I thought Miranda was going to play Ariel.

You see, if she had, I expect I'd have played Sylvia. I kept pretending to myself I'd be as good as she was. But inside I knew I wouldn't. It's that bit in the second act when she has to get all dramatic. I do my best at it, but you ought to see the stage manager's face at the understudy rehearsals when he watches me. As a matter of fact, though I wouldn't tell them at home, I was not a bit certain that if Miranda gave up the part they wouldn't get somebody else and leave me as understudy."

"Don't you want to be an actress?" asked Sorrel.

"No. I started as a dancer but my legs got too fat. Then I understudied Wendy in *Peter Pan* with this management. I'm reliable. That's a thing understudies have to be, you know—always punctual, never ill, and always know their lines. If I could be certain the people I understudy would never get sick so that I might have to take their places, I wouldn't mind understudying until I grew up."

Sorrel was quite incapable of believing there could be a person who felt like that. "But it's so dull. Just to sit in a dressing room and knit."

"Oh, well," said Mary contentedly, "it's not so bad. I take my money home every Friday and that's a great help. And it's not as if I were going to do it always, because as soon as I'm old enough I'm going to be a hospital nurse." They could hear Miss Smith coming up the passage. Mary lowered her voice. "But, mind you, anyone who understudies Miranda and has to share her dressing room earns her money."

They had a strange tea. Sorrel, in spite of the

goodness of the sponge cake, could only nibble at it and look at Miranda out of the corner of her eye. Miranda had her cup of tea and a piece of cake at the dressing table and spoke to nobody. Mary, who was obviously quite accustomed to this sort of atmosphere, ate three slices of cake and obviously enjoyed every mouthful. Miss Smith kept talking and did not seem to mind because nobody answered. Sorrel was glad when overture and beginners were called for the next act.

Alice waited until Grandmother was safely on the stage. Then she took Sorrel's hand and led her through the pass door and down to the stage manager. He was following the play in the prompt book.

Alice gave him a nudge. "Here's the other granddaughter. You'll have no trouble with this one."

Sorrel found it fascinating to watch the play from the stage. For the first time in days she forgot all about Ariel. It was such fun seeing Grandmother and Miranda and all the other actors and actresses within touching distance, as it were. From where she stood, it sometimes seemed as if the people on the stage were speaking to her. And when Grandmama said in the play that Sylvia ought to be whipped, Sorrel felt a shiver run down her spine.

When Miranda went off to be whipped, she came down to the prompt side to await her end of act call. Sorrel moved nearer to the stage manager. After all, it was no good looking or smiling at a person who would not speak to you.

But Miranda was always surprising. "I don't suppose Dad will let you play Ariel. You're only rehearsing on approval, you know," she said now.

They had to talk in whispers, of course, and even that was a risk with the stage manager so close to them. Sorrel came right up to Miranda so that she could speak in her ear.

"Perhaps he won't but I'm going to try very hard to be good enough. I don't see why you should be hateful about it. It's not my fault that you aren't playing it."

Miranda looked at her in surprise. "Goodness, you have changed!" She said nothing more for a moment, then she drew Sorrel to her again. "I don't believe you're the sort to tell tales about people. What I'm trying to do is to get everybody feeling so sorry for me that they'll let me play it after all."

Sorrel thought that was pretty cool. "What about me?"

"I don't care a bit what happens to you. I'm always going to think about me and nothing but me. That's the way to get on." The act was coming to an end. Miranda straightened her frock preparatory to taking her call. "There's just one comfort I've got. If Daddy does allow you to play the part, you'll be simply awful in it."

The curtain came down and Miranda ran on with the rest of the cast. She stood in the center of the stage holding Grandmother's hand, smiling and bowing.

The audience whispered to one another: "Isn't that young girl sweet?"

Chapter XIX

Rehearsals

On Monday morning Miss Smith took Sorrel to the Education Officers' Department of the London County Council, which was in the County Hall on Westminster Bridge. Grandmother had already sent for an application for a license and this had been filled in by Grandmother on behalf of Sorrel, and by the manager of the theater where *The Tempest* would be produced, on behalf of the theater management. The application had then been returned to the County Hall and Grandmother had received a letter telling her to send Sorrel to the County Hall with the particulars of her birth, as she was to be examined by the medical officer and interviewed by somebody in the Education Department. Sorrel thought all this a lot of nonsense because she was perfectly well and she had been to a dentist since she came to London so all her teeth were in order. And she knew she was all right at her lessons. But Miss Smith said that the London County Council's rules for young people in the entertainment industry were all good.

"There's absolutely nothing to be frightened of, Sorrel dear. Just answer each question you're asked. That's all you've got to do."

Sorrel found this was perfectly true. The doctor was like any doctor whom Sorrel had ever seen and just as friendly. He prodded her all over and sounded her heart, and told Miss Smith that she was under-sized but a tough little specimen. And though she was thin, he could not find a thing the matter and supposed she was the thin kind. The Education man was just as nice. He scarcely asked Sorrel any questions because he knew Miss Smith. He was, however, very much interested to hear that Sorrel was going to play Ariel, and said that playing a part like that was an education in itself.

Miss Smith took Sorrel by the arm. "Well, if you've passed her we must be getting back. She's got her first rehearsal at twelve o'clock."

Uncle Francis at rehearsals was very much like Uncle Francis playing a charade. He was grand and serious and very aloof. For a whole week he was like that, quite calm and never raising his voice. To her great surprise, Sorrel enjoyed herself. She never saw much of the play or of the actors, because her scenes were taken together as far as possible. And when she was not wanted, she was sent back to her lessons.

Then suddenly, on the Monday at the beginning of the second week's rehearsals, Uncle Francis changed. He had said on the previous Saturday that no one would have a book on that Monday. And Sorrel, who knew her part by now, had not minded a bit. But on Monday she found that having no book meant a lot of other things as well. Uncle Francis made a speech. He explained what the play meant. He spoke in his big booming voice and used long grand words. And though Sorrel put on an interested face, she scarcely understood a word he was saying.

At the end Uncle Francis said, "That is what we have got to get over. And I want pace and, of course, full value to the prose. Clear, everybody?"

Everybody scuttled off the stage except the people who were playing the shipmaster, the boatswain and the mariners. The stage manager called out, "Thunder over" and then the rehearsal began.

Sorrel was standing beside the girl who was playing Miranda, the daughter. Her name was Rose Dean. Rose smiled. "It starts with a storm, you know. You'll see some terrific goings-on in the sound- and lighting-effects department later on — thunder and lightning, wind, and goodness knows what. There's a boat, too, being wrecked on the island."

In the previous week Sorrel had learned where she came on for her various entrances. So when Uncle Francis said, "Approach, my Ariel! Come!"

she was ready. She ran as she had been taught to do and knelt at his feet, then raised her head to speak.

Uncle Francis let her get to the end of her first speech without interruption. Then he told her to stand up.

"That, my dear, was said like a young girl at an elocution class. Tell me, what do you think Ariel is like?"

Asked directly like that, Sorrel forgot the listening cast and forgot to be shy with Uncle Francis. She had done absolutely nothing but think about Ariel ever since she had been told she might play the part. Except for her weekly rehearsals and broadcasts for the B.B.C. and the afternoon when she had watched Grandmother's play, she had thought of scarcely anything else, and a picture of Ariel had grown in her mind.

"It's something not real at all, like the wind, that you've caught and who does everything you ask him, but all the time is simply longing to be up in the air again where it belongs."

Uncle Francis took her chin in his hand. "Is that your idea or Miranda's?"

Sorrel was surprised at the question. "Mine. Miranda never said anything about Ariel. We didn't know she was supposed to play it till she wasn't going to."

Uncle Francis's voice became even more caramel than usual. "It." He turned to the cast who were sitting around the stage. "You notice she uses the word 'it.' My conception entirely."

Sorrel had no idea what the word "conception"

meant and only hoped that it was intended to be complimentary rather than otherwise. "Is it a he or a she?" she asked, timidly.

"Neither," boomed Uncle Francis. "It. And how do you suppose you look?"

Sorrel had no idea. Miss Jay had said there were innumerable ways of dressing Ariel, and that the last time she herself had seen the play Ariel wore a tunic of rainbow silk. Sorrel thought that would be gorgeous.

"Rainbow silk?"

Uncle Francis roared. "Rainbow silk! Rainbow silk! And what else did you plan? A wreath of roses round your hair? No, my dear, Ariel is a strange shape, almost terrifying in the way nature is terrifying."

Sorrel, though very disappointed about the rainbow silk, tried not to show it. "Do you mean with a long nose and big ears?"

Uncle Francis looked for a moment as if he were going to burst. At the same moment the cast began to laugh. Uncle Francis wavered between bursting and laughing. The laugh had almost won when he turned to the stage manager.

"Are the designs there?"

The stage manager fumbled among some sketches and then brought a bit of paper to Uncle Francis. "Here's the rough."

Uncle Francis showed the picture to Sorrel. It was of a strange creature with weird hair that had little curls at the ends. It was wearing a very tiny piece of stuff and at the back it had stiff wings rather like a beetle's. It was so unlike what Sorrel had pictured that for a moment she could only stare at it. And while she stared she tried to think of something polite to say.

Words came at last. "It's very unusual."

"Your face and arms and legs are faintly blue," said Uncle Francis. "The wig and the dress and the wings are silver."

Sorrel went on staring at the picture. Blue! After a minute she said, because she could not think of anything else and that was what she was truly thinking:

"'Their heads were green and their hands were blue and they went to sea in a sieve.'"

"Now," said Uncle Francis, dismissing Sorrel's quotation as if it had never been made, "you will go off and make that entrance again and don't forget there's nothing real about you. Magic, my dear, magic, magic, magic!"

Sorrel, running to the side of the stage, thought to herself:

"It's all very well for Uncle Francis to talk like that, but it's very difficult to feel as if you're magic and blue all over and dressed in silver when you're wearing a school tunic which you've outgrown."

Sorrel was given the part of Ariel. Not, of course, just like that. There were desperate days when both she and Uncle Francis were in despair, and almost worse days when he did not look despairing but grieved. Yet somehow the days of rehearsing on approval came to an end and she knew they had come to an end because Miss Smith was told to take her to

Garrick Street to have her wig fitted, and to see Mrs. Plum, the wardrobe mistress, about her dress.

The situation with Miranda got worse, of course, as Sorrel's rehearsing of the part got better. Miranda had hoped to hear her father tell her mother how shocking Sorrel was. Instead she heard the very things she most hated to hear. Her father would discuss Sorrel at meals.

"Sorrel has a quality. She is inexperienced, of course, almost amateurish, but she has a miraculous gift for getting about the stage quickly and always being in the right place, almost without appearing to move. Then, of course, there's that queer little voice of hers. Quite definitely she has something."

"How does she sing the song?" Aunt Marguerite asked.

Uncle Francis very consciously acted when he was acting and so, in spite of being pleased with Sorrel, he thought there must be something wrong with a performance which came so naturally and easily.

"Just sings it, true and clear as a boy. Sometimes I say to myself that I'd like it this way, or that way, and in the end I leave it. It seems very right as it is. Extraordinary!"

Miranda's anger with Sorrel and her wish to hear her criticized did not spring from real jealousy. She was jealous of her for having the luck to play the part, but never once did it cross her mind that Sorrel might be as good an Ariel as she would have been. Miranda knew that her own speaking of Shakespeare was outstanding and that she had only to appear in a good part for her gift to be admitted. She had heard Sorrel recite Shakespeare and knew she was not in the same class as herself.

Her jealousy was entirely professional. Somebody else was getting the chance that should have been hers. She really minded so much that she got pale and quite ill looking. And when she found that her father and mother were looking at her anxiously, she added to the effect of illness by acting as though she were much worse than she was. She had her reward at last. One evening when she came in from the theater her father called her to him. He stroked her hair. He spoke in his most caramel voice.

"Your management have consented to allow you to play Ariel at a few matinées. Will that bring the roses back into your cheeks, little daughter?"

Miranda was enchanted. She felt sure she could trust her father to see that some influential people were present to see her play. And apart from that, she would at least have the occasional pleasure of acting the part in the way she knew it should be acted.

"Poor Sorrel," she thought. "I'll show them what's what."

Miranda arrived in the wardrobe for her lessons the next morning with shining eyes. Miss Smith was talking to Mrs. Plum about Sorrel's dress, so Miranda drew Sorrel into a corner.

"Have you heard? I'm going to play Ariel at some of the matinées."

Sorrel remembered the conversation she had had with Miranda on the side of the stage. "So you've won."

Miranda shrugged her shoulders. "As far as I could. If my management won't release me, they won't, though I think it'll be pretty mean of them. But even a few matinées are better than nothing. I'll always get my way, Sorrel, because I know what I want. You'll see."

What with Sorrel's rehearsals and broadcasts and her lessons, she did not know that anything else was going on in the world. But, of course, quite a lot was. Mark sang in a children's revue on the air and got immediately, or rather the B.B.C. got, the most enormous fan mail, particularly from old ladies and clergymen and inmates of hospitals and nursing homes, all of whom said Mark's voice had done them good. Mark himself was not very much interested in the broadcast except that after it he had received two letters from boys who had been at school with him at Wilton House. They both said they had heard him sing. One said it had made the matron's cat sick and the other that the headmaster's radio had broken in half. But they also told him all about what was going on, about cricket and school rows and how somebody or other had cheeked somebody else.

Mark, drifting along at the Academy, had accepted life as it was, partly because it was new, partly because he had enjoyed being a polar bear, and partly because there did not seem to be anything else to do. But getting those two letters brought Wilton House back very vividly, and he liked what he saw of it in his memory. Moreover, he did not think much of the summer term at the Academy. It was hot in London and nobody played any proper games. He never had cared for his dancing classes and now he pictured what the boys at Wilton House would say if they could see him in a bathing dress and white socks and sandals dancing every day.

When Mark had come home from his broadcast, he had been quite pleased that Hannah had said:

"You ought to be in a church choir singing 'Oh, for the wings of a dove' like the boy I heard once in cathedral."

And the next morning he had been charmed when Grandmother had said: "I heard you yesterday, Grandson. It was beautiful."

But when he got his two letters and heard about the cat being sick and the radio broken in half, he knew that was the real way to think about singing, and precisely how he himself would feel if he heard any of the boys at Wilton House caterwauling over the air. Because Sorrel had always been the leader of the family since their father went away, Mark went first to her.

"I do wish I didn't have to go to that awful Academy," he told her. "I wish I could go back to Wilton House."

He was standing at Sorrel's bedroom door. Sorrel was crouched on the floor, practicing moving her shoulder blades to give the effect of keeping her wings continually on the move. She gave Mark only half her attention.

"So do I," she said absentmindedly, "but I shouldn't think you could. You'll go somewhere different in the autumn, though."

Mark glared at her back view. "Ever since you

started to act in that awful old Shakespeare, you don't pay any attention to what anybody says."

Sorrel gave her shoulder blades another twitch. "Mark, just look at my shoulders. Am I moving them just a little, so that I'll make my wings tremble, or am I jerking them up and down?"

Mark shot his chin into the air. "I couldn't care less."

There seemed to be only one other person besides Sorrel who would understand about Wilton House, and that was Hannah. Mark heard her before he saw her. She was singing while she ironed and her voice came rolling down the stairs.

> "Do no sinful action
> Speak no angry word;
> We ought to spend our points today."

Mark leaned against the table on which Hannah was ironing.

"I do wish I could go back to Wilton House. It's where I ought to be."

Hannah held the iron up close to her cheek. "You never spoke a truer word."

"Well, can I?"

"Now, don't be silly, Mark dear. You run out and play in the garden. Pity to waste this nice sunny evening."

"But why can't I?"

Hannah shook her head. "There's things beyond your or my understanding, Mark. And what I say is, what you don't understand take on trust."

Disconsolately Mark hung over the banister and slid down. How hateful everybody was! Why couldn't he go to Wilton House? Surely somebody besides himself must see what a sensible idea it was. The word "sensible" brought somebody to mind. He and Petrova had kept up a short but entirely sensible correspondence. Grandmother, he knew, was at the theater. So he slipped into her drawing room, opened her desk, found a sheet of paper and a pencil and, breathing hard through his nose, because he hated writing, he wrote Petrova a letter.

Holly and Miriam were sent with Hannah to Sorrel's dress rehearsal. Mark was asked too but nothing would induce him to go.

"If Sorrel is going to act in that awful Shakespeare she can act by herself. I don't want to see her," he declared.

As a matter of fact, neither Hannah nor Holly nor Miriam enjoyed the play very much. At one point Holly even went to sleep. Hannah was so appalled by Sorrel's clothes and general appearance that she made Holly nudge her each time Sorrel came on so that she could shut her eyes. And that, of course, is not a very good way to enjoy a play.

When Sorrel came in that evening after the rehearsal, Hannah did not even try to be polite. "Shocking! What Mr. Bill would say if he could see you, I don't know. No more on than some poor savage! I was so upset my stomach hasn't settled yet."

Holly was frank. "Well, of course I think it's a dull play, but I thought you were most awfully good. You were just like that bit of silver stuff we had in a puzzle—you remember, it had to break up into five pieces to make buttons for a man's coat. But the worst thing was that girl who played Miranda. I'll show you."

Rose Dean was a good actress in ingenue parts, but she was not well cast as Miranda, and she had been so bullied by Uncle Francis that she was in a state of nervous twitter. Holly, without of course using the right words, gave an imitation of her that was so funny Sorrel forgot for several minutes that tomorrow was the first night.

Then Hannah came, still looking very disapproving, and fetched Holly off to bed. Sorrel, left alone, suddenly felt as if something were spinning in her middle. She clutched at her stomach with both hands and said out loud, although there was no one to listen:

"Oh, goodness! I do wish tomorrow was over."

Chapter XX

Plans

Sorrel's performance of Ariel created a good deal of interest. It is difficult for anyone to be a success in Shakespeare because there are so many people who love all Shakespeare's work and have strong ideas as to how the different parts should be played. There were a large number of people, therefore, who were angry because Ariel was played by so young a girl as Sorrel. Of course that was not Sorrel's fault; it would have happened just the same had Miranda played the part. There were a few critics who wrote about "little Miss Forbes tripping and posturing," but they were the kind of people who hated the sort of Ariel that Uncle Francis imagined. What was encouraging was that there were a large number who wrote in a very complimentary way: "Silvery-voiced little Sorrel Forbes"; "Little Miss Forbes spoke Ariel's lines in a way that is a lesson to far more experienced actors"; "Sorrel Forbes, as Ariel, gave a quicksilver performance and her young, piping voice, together with her weird blue make-up, gave an ethereal effect which was curiously moving."

Sorrel herself had thought that once the first night was over everything would be lovely, and that she would have all the fun and excitement of playing Ariel with nothing more to worry about. But acting for Uncle Francis was not a bit like that. Almost every performance, every actor did something he did not like. And when the curtain came down he saw the company on the stage and gave them what he called "my little notes." He had little notes for Sorrel all the time and generally a great many of them, because as she played all her scenes with him, he could not help hearing and seeing anything he did not like.

One of the things that Sorrel learned that season had to do with getting fond of a part. She had first discovered this when the serial finished on the Story Hour at the B.B.C. She simply hated to think she would not be Nancy any more. Indeed, it seemed odd to think she would not be. Now, though it was nervous work acting with Uncle Francis, she had gotten to love Ariel and to feel she was Ariel. And it was with dismay that she heard Miranda was to play at the next Wednesday matinée.

From the moment they knew that Miranda was

going to play the Wednesday matinée, the relationship between the two girls changed in a queer way. Miranda grew gay and excited, Sorrel silent. It was not that Sorrel wanted to be mean. It was only fair that Miranda should play Ariel a few times, she told herself. But Ariel was *her* part. She hated having somebody else do it. And she particularly hated having somebody else wear her dress and wig.

Sorrel had not known what was the proper thing to do when somebody else was playing your part. Did you go to the theater or not?

Miss Jay settled that question. "I've two seats for us in the dress circle, Sorrel. I'm very anxious you should see Miranda's performance."

Miranda had been quite right when she said that her father would not let her performance pass without having some interesting people in to see her. She was a success and she was Uncle Francis's daughter and she was a Warren. Though Sorrel had done very nicely as Ariel, it had been because of the very simple, almost childlike way in which Uncle Francis wanted the part played. Miranda had done well as an actress as Sylvia and people had talked about her as the latest sprig off the Warren tree. Sorrel was a sprig but there was not so much fuss about it.

Sorrel found it interesting seeing the play from the front of the house. It was fun knowing all the actors, and the comedy scenes were much funnier from where she sat. The scene where the goddesses appeared was really quite beautiful. Then there was Miranda, who looked so much the way she, herself, had as Ariel that it was quite odd. The wig and the blue paint would make any two girls look alike. But there was any amount of difference in the way Miranda played the part—different inflections on different words, a different way of moving, different everything.

During the first intermission, Sorrel was very careful not to say anything to Miss Jay to show she wanted to know how good she thought Miranda was.

Then two men in the row behind them began to talk. "Francis's idea of Ariel and mine are worlds apart anyway, but at least in the wisp of a girl who normally plays the part he had what he wanted. This Ariel is a budding woman with a pronounced personality and bursting with talent. I would stake anything I had that she has an enormous career in front of her in the great parts, in the great way. But if you want to see Francis's conception of Ariel see the other one." The two men went out then to get some tea.

Miss Jay turned to Sorrel. "Did you hear what that man said?" Sorrel nodded. "Did you understand it?"

Sorrel nodded again. "I think so, except about Miranda's being a budding woman."

"Miranda's older than her age and you're younger than yours. But that part's not important. It's what he said about the playing of the part that is. Miranda's brilliant and yet, as Ariel, you give the better performance; and that you'll find all the way through your stage career. It's getting inside the part that matters, and I think you've got inside the part as your uncle wanted it and Miranda hasn't."

"But he said he would bet Miranda would be a great actress," protested Sorrel.

The attendant brought their tea. Miss Jay took the tray and balanced it on her knee. "So she will. Great like Edith Evans, perhaps, if she works. But you won't have that sort of career and you wouldn't aim at it."

"No," Sorrel agreed. "What I would like would be to act something like Pauline Fossil. I would most awfully like something like that."

Miss Jay poured out Sorrel's tea and passed her the cup. "Well, we must see if we can manage it. Perhaps in a few years' time somebody else who is thirteen will say to me, 'What I would like is to be able to act like Sorrel Forbes.' Wouldn't that be fun?"

Mark had put on the envelope to Petrova, "Strictly private and conferdenshul." When Petrova's reply came, she had written the same thing on her envelope only she had spelled *confidential* correctly. Like all Petrova's letters it was strictly to the point.

> *Dear Mark,*
>
> Of course you must go to Wilton House. I have written to Madame and she says that what you want to be is a sailor, like your father. But she thinks it is difficult to arrange because at the moment your grandmother's looking after you and she wants you to go on the stage. She has suggested that Pauline

271

have a talk about it with your Uncle Henry, and I have cabled Pauline and asked her to do this. Madame says that your Uncle Henry is the right person because your grandmother does anything he says.

Gum says he would like to adopt you until your father comes home. We will see about this when we hear from your Uncle Henry.

Yours,

Petrova.

P.S. I am sending you a screwdriver. It's always useful to have a good one.

Holly and Miriam were great friends and almost every week Aunt Lindsey would come around on Saturday and fetch Holly to spend the afternoon. One day at the end of July, she fetched Holly to spend not only Saturday but the whole weekend. To Holly spending the weekend with Miriam was all fun.

It was anything but fun to Hannah. "And your pajamas that threadbare I'm ashamed to pack them, and no bedroom slippers, and only your house shoes to wear. But there, humility's good for us, they say. But my cheeks won't stop flaming the whole weekend, every time I think of your aunt's face when she opens your brief case."

It was a lovely weekend. Aunt Lindsey took them to the zoo and to tea in a shop, and the best thing of all was that on Saturday night Uncle Mose came home. Uncle Mose had been doing a two months' tour of the Middle East, and he was not expected back for another week, but somehow he had wangled his way onto an airplane instead of a boat. And there he was, with a little red fez on the side of his head, sticking his head around the door and grinning at Miriam and Holly, rubbing his hands and saying "Vell, vell, vell!" He brought back some presents—nothing big, as they had to go in his pockets—but the most exciting were two bananas. They ate the bananas on Sunday and afterwards Holly, carried away by the excitement of having a banana, gave an imitation of how all the staff at the Academy would react to seeing a banana.

Aunt Lindsey and Miriam laughed a great deal at Holly's imitations. But though Uncle Mose laughed, he had a look on his face as though he were being serious as well.

When Holly had finished he said, "Let's see some more of your imitations, young woman. What else do you do?"

Miriam was exceedingly proud of Holly and bounced with excitement. "Do Dr. Lente at music, that's much the funniest."

Holly did Dr. Lente and then Madame, and then Miss Sykes and, finally, she wound up with Uncle Francis being Prospero. This last took all the thoughtfulness out of Uncle Mose's face and made him roar. When he had stopped laughing, he beckoned Holly to him and took her on his lap.

"So you're going to be a comedienne, are you?"

Aunt Lindsey had laughed so much, the stuff on her eyelashes had run down her cheeks. She mopped her face. "Addie was a mimic, you know, Mose. We

273

always said she ought to have gone in for it."

Uncle Mose gave Holly a kiss. "I take a great interest in your career, young lady. We always wanted a comedienne in the family, didn't we, Miriam?"

Miriam took a deep breath and, dashing forward, pushed Holly aside and sat on her father's other knee. "I've thought of something. Let Holly be a comedienne instead of me. I mean, I never was going to be a comedienne. But let's stop making me train all round to see which way I shape. Let me do nothing but dance. Please, Dad, please."

Uncle Mose raised his eyebrows in a question mark over Miriam's head and looked at Aunt Lindsey. And Aunt Lindsey gave him a funny sort of smile.

"I never did think it was going to be any other way, Mose. But it's funny we should have a dancer."

Uncle Mose was a man who came to decisions and stuck to them. Now he got up and stretched himself. "Well, I'm going for a walk. Who's coming with me?"

Miriam flung herself at him again. "But you can't just leave it like that, you must see Madame about me."

Uncle Mose gave her hair an affectionate pull. "And who said I wasn't going to? As a matter of fact, I'm going to see Madame tomorrow. But not only about your future, young woman — about the future of my niece Holly, as well."

Chapter XXI

The End of the Story

Uncle Henry cabled to Grandmother and told her that he wished Mark to be sent to a boarding school, preferably the one in which his father had placed him, and that he would be responsible for the school fees. Grandmother sent for Mark the moment she received it.

"Read this, Grandson." Mark read the cable and beamed at her. "And why is it necessary for you to go to your Uncle Henry when you want something instead of coming to me?"

Mark was quite unmoved by her tone. "As a matter of fact, if you want to know, I didn't. I wrote to Petrova and she cabled to Pauline, and Pauline talked to Uncle Henry."

"Of course it's absolute nonsense," said Grandmother, "your uncle saying that he will pay the school fees. He's never paid for anything in his life."

Mark looked proud. "I've arranged for that, too. I have been adopted by somebody called Gum."

Grandmother snorted. "I've never heard of such behavior. Here I take you into my beautiful home and bring you up in the lap of luxury and have you educated at the very best stage school the world can provide, and this is how you repay me."

Grandmother was lying on her chaise longue and Mark was standing beside it. Now he made room for himself to sit.

"I don't exactly know what the lap of luxury is, but if that's what we've got I still would rather be at Wilton House. And though I think the Academy is all right for girls, it isn't all right for boys at all. I haven't played cricket once this term. I'm made to dance in white socks and I simply hate it."

Grandmother fixed him firmly with her eye. "And what about that beautiful voice? Is that to be squandered at a horrid little boys' school?"

Mark's eyes were every bit as firm as Grandmother's. "As a matter of fact, if you want to know, we sang a concert of Gilbert and Sullivan at Wilton House, and that's a very important sort of singing. And our singing master was just as good as Dr. Lente."

Grandmother looked at him a little while in silence. Then her eyes twinkled. "Go to your horrid little boys' school. I've one great comfort, Mark.

What an atrocious nuisance you will be to the Royal Navy." She made an imperious gesture. "Go away, Grandson, go away."

To Sorrel it seemed a long, dreary autumn term. *The Tempest* came to an end and she was not asked to do another broadcast. And though she had "m'audition" ready, including a dance in which she got on her pointes, nobody seemed to want to see or hear her do it. She even had an audition frock ready, for Hannah had decided that she must have a new utility frock. Hannah had been very reasonable about it, too, and had not made any fuss when Sorrel had chosen coral color, saying only that with the winter coming on they could do with a bit of brightness.

But for one reason or another Sorrel felt terribly flat, and because she felt flat she was a prey to miserable thoughts. And the most miserable thought of all was that there was no news of her father. News was coming through now about other prisoners in the hands of the Japanese but nobody ever wrote and said he had seen or heard anything of her father. Sorrel tried terribly hard to go on hoping, but little by little a horrid snakelike fear was settling down inside her.

The autumn was depressing for everybody else as well because the weather was so nasty. Alice said:

"When the fog gets into my old north and south and I can't see anything in front of my meat pies, I feel a bit off and I don't care who knows it."

In spite of the special matinées for the forces the Academy term dragged and dragged. Almost every day groups of pupils were waiting in the hall in their best clothes and everybody called out "Good luck," "Good luck." But Sorrel was never among them. Mark and Holly felt this shame as keenly as Sorrel did. They took a truculent attitude about it.

Mark said, "I wouldn't want to act in an old pantomime anyway, and that's all they're going to the audition for."

Holly said, "It's just because they've all done dancing longer than you and that makes a difference. But who wants to dance anyway?"

They were ashamed, though, no matter how hard they pretended they were not, and felt that the Forbes family had been let down.

Then early one morning just before the end of the term, the telephone bell rang. Alice ran up the stairs beaming from ear to ear.

"Put Sorrel into that new frock, Hannah. Her Miss Jay has just rung up. She's to go for an audition. Somebody's ill in some show and they want another girl to take her part."

Sorrel was the only girl going to an audition that morning. She felt very self-conscious as she stood in the hall waiting to be inspected, though she knew she had nothing to be ashamed of. Mark and Holly were so proud of her that they made a point of seeing that everybody in the Academy had a look at her and wished her good luck. Mark raced around, raking out anyone who might possibly have missed her.

"Go and see Sorrel, she's going to an audition. She looks all right, she ought to get it."

Sorrel came back from the audition, her face radiant. Someone was putting on the pantomime *The Babes in the Wood,* and Sorrel had been given the part of the girl babe. The part was written in verse and quite easy to learn, but, there was a song as well and there should have been a good deal of dancing. But fortunately the boy babe danced very well so Sorrel's dancing could be simplified, and she had learned quite enough by now to manage what was required of her.

As they went home on the night of the audition Mark summed up their general pleasure. "There's Sorrel with a big part in a pantomime, and me going to Wilton House next term, and there's Holly playing the Dame in *Dick Whittington.* She's the youngest pupil in the Academy who ever played a Dame. And besides, it's almost Christmas. I should say we were pretty lucky."

Christmas was much more difficult in 1943 than it had been in 1942, even though the Forbes family had far more money to spend. At first, it seemed presents were absolutely hopeless. There was hardly any choice and what could be bought cost so much.

Sorrel bought books for everybody, but books were as scarce as everything else if you wanted a special book. However, if you went with an open mind, prepared to take anything that was suitable, you could get some good things.

Mark gave another set of useful presents. For Hannah nails, thumbtacks, wire, everything for mending. Holly gave everybody notepaper. Plants were even more expensive than they had been last Christmas, so instead they bought flowers. These cost enough, Hannah said, to make the hair on a saint curl. But Sorrel and Mark and Holly said Christmas was Christmas and should be properly kept. So they bought flowers not only for Grandmother but for Aunt Marguerite and Aunt Lindsey as well. Nobody gave a present to Miriam, though they would have liked to, because nobody wanted to give one to Miranda and it might look pointed.

Christmas morning started as usual, except that Hannah seemed queer. She kept saying she felt all of a jump and she made three false starts before she began her carol.

All the Forbes family took enormous breaths to start to blow into their instruments, when suddenly the door opened and who should come in but Uncle Mose. He looked messy for him, and he needed a shave. But he was his usual gay self.

He rubbed his hands. "Vell, vell, vell! Happy Christmas, everybody."

The three of them hugged him and asked what on earth he was doing there at that time in the morning. He rubbed Mark's hair the wrong way and played with Holly's curls before he said:

"I've traveled all night because a present for you three had gone astray. It went down to Martins by mistake and I've been to fetch it back to get it to you in time for Christmas morning."

They all spoke at once.

"What is it?"

"Where is it?"

"Is it for all of us?"

"You shall play it in," said Uncle Mose. "Come on, start again."

So Sorrel and Mark and Holly hummed down their trumpets and Mark beat with a free hand on a drum and Hannah kept time on a triangle.

"Noël, Noël, Noël..." And then they all stopped because someone was singing, a big cheerful voice coming up the stairs. Then the door was opened and there was their father!

Such a lot of talking went on! Luckily their father had been able to gossip to Uncle Mose on the train or he would never have sorted out the jumble about *The Babes in the Wood*, Wilton House, the Dame in the pantomime and the Fossils, but as he knew it all already he was able to sit on the bed among them and tell them with absolute truth that he was proud of them all and thought every arrangement splendid. Then he told them a little about himself, how he had been wounded and hidden in a native's hut, and finally escaped across India. And how they were meant to have had a cable and he did not know why they had not. While their father was talking, Hannah and Alice went away.

Uncle Mose was following when he popped his head back through the door. "See you tonight, everybody. What's the betting this is the best Christmas night this house had ever had?"

Also by Noel Streatfeild

Ballet Shoes

When three orphans—Pauline, Petrova, and Posy—vow to make a name for themselves in the world, they have no idea that it's going to be such hard work! With the help of a kindly benefactress, they launch themselves into the world of show business, complete with working papers, the glare of the footlights . . . and practice, practice, practice.

Each girl quickly finds her own special talent. Pauline—with a flair for the dramatic—seems destined for the movies. Posy is a born dancer. Practical Petrova, however, discovers she'd rather pilot a plane than do a pirouette. . . .

"Original, amusing, first-hand account of three young girls who study for ballet and the stage."
— *The New Yorker*

". . . most interesting of all is the account of the flowering of Posy's unselfconscious genius."
— *The New York Times Book Review*